To Gene,
My purpose, as always . . .

Some days all you can do is smile and wait for some kind soul to come pull your fanny out of the bind you've gotten yourself into.

—Anonymous

1

Florida's Panhandle

On the sultry summer day that Vonda Kay Thayer turned fifty, she celebrated her birthday unlike any other.

She took off her thirty-year-old wedding band, packed a bag and a light lunch, and drove to the Grand Motel where, with a little help from Andrew Jackson, she persuaded the sweaty clerk in the flip-flops and Speedo to give her his discretion and his Frederick's of Hollywood catalog. The clerk, a Hair Club candidate named Dirk, palmed the twenty while Vonda registered into the bridal suite.

There for a second, it appeared as if Dirk was staring at Vonda's chest, but he soon set her straight.

"What's with the binoculars?" he said.

The compact camo Leupolds hung around her neck like a string of cheap pearls.

"Bird-watching," she said. "I'm trailing the dodo bird."

Dirk snatched up the swimming pool pole brush he'd left leaning against the counter and raised a dubious eyebrow.

"Ain't it extinct?"

"Not yet he isn't," Vonda said, and then spoiled the deadpan answer with a cackle. "But we live in hope."

Up in the bridal suite—the only room within clear sight of both the motel entrance and the sprawling parking lot—Vonda was so accustomed to the heat and constant humidity, she paid little notice to the musty smell belching out of the drippy window air conditioner. First, she set her bag down atop the bed, then whipped out a tea cloth, which was little bigger than the wall calendar Jerome's real estate company gave away every Christmas to preferred clients.

Next, she spread the makeshift tablecloth over the lone table in the room, and topped that with her cheese sandwich and a newly uncorked bottle of California Pinot Noir. A ripe burst of cherry, plum, and a hint of spice wafted into the air.

Jerome had a more refined palate and stocked older wines in the cooler, but this was the last bottle of the silky-textured Bellisimo they'd bought together in Sonoma. The choice seemed apropos.

Out of habit, Vonda flipped on the television to fill the room with the sound of more than just her own thoughts.

Someone had left the dial set to the Weather Channel, and Vonda caught snippets of the nipped-and-tucked anchors reporting a storm forming off the west coast of Africa. It sounded like a slow weather day as they hashed and rehashed the chances of a major blow possibly sweeping into the warm waters of the Gulf over the summer.

Finally, Vonda dragged a chair next to the window and settled in to peruse the clearance issue of Frederick's.

Only now was she set for her vigil.

The Grand Motel lay on the outskirts of town, just off Interstate 10, in a sleepy area frequented by bleary-eyed travelers, anonymous truckers, and unfaithful spouses. Gauging by the moans, groans, and bangs filtering through the thin walls from the room next door, somebody had swallowed enough Viagra to shoot bullets into the headboard all afternoon long. The lurid racket hadn't slowed up one iota since Vonda had eased into the suite.

A bubble of giddiness had carried her to the motel but had quickly dissipated in the sullen quiet of her musings. Now her thoughts were a gloomfest, an emotional boa constrictor that threatened to strangle her.

All right, already! What she was doing was against the order of nature. She admitted it.

A wife and mother in the vanguard of baby boomers didn't prance about strange motels. No, they looked after home, kids, and elderly mother-in-laws, while über-sexy lustbots pranced about with geezers coasting toward retirement, the seasoned men, if you will, the ones trying unsuccessfully to preserve a youthful self-image.

Geezers like Jerome Thayer.

It wasn't long before Vonda caught a gander of her husband's champagne-colored Escalade through the binoculars. The shiny urban truck whipped into the motel's entrance just as her cell phone chirped. She recognized the number as belonging to her big sister.

To answer or not to answer, that was the icky question.

To answer meant listening to an earful. Not to answer meant listening to an earful *after* her sister called 911 to report Vonda as dead, buried, or both for not answering when everyone knew she always answered her cell phone.

Crap.

Vonda flipped open the phone without tearing her gaze away from the progress of Jerome's truck.

"Chez Thayer."

"Don't hand me that," a familiar voice said without preamble. "Here I am, standing on your front porch with a birthday present and chocolate cupcakes that I slaved over and which are now melting—thank you very much—and you're not home. And why aren't you home where you're supposed to be? Lord love a duck, I couldn't believe my ears when I heard where you were. Y'know, sis, there's a name for what you're doing. It's called stalking."

"No, I'm sitting down," Vonda snapped back, "so I'm a voyeur. It's called . . . *voyeuring.*"

The voice arguing on the other end of the phone belonged to Lurlene—dubbed Lolo early on by a toddling Vonda—easily the oldest living mammal in town, if you believed every tale of woe she spouted. Lolo was the most opinionated of Vonda's elder twin sisters, but Vonda figured she'd be narrow-minded, too, if she were stuck married since the flood to a friend of Bill W.'s, a buzz-cut redneck with a wooden leg and teeth that were a train wreck.

"What if someone we know catches you *voyeuring*?" Lolo said.

"No way that'll happen. My binocs are camo-colored; no one can see me. So how did you know where I am?"

"Dirk's in Twyla's Pilates class," Lolo said, speaking of her twin. "He called her. She called me."

Vonda rolled her gaze heavenward, and said, "Son of a bitch. After I forked over twenty bucks to him, too."

"It's not like you can't afford it. Listen, since I have you on the phone . . . happy birthday."

"Thank you. I appreciate you reminding me I now have one foot in the grave."

"Nonsense. Now you can join AARP and get early-bird specials and senior discounts."

"Senior?" Vonda muttered, rolling the word around on her tongue. The taste wasn't for everyone. But then, that was the whole point. "My God."

"Am I to assume you feel justified lyin' in wait in a strange motel?" Lolo said, back to her effort to spread good cheer wherever she went. "What's lover boy gone and done this time?"

Vonda could see Jerome wasn't alone and said so.

"He's turned in the front seat," she said. "Appears to be attemptin' to storm the fortress of a shaggy blonde. Guess that's one way to get rid of the new-car smell."

"Vonda Thayer!" Lolo shrieked.

"I'm just sayin'," Vonda countered. "Aren't the cupcakes meltin'?"

"Forget the damned cupcakes! What in heaven's name do you think you're accomplishin'?"

"You mean, other than watchin' a dharma bum stroll down memory lane with the Whore of Babylon?"

"Vonda, you have a beautiful home, beautiful children—"

"An unfaithful husband."

"Oh, suck it up, little sister. Who promised you perfection? Thirty years is worth overlookin' a few peccadilloes. Think. How many women wouldn't give their left ovary to have a man who's a good provider, a good father, and not bad-lookin', to boot? In this day and age—"

"Now I'm a fuddy-duddy?"

"I didn't say that, did I? But just look at Marcel and me—"

"Must I?"

"We don't always see eye-to-eye," Lolo continued, "but we manage to work things out."

By now, Jerome and the blonde had scrambled out of the Escalade. She was petite and, because Vonda's life didn't suck enough, she wore a figure-hugging halter dress obviously made for less generous curves.

He was easy to recognize, duded up in his creamy white Palm Beach linen suit and Kenneth Cole sunglasses. Jerome possessed an innate sense of style. All he lacked were a fedora and an unfiltered Camel to complete the Southern planter power-and-money look.

A clotheshorse, that described Jerome Thayer. Elegant and

sophisticated, he projected an image of a man at ease in his own antique beige-and-white leather spectator shoes. Those were definitely not his father's Pat Boone white bucks.

"Biology does love variation," Vonda said.

"When you embrace diversity, you embrace God."

"Where did you hear that?"

"Didn't. Saw it on a billboard."

"Oh," Vonda said and then muttered, "and she's a midget, to boot."

Vonda watched while Jerome hesitated in one of the motel's first-floor doorways and checked an angle over his shoulder, the sleepy blue eyes she knew so well still camped behind the dark shades.

"A midget?" Lolo echoed, then dropped her voice to a conspiratorial whisper. "You can't say 'midget' anymore. It's 'little person.'"

"Well, it's obvious she's little," Vonda said just as low. "But I think she's a dog more than a person. Woof-woof!"

Lines of confidence and determination were mapped across Jerome's face in that instant before he turned and followed the blonde inside an out-of-the-way room on the first floor, vanishing behind a closed door. Vonda pushed back from the plate-glass window, then lowered the binoculars and contemplated her husband's cornucopia of extracurricular activities.

"There should be a mandatory waitin' period on buyin' the bullshit of a guy who lives with his mother."

"Speaking of which," Lolo said, "what thoughts have you given to your monster-in-law?"

"Miss Ludie?" Vonda snorted. "Not everything at home re-volves around Jerome. Oh, wait. Yes, it does."

"This may be her last summer, y'know."

"I should be so lucky," Vonda said. "I've put up with her crap for thirty years. She's his mother. He can play fetch-and-carry slave for her for a change."

"Now, you're really talkin' nonsense. Listen, Von, it's a fact of life: Sometimes people disappoint. Get over it. Go home before you make a worse mistake than when Ivana dumped the Donald."

"Me? Wait a minute. I'm not the one screwin' the pooch."

"Have you been drinkin'?"

"Just a little wine—"

"I knew it! Marcel's goin' to a meetin' tonight, and I'm sure he wouldn't mind pickin' you up on the way—"

"For the last time, I don't have a drinkin' problem."

"Denial is one of the signs, y'know."

Vonda paused to stifle a burp, and then said, "When did life become a one-way street?"

Better yet, when had she become Walter Mitty, plastering on a vacant smile for the world while she retreated to her inner happy place?

Jerome's antics never used to bother Vonda. They bothered her now, she guessed in a moment of clarity, because today . . . well, today she'd gotten old.

Looking back, it was all too obvious.

She could pinpoint the exact day Jerome had closed the deal with her, only then she'd been too naïve and foolishly infatuated to believe that marrying the boss's youngest daughter was just one rung up the career ladder for him. Jerome was handsome, sexy, and romantic—a man she could trust.

Or so she'd thought.

So she'd said yes before his mother could sabotage the wedding. However, when Miss Ludie immediately moved in with them and never left, Vonda quickly learned that it was easier to wash the stripes off a zebra than it was to pry Jerome away from his mother.

In response to Vonda's question, her sister made a noncommittal noise.

"Lolo, you don't understand," Vonda said.

"Try me."

"Now that I've got one daughter grown and married off and the other two are close behind, I want more out of my golden years than television and yard work and trips to the post office." She sighed. "I'm tired of the monotony, of settlin' for a mediocre life and a routine relationship. I want passion. Excitement. I want a love affair for the rest of my life."

Lolo huffed and said, "What you want is a pipe dream, Vonda. When are you gonna wise up? You're a housewife, a *middle-aged* housewife, mind you. The reality is you don't know how to do anythin' besides be what you are."

All of which were distressingly accurate, Vonda sadly admitted to herself. That truth was tough to acknowledge, but this was a day for firsts, wasn't it?

"Maybe you should try lookin' at this from a different angle," Lolo was saying. "The more you give, the more you get. Maybe you're bein' tested."

Tested?

Turning fifty—the mere act of owning the thought that this ship really was sinking—had a way of goosing the inner child into dashing for the lifeboat. Looking at it another way, today marked the first day of the rest of Vonda's life.

She took a deep breath.

Change was coming. It was in the air. She could smell it.

And now it had arrived.

In the expectant silence that followed, Lolo's unsolicited advice fueled a very reckless idea in Vonda.

2

Meanness doesn't just happen overnight.
—Old Farmer's Advice

Fifty years ago, when Gum Creek was little more than a jerkwater town, Ludie Estelle Varner won the coveted title of Sweet Potato Queen for three years running.

Every boy in Beulah High School's senior class sniffed at Miss Ludie's skirts, and she could have had her pick of the litter. But no. She set her sights—and her heart—on Cletus Thayer, a cigarette-smoking high school dropout with a youthful zeal for liquor, an air of pained ennui, and a restless charisma so like James Dean.

Every girl practically swooned over Cletus, and it was no tale out of school to say Miss Ludie enjoyed being the object of their envy. To his credit, Cletus warned Miss Ludie then and there he wasn't worth her time.

Barely six months into their stormy marriage, Miss Ludie

finally admitted Cletus hadn't lied. A bevy of well-fed Varner relatives, filled to the brim with moral indignation and seated in accusatory silence, breathed down the couple's neck at the Beulah County Courthouse on the day of their divorce.

Jerome was born seven months later.

If ever a woman had misread a man, Miss Ludie had sorely misread Cletus. He stripped away her schoolgirl edifice, his every word and deed flushing her white-picket-fence fantasy so far down the reality plumbing there was no pulling it back.

And she'd hated him ever since for that.

So had Jerome.

Who knows how different growing up with Miss Ludie might have turned out for Jerome, if only she'd gotten laid once in a while? Fat chance of that happening, though.

The nun's habit she donned most days worked better than a string of garlic to ward off any man's interest. Not that Miss Ludie was a nun. She wasn't. She just liked the outfit.

The penguin look was her statement of martyrdom to the world, although many a school day saw young Jerome wishing his mother didn't have quite so much to say. It was no exaggeration that Miss Ludie single-handedly all but turned sainthood into a cottage industry.

But it wasn't a question of clothing preference temporarily crippling the mother-son relationship; instead, her parental chill was inevitable. Year after year, her slow, festering resentment at life's unfairness bled out all humor and warmth, leaving her a snide, temperamental, sarcastic pain in the ass, and generally mad at God and man.

As Jerome matured and the breadth of his social experience widened, his neglect served only to throw Miss Ludie's dependency upon him into high gear. For Jerome's part, he reacted to his mother's overbearing, bug-eyed rants as any son of his father would: He ignored them with increasing indifference.

College never suited Jerome. He'd felt caged and reckless there, didn't care about academic recognition, and thought studying sucked time like a Hoover. Instead, using his hard-sell charm that played so well with the local audience, he lit upon his calling.

Jerome found he had an uncanny aptitude for successfully closing real estate deals.

Marrying the boss's daughter hadn't slowed down his fast track to success, either. In fact, the reflected glow from Vonda's family shone brightly on Jerome and ensured his social standing in the community.

When his father-in-law died, Jerome inherited the company. He juggled the multiple responsibilities of family and work, and soon discovered that, along with the pressures, there were quite a few perks to being the head honcho of a successful business.

And he'd be buried to the hilt in one of his favorite perks at the Grand Motel that very moment if his cell phone hadn't struck up the Florida State fight song and interrupted his rhythm. Available to clients twenty-four/seven and never one to pass up any potential business, he reached over the naked blonde spooned in bed with him and answered the phone in his smooth-as-dark-chocolate, I'm-working-and-not-really-screwing-around voice.

A second later, his hard-won erection shrank lickety-split and he bolted upright in the motel bed, elbowing the blonde onto the floor in the process, and barking into the cell phone, "Whaddaya mean? Who's gonna take care of Mom? Dammit, Vonda, I have to work. I can't laze around the house all day like you can. Someone has to support this family. I work and you tend to everythin' else—that's how it's been divvied for thirty years, that's how it'll stay divvied."

As the frowzled blonde clawed her way up the side of the rumpled bed to shoot him a damning glare, Jerome's little wife's quiet reply surprised him speechless. And as her meaning slowly sank in, he felt an awful trembling deep in his bowels.

Remy Broussard woke up and immediately noticed the bathroom floor tiles were cooler on his face than usual.

They were stickier, too, and smelled faintly of ammonia. Guess some jerk took a leak and missed the mark. With good reason, he didn't care to contemplate who.

Today, nothing was going to spoil his good mood. He'd won a major tourney yesterday—Remy was a pro bass fisherman—and he'd been out with his bubbas celebrating the end of a long dry spell between wins.

Gauging by the chill bumps goose-stepping across the tribal tattoos that wrapped from his biceps to his shoulders, he'd also misplaced his T-shirt somewhere. How he'd managed to lose his shirt, he hadn't a clue. But at least his jeans were still on his butt.

Thank you, God, for small favors.

That is, Remy hoped the jeans were his—Amelie had many gifts, but overlooking her husband's tomcatting wasn't one of them. In that respect, Remy's frail-looking, waifish bride of one year was the spit of her father, Jerome, more than her mother, Vonda, especially now that Amelie was pregnant and channeling the *Exorcist* most of the time.

Up on your feet, old boy. Got to stand up and greet the day.

That much good sense ricocheted through Remy's brain, along with a teasing image of imitating some vanilla S and M stuff with a lap dancer the night before. The rest of his thinking was a mite fuzzy.

One thing for sure: Remy had no wish for Amelie to catch him sprawled at the foot of the porcelain god . . . again. He counted his blessings for getting out alive the last time and wasn't into tempting fate by reminding her that he and the word "no" enjoyed a long-distance relationship.

Apparently, the fuzzy part of Remy's brain decided he had nothing to live for, because Remy foolishly rolled into a sitting position without checking first to see if he was alone in the bathroom.

He wasn't. Lately, he never was.

Between Amelie having to pee at the mere suggestion of a sneeze and the smelly stray cats she refused to leave to Mother Nature's good graces, Remy couldn't recall the last time he'd had the throne room all to himself. For the life of him, he failed to see why the critters felt inclined to congregate in the smallest room of the house, but it was damned unnerving always showering in the company of an overly attentive audience of carnivores of questionable loyalty.

Sure enough, a couple of Amelie's mangy cats threw Remy the yellow-eyed glare from atop the toilet. A long-haired gray hawked up something nasty while claiming squatter's rights on the back of the tank, and a black one perched on the closed lid of the seat like a vulture eager to alight on a day-old carcass. When Remy moved, both felines adopted a suspiciously superior air.

"Lookie here," Remy said to them. "I'm the breadwinner in this here house, and don't you forget it."

Not that Remy didn't like cats. He did. In fact, he often supposed they might be particularly good sautéed and étoufféed.

The wild Cajun in Remy was game to try. Too bad Amelie wouldn't hear of it. Wherever an Amelie cat was, you could count on Amelie herself being nearby.

So Remy shoved his nose into the hanging bath towel to dry his unshaven face. Then he heaved himself to his feet and staggered against the doorframe, his foggy gaze searching down the mobile home's short, cluttered hallway that ended at the compact kitchen.

And there she sat.

Amelie read the paper at the chrome-legged Formica table. The sunlight streamed through the storm door beyond her and created a halo around her profile.

He sighed to himself—no more skimpy, lacy numbers. But he had to admit she did look adorable in a blue gingham sundress with her rounded stomach resting on top of her thighs and her sandy-blond hair falling in a neat braid down her back.

The mystery of his missing shirt was solved, too. The new red T-shirt Remy wore last night hung from a wire clothes hanger angled off the padded corner of the banquette Amelie sat on. Except . . . Remy squinted . . . This morning the shirt looked to be riddled with nasty holes.

All at once his tongue tasted much like a bar rag smelled.

He braced his bare back against the cool bathroom door, mustered his most disarmingly toothy smile, and practically purred when he said, "Hey, there. Mornin', sweetheart."

"That ship has already sailed, babe," Amelie said without looking his way. "It's two in the afternoon, and you're still piss-ass drunk." She flipped the page. "Have y'ever perused the obits?"

Her eerie calm was a bad sign.

Remy cautiously said, "Not lately, sugar. Can't say as I have."

"Must be the same person writes every one of them," she said, her attention still focused on the page, "because they all say the same thing: 'So-and-so went home to be with the Lord.' " She snapped her paper shut and dead-on sober looked Remy straight in the eye. "Just once, I'd like to see one that says the sonovabitch went straight to hell and good goddamned riddance." Then she smiled, inexplicably reminding Remy of one of her cats. "What are the chances of seein' that in print, y'think?"

If there was any doubt Remy topped her fecal roster, those doubts were quickly disappearing.

He winced and ventured a guess. "Probably better today than they were yesterday?"

Amelie nodded to show her agreement. Then she held up the holey tee.

"Any idea what this is?" she said.

Her eyes glimmered, round, brown, and innocent. A really bad sign.

If Remy had a lick of sense, he wouldn't give his troubles to the Pope's ugly dog. He'd worry what Amelie was up to and drop to his knees for good measure to beg forgiveness.

But Remy was hungover and came a bit late to that party.

"C'mon, sugarplum," he said. "Is that a trick question?"

"Not at all, sweet cheeks. It's a perfectly legitimate question. No idea? Go ahead, take a guess."

Remy squirmed, tried to rake his fingers through his unruly dark hair, and that was when it finally registered that his wrists were loosely interlaced with plastic flex cuffs.

"Uh, sugar?" Remy said, squirming even more now. "I seem to be stuck." He held up his latched hands, his blue eyes gone soft and beseeching as he attempted to tear the thick white plastic with his front teeth. "Could you help me out here? Get some scissors, will you?"

"First things first, Remy: your shirt." Amelie ignored his request and waved the wilted red cloth like a flag. "No guesses?

Then let me enlighten you. It's a message from Malone. You do remember him, don't you?"

Remy prided himself on being an easygoing, lovable cuss, one with a healthy lack of ambition, along with occasional detours into sobriety. He also enjoyed a fondness for playing the ponies.

Despite what his trailer park neighbors and his inlaws thought, betting wasn't his problem.

Losing was.

"Oh, shit," he said.

"Well put, darlin'." Amelie rose to her feet as fast as her stomach allowed, ripped the ratty shirt from the hanger, and wadded it around her fingers, and then zinged the ball of ruined cloth at Remy's head. "His rent-a-thugs said to tell you that if he doesn't get his money pronto, next time you'll be *in the shirt.*"

"I can explain—" Remy dodged the flying bloodred shirt, and then had the effrontery to look annoyed. "Now, now, sugar. Mind your condition. Don't upset yourself over this little—"

"Oh, I'm not upset, darlin'."

Remy's sigh of relief was short-lived.

"I'm way past upset," Amelie finished in a voice sharp with authority. "I passed upset at six this mornin' when you were dumped in the front yard like a load of ripe manure. Now how much?"

"How much what?"

"Don't play innocent."

"Ain'tcha sleepin' well, sugar? You're certainly cranky."

"How much did you lose⸮"

"Not *that* much."

"How much is *not much*, Remy⸮ C'mon, speak the truth and shame the devil."

"Only five thousand."

After a quick indrawn breath, Amelie said, "Only⸮ *Only*⸮ You'll never change, will you⸮"

She marched into the living room of the double-wide, and Remy padded after her in his bare feet. Well, hell, if he hadn't lost his flip-flops somewhere, too.

Amelie snatched up her car keys from the oval coffee table, and then grabbed a duffel-sized overnight bag off the recliner that sat near the front door. Remy digested the scene and searched his mental calendar for a Lamaze class they were to attend but he'd forgotten about.

He came up blank.

"Goin' somewhere, sugar⸮"

"You're good, Remy," she said, throwing open the door. "Nothin' gets past you."

His attention was diverted when the black and gray cats seized the opportunity for freedom and skedaddled outside. Amelie followed on their heels.

"Hey, wait a minute—you leavin' me here like this⸮"

Remy jabbed the air with his cuffed wrists and struck his most hapless pose, which, in his miserable state, came out as looking more constipated than someone in need of sympathy.

But the pose worked . . . to a degree.

Amelie halted midstride, blew a heavy breath, and gestured

toward the kitchen, saying, "There's meatloaf in the freezer. That ought to last you a few days. After that you're on your own."

Remy's face twisted into a scowl. "I hate meatloaf."

Amelie flashed him a tired smile and said, "I know."

Then she cat-footed it down the stairs and into the carport.

"Sugarplum, wait up. Can't we discuss this?" Remy had no choice but to shuffle out onto the front porch for God and everyone in the trailer park to see. A lively cross-breeze filled with barbequed burger smoke and hot, humid air hit him in the face. "What if I dropped dead or something? Or am I stupid for askin'?"

"You're not stupid for askin', Remy. You're stupid for askin' *me*."

He tried a different tack, saying, "Okay, forget me. What if somebody calls? Your aunties, maybe. Or your grandmother. How are they supposed to get ahold of you? Do I tell them you vanished into thin air?"

Amelie hesitated a moment before finally conceding. "Oh, all right—Mama's. Anyone asks, they can reach me at Mama's house."

Then she chucked her bag into the backseat of her ten-year-old Volkswagen, where it landed with a *thud* of finality.

Taking her answer as a victory of sorts, Remy forced back a chuckle and ignored the stares of his nosy gray-headed neighbors. He raised both cuffed hands and dismissed them with a careless wave, then waggled his fingers good-bye at Amelie.

A couple or three days listening to the bleats of Mother

Vonda and old Miss Ludie, and Amelie would be chomping at the bit to come back home.

Gar-ron-teed.

"Take your time, sugar," he called after her. "We'll talk later. And don't worry your little heart about all them little kitties. I'll be sure to give them the care they deserve. You just enjoy visitin' with your mama and come home when you're ready."

The last view Remy had of his wife was of her shaking her head as she peeled out of their driveway.

3

Sometimes you get, and sometimes you get got.
—Old Farmer's Advice

*N*ote to self: *Never use medicated powder near privates.*

Fresh from a cool shower that turned his sun-spotted skin pruney a zillion ways from Sunday, Cletus Thayer alternately hopped on one flat foot and danced on the other, barely giving a nod to modesty while loosening tiny clouds of talc into the air.

Burning cojones or not, he wasn't to be deterred. Cletus was on a mission from God to step his rangy legs into the nut-hugging tighty-whities that the day orderly held open for him.

Cripes. Just Cletus's luck, they assigned him a sprout who couldn't count to ten if he used all his teeth.

So what else was new? It wasn't as if emptying bedpans in the Sit-in-Shit nursing home had the cachet of, say, a brain surgeon.

Cletus was a lanky lothario, once considered handsome and virile in his youth but was now stooped-shouldered and leeched of all color, and chronically short of breath and patience.

He clamped his arthritic hands on the orderly's square shoulders and barked in his face, "Can't y'hold the damned things still? What am I paying you for?"

"Y'*don't* pay me, Mr. Thayer," the orderly said, steering one hairy leg into an opening in the drawers. "The nursin' home does that."

When had bathing and dressing become a chore?

Cletus couldn't recall exactly, but lately the task had morphed into a gruesome display of endurance. It seemed the nursing home staff and Cletus's popping kneecaps had both adopted a no-surrender doctrine.

The newest torture device thrust upon him was an ugly green portable oxygen tank, now parked haphazardly against the beige tiled bathroom wall, and leashed to Cletus by tubes shoved up his nostrils. Very attractive. And just how in the hell was a guy supposed to get girls with tubes stuck up his nose?

Better yet, how in the hell was a guy supposed to launch any kind of beginning when he was surrounded by people occupied with endings?

Cirrhosis, the doctors had diagnosed. Emphysema, too. A few months. Maybe a year.

But what did they know? Cletus felt okay, a little pain maybe, some fatigue, but okay. What did they know?

"Who do you think pays the bills *here*?" Cletus shot back.

"Medicare."

"Are you being a smart-ass?"

"No, sir. I wouldn't dream of it, Mr. Thayer."

" 'Cause I'll whale the tar out of you, if you are. Just wait and see if I don't."

Using moves that called to mind Jim Fowler wrestling the anaconda, the orderly proceeded to get Cletus into underwear, a pair of khaki shorts, and a white T-shirt emblazoned with a black-and-white picture of the Three Stooges beneath the phrase *Just Say Moe*.

A phlegmy wheezing fit took Cletus's breath for a moment before he shuffled down the sterile corridor and back to his uninspired digs, where he slumped into a worn leather chair to recover his sapped strength. All the while, his feet and ankle joints creaked like a coffin lid.

Officially, he was labeled as Bed B, one of the great unwashed claiming squatter's rights nearest the door, with only the walls for scenery. His roommate was Bed A, lavishly situated near a window with views of the great outdoors, albeit *outside* was a scrawny patch of concrete that surrounded a dead bush.

Who wanted to stare day in and day out at a dead bush, for cripes' sake? The most exciting thing to happen out that window occurred last summer when someone's lippy kid dropped a sparkler into a bag of firecrackers and July 4th was over in thirty seconds.

But, as they say in real estate: location, location, location. One day, when Bed A croaked—which, if the guy's watermelon-sized prostate could be counted on, would probably be sooner rather than later—Cletus intended to move up in the world and take over the coveted window position.

A man had to have goals, didn't he?

One glance at the rest of the building told its own tale of better times. Most of the current patients were babies when the two-story redbrick structure, with its gleaming white gingerbread trim, opened its doors, boasting twenty-five beds and heralding the town's first general hospital.

By the latter part of the twentieth century, the old hospital had reached the end of its useful life—and so had many of its patients—when the facility became too small to meet modern standards and justify the costly building upgrades.

So it was that Jerome's real estate company—owned by Cletus's only child—handled the sale when a law firm out of Houston forked over pennies on the dollar for the decrepit building. And judging by the interior, the cheap bastards then went on to hire a designer who was totally free of originality, surprises, or talent, for each patient room sported the same sorry look: two twin beds, two nightstands, two chairs, and two lockers, all done in perpetual-winter chrome and as cozy as dirty snow.

All the rooms were double occupancy, because that was what Medicare covered.

In Cletus's room, on the faded blue wall between the beds, hung a dusty paint-by-numbers picture that depicted the bucolic scene of a basketball grazing at the edge of a forest. Only a kindhearted person would mistake the paint glob for a deer.

Cletus Thayer was old, not kindhearted.

He hated that ugly picture. Hated the ugly wall it hung upon. Hated the ugly metal nightstand next to it, and the ugly metal twin beds. Hated the worn, brown-speckled vinyl flooring and the black vinyl baseboard, the fetid smell of urine and disinfectant that permeated the corridors day and night.

He longed to rip the picture off the wall. Fantasized about it. Composed odes to it.

"I've done time in jail cells that were cheerier," he said. "I need a smoke—"

"Oh, no, Mr. Thayer, don't go gettin' yourself in a pucker. That's how it started last time."

The orderly knelt at Cletus's feet, tying the laces on his doctor-recommended jogging shoes. And just how in the hell was a body supposed to jog strapped to a heavy metal cylinder?

Damned smart-ass doctors. What did they know, anyway?

"Don't get started or what?" Cletus said. "The moral police are going to come rip out my kidneys?"

"Y'know what admin said: Act up again and . . ."

"I could do with a cold beer, too."

". . . and you're out on your royal keister."

Cletus dismissed that possibility with a careless hand wave and a racking cough.

"Nurse Ratchet doesn't have big enough walnuts to toss me out," he said. "I'll sic my son on her. He'd be all over her like a cheap suit."

Or not.

Truth be told, Cletus didn't have the first clue what Jerome might do, if anything, for his old man, since they hadn't shared the closest of relationships over the years. The boy had been raised by his mama, after all. But for a threadbare man feeling the years rise above his chin, the boast shored up his morale.

"She can toss you," the orderly muttered, "and she will, y'old reprobate." He rose to his feet. " 'Specially if you and your frolickin' starts another ruckus."

Cletus pinched his index finger against his thumb and said evenly, "Son, you're standing this close to knocking on heaven's door and emptying St. Peter's bedpan."

Then he heaved up out of the chair.

"Where you headin'?" the orderly said, hooking a thumb over his shoulder. "The day room's thatta way."

"I want to get some air."

"Seems t'me they's plenty of air in here."

"I like a drink with my air." And fast on the heels of that not-so-original idea, came another one. Cletus jerked to a halt and whipped his chin around. "Hey, y'got any of them boner pills?"

The orderly shook his head, saying, "Sweet-talk the med nurse. That'd put my tit in the wringer for sure."

"And that's a problem? Cripes, son, you were looking for a job when you got this one. Now, I want some company prettier than you. Quit flapping your gums and go fetch me back a gal . . . one with a large trust fund."

"No, Mr. Thayer."

"A working gal'll have to do then, I guess."

"I meant I'm not your pimp."

"There's a hundred dollars cash money in it for you."

"You ain't got a hunnerd dollars."

"Not on me, but don't forget I've got a son who does. *Jerome Thayer?* Largest real estate firm in the county?"

The orderly wasn't without horse sense. His eyes widened for just a second, and Cletus could see him sifting through the possibilities, before he made up his mind.

"Make it two hunnerd," the orderly said.

"Done."

"Which would you be wantin', a blonde, brunette, or redhead?"

"Atta boy."

With one gnarled hand Cletus reached into the space behind the locker nearest to him and came back out with a half-finished stogie and a book of matches he'd stashed there earlier. The other hand he wrapped around the oxygen tank to steady himself, and smiled.

"Step right this way into my office," he said. "Say, isn't it about time for meds? Better send up a flare. I haven't seen the med nurse making rounds in a while."

4

*Lettin' the cat out of the bag is easier than
puttin' it back in.*
—Old Farmer's Advice

Experts say only two naturally round spring-fed lakes exist in the world: one somewhere in Switzerland, the other in the Florida Panhandle.

Back in the day—before oil and railroad magnate Henry Flagler opened the swamps of south Florida to real estate scammers and mob luminaries such as Al Capone, and it became the sixth borough of New York—well-heeled snowbirds flocked to the Panhandle to dot the perimeter of that pristine lakeyard with mansions and Sears and Roebuck houses.

One such snowbird commissioned a three-story gleaming white house in the Queen Anne style, at a time when labor and materials were abundant and cheap. In addition to the projecting bays, turrets, and wraparound verandah that were the apex of the Victorian era, he included a low, black wrought-iron fence that enclosed a manicured lawn edged in boxwoods and trimmed in pink and white azaleas. A breezeway at the rear of the house connected the double carriage house and four-room servants' cottage.

Years later, the carriage house morphed into a garage and workshop, the servants' cottage morphed into a pool house, and the original owner's last surviving heir exhibited a fondness for dancing in the buff in the middle of downtown Main Street. The latter's predilection eventually made it easy for Jerome to snatch up the entire choice property for a sum way below appraisal.

Five seconds after Vonda and the girls moved in to the Victorian with him, Jerome established the second-floor turret room as his study, his sanctuary, his office away from the office. Mostly, though, Jerome holed up in the study to smoke Cohiba cigars and hide from his mother.

So it was to the gracious house on the lake that Vonda retreated after her morning of discovery at the Grand Motel.

The afternoon at the Thayer household started out as predictable as trail mix, an afternoon when summer seemed infinite, when winter and chilly weather seemed way too far away, when the lazy air was heavy with the fertile smells of newly cut yards and the burp-gun volleys of the neighborhood's prickly mutts . . .

And some jackass singing?

Vonda rested her paint roller in the pan and hurriedly tossed on a black beach cover-up to run downstairs and answer the front door for yet another in the teeth-grinding series of humiliations awaiting her today.

There, under the shade of the verandah, stood her two best friends in the world, Donna Lily Wagner and Tata MacKnutt. They were both decked out in wide straw hats, studio tans, designer casual floral sundresses, and performing their best duet warble.

Vonda threw open the screen door in the middle of their off-key voices belting out a sorry rendition of "Happy Birthday." The way the old gals hung on like a tick to the final note you'd think they were on the Broadway stage and singing to the cheap seats way up in the balcony.

Beyond Donna Lily and Tata, a gruesome flock of black plastic crows littered the front yard. The display of little beasties surrounded an obnoxious shroud-draped sign that advertised Vonda's old-age status to the world at large. Vonda swallowed a mewling noise stuck at the back of her throat.

Well, crap, crap, crap, crap . . .

Guess it could have been worse, but she wasn't sure how. This birthday was spiraling into the eighth circle of hell.

And was that a cake carrier in Donna Lily's hands?

Vonda froze like a hound on point and couldn't have been more surprised if her staid Republican sixtysomething friend had whipped out a basket loaded down with glow-in-the-dark condoms.

Donna Lily was a platinum-blond widow, with a Tallulah Bankhead what-the-hell joie de vivre and a comfortable nest egg, thanks to thirty-seven years of marriage to an incompetent gasbag who had specialized in ear, nose, and wallet. But unlike Tata, who was a thrice-divorced full-figured woman of independent mind and means, Donna Lily was a size-two perpetual dieter for whom "cake" was a four-letter word indeed.

"Nifty, nifty, look who's fifty," they said in unison, both talking with the unhurried attitude and cadence of those born, reared, and destined to die in the deep South. They giggled and then grinned like fools as Donna Lily offered up the sheer, plastic-domed cake plate. "It's red velvet—your favorite. And, no, we didn't bake it."

Vonda's mouth practically watered as she said, "Do y'all really think you can buy my forgiveness with cake?"

"Not just any old cake," Tata said, straight-faced. "A *Jay's Bakery* cake." Then she added in a singsong voice, "Cream cheese frostin'."

As if that blatant appeal to Vonda's sweet tooth would tip the scales . . .

"Okay, you win," Vonda said, breaking out into a lopsided grin. She stepped away and waved her friends in the door. "C'mon back to the kitchen, I'll fetch some plates. Y'all want coffee or sweet tea?"

"Make my tea a Bloody Mary," Donna Lily said, to which Tata chimed in with, "Screwdriver for me, easy on the orange juice."

Sharing nearly the same thought bubble, Vonda pivoted on her heel, a slow, wicked smile taking over her face.

"I know. Why not mimosas all around?" she said, proud of

herself for thinking of it. "There's a bottle of Cristal Rosé in the bar fridge."

One small step for jerk magnets. Take that, Jerome Thayer.

"My God, five-hundred dollars-a-bottle champagne!" Tata clapped. "You're my hero."

"Only if you promise to clear the front lawn of crows when you go," Vonda said.

"Deal."

"Signage, too."

"You drive a hard bargain."

"Is that a yes?"

"*Yes.* Are you sure the coast is clear?"

Vonda nodded. They could hear Miss Ludie's radio, coming at them from somewhere back of the house. She had the channel tuned to the funeral home report broadcast every day except Sunday by the local mom-and-pop station. The disembodied voices droned through the house, riding on the smell of pine cleaner.

Celebrate life's journey . . . join us this weekend at your locally owned and family-operated Rayburn Funeral Home for the grand opening of our new crematory . . . a lighthouse in your hour of darkness . . .

The attention-getter was the offer of guided tours and refreshments. No doubt Miss Ludie would expect to be carted down there for the ribbon-cutting and sandwiches.

"The girls are workin' the lunch crowd at the Tastee Freeze," Vonda said, "and Miss Ludie's soap starts right after the noon news."

"So that gives us what?" Tata said, checking her diamond-bezeled wristwatch. "Forty-five minutes to ourselves?"

"At least."

Tata followed Donna Lily inside, letting the wooden screen door slide shut behind her. She swept off her straw hat, revealing a glossy black bob underneath. After she bussed Vonda on the cheek, she watched her snatch the cake carrier by the handle and all but sprint back to the granite and stainless steel kitchen.

"Somethin's different," Tata said, studying Vonda as she moved about.

"Different how?"

"I can't put my finger on it. There's an aura about you, of, of—what's the word I'm lookin' for?"

Over-idealistic? Spineless? Fed up? All emerged in Vonda's mind, but she simply tilted her head and offered her friend an indulgent grin.

"I can't think of it," Tata said, shaking her head. "God, I hate when that happens. Gettin' old really sucks. Did you get a new trainer?"

"Me?" Vonda quickly pooh-poohed that idea. "I'd rather eat fried liver á la mode than exercise."

"I knew that. Sorry. Can't imagine what got into me."

"No cake for *moi,*" Donna Lily called.

"Like hell," Vonda said, rummaging in cabinets for mugs and flatware. "If I'm feedin' my face, so are you. Misery loves company. You're havin' a slice with me." She held up a free hand to stem the rising objection. "And I don't want to hear any more about it."

Donna Lily tossed her hat atop the glass-topped breakfast table that overlooked the lanai and swimming pool. She paused in front of the French doors for a second, and Vonda surmised she was admiring the half-naked pool boy at work.

He was a young one. Maybe early twenties. Nice ass. His bare back and arm muscles bunched and expanded as he leisurely drew the long-handled pool broom back and forth through the blue water. Bet if Donna Lily stood on her toes and stretched, she'd barely reach his shoulder. Vonda visually traced the firm curve of the high-set cheeks displayed so well by his tight cutoffs and then down well-tanned calves.

An eight. Maybe a nine? Back and forth, back and forth he drove the broom through the languid water, beads of sweat glistening on the corded muscles in his forearms and biceps until she could almost hear Ravel's "Boléro" playing in the background.

Then the young man turned around and revealed a chest so hairy he resembled a Chia Pet, and Donna Lily lost all interest.

"Make mine a sliver then," she said, angling back to the kitchen. "I'm tryin' awful hard to lose ten pounds."

Vonda paused with the cake knife in midair and gave her slender friend the once-over.

"From where?" she said. "Your eyeballs?"

"She's been losin' the same ten pounds since the Nixon administration," Tata said.

Donna Lily patted a nonexistent tummy pooch and said, "For your information, my tennis skirts are gettin' a mite tight. So there."

"Oh, please." Vonda rolled her gaze toward the ceiling. "Have three kids, then talk to me."

"Speakin' of kids," Tata said, bringing a finger full of creamy white icing to her mouth. "Y'all will never guess what I read the other day about John Wayne."

"He couldn't ride a horse?" Donna Lily said, making herself at home at the wet bar. She perused the liquor cabinet that sat on the same wall with a few old photos and some books nobody read anymore.

"Worse."

"I was jokin'."

"I wasn't." Tata licked her gooey fingertips, while Donna Lily fixed their drinks. "Get this: He never served in the military. Whaddya think of that?"

"Go on, of course, he did," Vonda said, serving up cake onto three pumpkin-shaped paper plates that she'd bought after last Halloween for seventy-five percent off.

"Usin' the good china, I see," Tata said.

"Nothin' but the best for my friends." Then Vonda returned to her previous thought. "How can you say John Wayne wasn't in the military? He made all those war movies and was a patriot and everythin'."

Tata shook her head and accepted the dessert plate Vonda passed to her.

"Surprised me, too," she said. "But I read he opted for a hardship deferment on account of bein' in his thirties and havin' three kids when the war broke out. He never served a day. Can you believe?"

Donna Lily disguised the mimosas by pouring them into brown *Thayer Real Estate* coffee mugs, her one concession for rushing happy hour.

"Well, I, for one, am thoroughly bummed," she said. "First Santa Claus, then Rock Hudson, and now John Wayne." She tsk-tsked under her breath, set the mugs on the table, and slid into a cane-backed chair. "Is any man what he pretends to be anymore?"

Before the three of them sat down for a champagne-fueled chat over cake, they offered a reverent moment of silence to the outrageously expensive bottle they were about to swill like soda pop.

The moment over, they raised their mugs and toasted the birthday girl.

Clink, clink, clink.

Then they drank and talked their heads off. Tata's manicured red fingernails tapping gently, gently on the glass top accompanied the chatter.

When Donna Lily came up for breath, Tata pointed to the crinkled cotton cover-up Vonda wore and the neon green plastic water misting fan that enjoyed a prominent spot within easy reach at the end of the counter.

"Headin' to the beach today or layin' out by the pool?"

"Hot flashes," Vonda said. "I couldn't wait to strip down to nothin' the moment I walked in the door. Feet are the size of a Hobbit's, too."

And she swung her legs out from under the table, wiggling her swollen bare toes as confirmation.

"Welcome to my world," Tata said, spearing the last bite of cake with her fork. "Y'know I heard some women suffer hot flashes for the rest of their lives. How about them apples?"

"Oh, shoot me now," Vonda muttered.

Donna Lily murmured in agreement, then said, "Besides the fat feet, what did you get now that you're the big five-oh? C'mon, spill. Did Jerome pick out somethin' outrageously expensive? I'll bet he did, didn't he?"

While they waited, Vonda let out a subdued sigh.

"In a manner of speakin'," she said, thinking of the petite blonde with lush curves.

For the briefest second, she also considered spouting an absurd lie to keep the family peace. Then she decided, what the hay.

This was a new day. These were her dear friends. The Cristal was a tasty bottle of champagne.

She might as well head straight into the belly of the beast.

"I picked up a couple of gallons of paint this mornin' while I was out and about." She set her mimosa-filled coffee mug on the table and then quietly dropped her bomb. "I'm paintin' over Jerome's study. Peach walls, white trim. It smells better in there already."

Tata halted with her fork in midair.

"Really?" she said.

"Really."

"You? I mean, you're doin' the work yourself?" she added, apparently anticipating a punch line that was slow in coming. "Wait. You're serious?"

"Of course. Why wouldn't I be? I like color."

"It's just, well, D.I.Y. is so not you, Von. You hire people for that kind of stuff, that's all."

"That explains the smell when we walked in," Donna Lily said.

Tata nodded. "And here I figured Miss Ludie was usin' some new arthritis rub."

"Jerome must be mellowin' in his old age," Donna Lily added. "I can't believe he agreed to let you touch a dust bunny of his sanctum sanctorum, let alone color it a girlie peach."

"I didn't ask him."

"What?" Donna Lily waved her hand in a windshield wiper movement with her increasing disquiet. "What's goin' on, Von? Somethin's gotten into you. C'mon, throw us a bone."

Then she shoved a bite of cake into her mouth and waited.

"What's goin' on?" Vonda repeated and shrugged. "Not much, other than confirmin' my husband's must-have accessory du jour is layin' the wood to a blond young enough for him to adopt."

A fat second later, Tata's face folded in on itself, her expression that of a true believer who no longer believed.

"Great day in the mornin'," she said. "That is just wrong."

"Which one?" Vonda said. "Him screwin' around, or me knowin' about it?"

"Both," Tata muttered.

But she was hard to hear because Donna Lily exploded then,

using language that would send her genteel Baptist mother running for the smelling salts, if the dear woman weren't already spinning in her grave faster than a gyroscope.

"Are you shittin' me?" she said, red velvet cake crumbs flying in all directions.

Vonda calmly slapped crumbs off her chest and said, "No, sweetie, I shit you not."

"What a turd."

"Hold the phone," Tata said. "Are you sure?"

"Banged her like a cheap gong," Vonda said, nodding, and then went on to describe her morning sightseeing trip to the Grand Motel off of I-10.

Tata listened with her mouth hanging open.

"I know that place," Donna Lily said, to which her two friends silently prodded her with raised eyebrows. "By reputation, you understand . . . I've heard all kinds of stuff goes on . . . not that I would ever . . . Pass the napkins, please."

Returning her attention to Vonda, Tata set down her fork and said, "My God, girl, did you catch them in bed? Together? You didn't, did you?"

"Not exactly." Vonda picked up a napkin to pass, then forgot why she was doing that and set it back down again. "I didn't barge in on them, screechin' like a banshee, if that's what you're getting at."

"Civil," Tata said, nodding. "Bein' adult about it's a step in the right direction, I guess." She shifted her gaze to the back of the house and lowered her voice. "Who else knows?"

Vonda correctly read the direction of Tata's thoughts.

"I haven't mentioned anythin' to Miss Ludie," Vonda said, "and I seriously doubt Jerome has called her—"

Tata sucked in a quick breath. "You confronted Jerome about this?"

"Which leaves you two and Lolo," Vonda finished. "And, probably my sister Twyla, too. Now that I think about it, more than likely Lolo's spilled the beans to her, so I figure the news'll reach everybody in the Garden Club before breakfast. Actually, it's a wonder my cell phone isn't ringing off the hook already. And, no, I haven't confronted him, but he knows I know."

Donna Lily crinkled her brow.

"How does he know you know?" she said.

"Who cares?" Tata said. "The cat is out of the proverbial bag." She turned to Vonda. "So what are you gonna do now? Besides play Picasso on the study walls, I mean."

"Honestly?" Vonda said.

"No, hon, lie like a rug to us. Of course, be honest. We're your friends. We love you."

"I don't know yet." Vonda shook her head. "I haven't decided."

"And Jerome? What does he think you're going to do?"

"Take half. For starters."

"Atta girl!" Donna Lily said. "I like how you think."

"And are you?" Tata said. "Settling for half, I mean."

"Like I said, I haven't really decided."

Donna Lily reached for her friend's purse. "Let's find you the number to Tata's lawyer right now. She'll cut off his balls and feed them to the buzzards. Florida's a community property state, y'know."

"What—no!" Tata stayed Donna Lily with a firm hand. "Don't give her any crazy ideas. Von isn't talkin' divorce." She swung her gaze back to Vonda. "You aren't, are you? What you said to Jerome, that was a bluff, right? You can't be thinkin' of throwin' away thirty years just like that." And she snapped her fingers.

"Why ever not?" Donna Lily returned. "Jerome did, didn't he? What's good for the goose . . ."

"Just because he's a walkin', talkin' cliché," Tata snapped, "doesn't mean she has to be."

"That's certainly a different take on it," Donna Lily said, "comin' from you."

"What do you mean, comin' from me?"

"Be real. You're not exactly the Dr. Joyce Brothers of relationships."

Having survived three shrewd marriages, Tata took no offense. "There's more to be considered here."

"Like what?"

Even Vonda couldn't see where Tata was going with this.

"Yeah," Vonda said, leaning forward, elbows on the table, fingers steepled together. "Like what?"

Tata turned to her. "Like goin' against nature and against family. Love 'em and leave 'em—that's my M.O. But that's not you, Von, not by a long shot. You can't just pack up and leave."

"It could be me," Vonda insisted.

Tata shook her head. "What about the girls?"

"They're old enough to understand," Donna Lily said. "They'd get over it."

Tata shook her head again.

"You're a lifer," she said to Vonda. "For better or worse. Sacred institution and all that. A death-do-us-part kind of girl."

Thinking out loud, Vonda said, "Whose death?"

Donna Lily pursed her lips at Tata. "I suppose *that's* a good idea to put in her head?"

"Did I say *death*?" Tata slapped the air. "Never mind. Let's not even go there. Where was I?"

"Better and worse," Vonda said, popping a smidgen of cake into her mouth. "As in, he gets the gold mine, while I get the shaft."

"Wasn't that a song?" Donna Lily said, smiling.

"I knew I heard it somewhere," Vonda replied.

"By the guy with the race car? What was his name?"

"No, no, he was the friend. The guy with blond hair, nice eyes sang—"

"Yes, well," Tata said, staring at them with varying degrees of impatience to bring them back to the topic at hand. "What I'm hearin' is that you didn't actually catch them boinkin'. What you saw could've been innocent, right?"

Vonda wasn't sure who groaned louder, her or Donna Lily.

"I mean, what you're saying is a nice theory," Tata continued. "It fits the facts, but, face it, has little in the way of evidence."

"Where did you hear talk like that," Donna Lily said, "the cop shows on TV?"

Tata shrugged. "As a matter of fact . . ."

"Oh, brother—"

"Don't knock it," Tata said. "They're very informative. Have you thought maybe this woman's a client? Maybe the motel's up for sale?"

"And maybe," Donna Lily said, "Jerome'll gain religion and come clean about all the clandestine activity he ever engaged in." She leaned back in her chair. "But then, I believe sinners will burn in hell for all eternity, anyway."

"Am I sensin' some hostility here?" Tata said.

At the same time, Vonda cut her gaze to Donna Lily and narrowed her eyes, her brain swirling in a heady fog of confusion.

"All the clandestine activity?" she said. "What *all?*"

But fate robbed her of an answer when a movement outside the French doors caught their attention and the three women instantly clammed up.

To their surprise, Miss Ludie crossed the patio toward the kitchen. They hadn't heard her leave the house.

Little wonder, for she never walked. Instead, she shuffled, as if she were part of a chain gang and had to be careful not to trip on the feet of the convict shackled in front of her. The sight reminded Vonda to confiscate Miss Ludie's stash of Paul Newman movies.

Gonzo though Miss Ludie was, no one could deny she had presence. Besides being a strong-featured woman with skin aged to vintage patina that was now moist and flushed with the summer heat, she captured all the zeitgeist of a wilted chapter house prisoner.

Holy crap. Ninety-eight hot, humid degrees, and the woman was draped neck to foot in a white habit. Capping her head was a heavily starched cornette that looked more like a Nazi helmet with wings.

"Mark my words," Tata said, "Mother Mary Margarita there's gonna suffer heatstroke before the summer's over."

"You think?" Vonda mumbled, probably going straight to hell for the hope in her voice.

"Very retro," Donna Lily whispered out of the side of her mouth, "in sort of a demented kinda way. Where does she get those outfits?"

"She's an Internet shopper," Vonda whispered back.

Miss Ludie entered the cool kitchen on a furnace blast of hot air and acknowledged Vonda with the briefest of nods. She passed by Tata and Donna Lily, muttering, "Our Lady of Perpetual Punishment dot com."

Donna Lily winced and mouthed to Vonda, *Sorry,* then said aloud, "How are you, Miss Ludie?"

"Why?" she said, stopping short and whipping around. "What have you heard?"

"Nothin'," Tata said. "Not a thing."

"She was only sayin' you're lookin' well today," Vonda offered.

"Oh. Of course, I'm well. Why wouldn't I be? What're you now, a goddamned doctor?" Then Miss Ludie stared at Vonda's friends as if just realizing they were there. "*Quelle surprise,* if it isn't Frick and Frack. How's tricks, girls?"

Vonda felt heat gathering behind her eyes. The need to speak her mind lumped in her throat, but a pattern of thirty years was hard to break on such short notice. She had to live with the woman, and living with her meant someone had to keep the peace.

Unfortunately, fate had appointed Vonda as that someone.

She opened her mouth to smooth things over, but Donna Lily cut her off, saying, "We're just peachy, Miss Ludie. Business has really been improvin' since we got the sex-offender ankle bracelets off. How did you say your soap was today?" And she finished with the cheesiest smile.

Miss Ludie drew the wrinkles on her forehead into a why-is-this-person-still-alive frown.

"Damned network shitbirds," she said. "Cut my program short for a goddamned weather report."

"Are we expectin' bad weather?" Tata said.

"Not the hell today. Not when Veronica was ready to plug that lying bum she married and his bimbo smack between the eyeballs."

"Men are dogs," Donna Lily said.

"Y'got that right," Miss Ludie snapped.

"They should be pilloried."

"Ain't that the truth?"

"Strung up by their nuts and their hair set on fire—"

Tata jumped in then, before Donna Lily defected to the dark side completely.

"Have some cake, Miss Ludie? Maybe it's not all lost. Maybe they'll rerun your program tomorrow. Wouldn't that be nice?"

"They damned well better," Miss Ludie said. "I don't wanna miss them two gettin' blasted to smithereens."

And she imitated a series of finger pistol gestures worthy of Machine Gun Kelly.

That was the point at which Tata's forehead hit the table.

5

Don't judge folks by their relatives.
—Old Farmer's Advice

If Amelie were to get married all over again—knowing then what she knew now—she'd walk down the aisle wearing burlap rather than wasting the Cinderella ball gown and poufy tulle she'd chosen at the time. After all, the gunnysack motif was more in keeping with what life with her prince turned out to be like.

But on the sweaty drive over to her mama's house, it was hard for Amelie to sustain her outrage at Remy Broussard.

Like most women, she'd waded through her share of turkeys on the way to the altar, but face it, she liked the bad boys best. Always had. For some unexplained reason, her libido set its sights for the more virile side of masculinity, for men who never lived a working stiff's life.

And look where it had gotten her.

Why couldn't she go for a more stable, less sexy face?

Crude and studly, with hair the color of licorice, Remy Broussard was all that and a bag of chips. He was the man of her dreams, and the biggest mistake of her life.

So what to do about him now?

That was the nagging unanswered question, wasn't it?

As she saw it, her choices were pitifully few.

Among them, she could admit defeat. Kick him to the curb. Struggle to raise her baby without a husband.

And then what?

Become like Miss Ludie? Or maybe turn into one of those embittered women who went home every night to a house full of long-haired cats and empty wine bottles?

Neither of those options was appealing long-term. In the short term, the absolute last thing Amelie wanted tossed in her face right now was an I-told-you-so from Jerome Thayer.

When Amelie was growing up, her daddy made no secret that he fully expected to marry off his daughters—especially his firstborn—to men with strong business savvy, strong personalities, and the potential for excellent careers. A man who violated standards faster than he could lower them wasn't noted among the criteria.

But Amelie had turned a deaf ear. She was in love, and love made people know all and forgive all.

Now she found herself married to an unreliable but lovable rascal, and wondering how she got there.

So it was that Amelie did what countless new brides before

her had done: She went home to Mama. Mama would know what Amelie should do.

And Amelie knew this to the marrow of her bones simply because she knew Vonda Kay Thayer.

Her grandmother might be unconcerned with the details of everyday living, but Mama wasn't a thing like her. No, sirree. Mama wasn't one of those helpless women who sailed through life using neediness to fine effect or one easily persuaded to stick her head in a gas oven.

On the contrary, no matter what crisis reared its ugly head, Mama was a fountain of strength and good advice. A rock. An anchor. Living with Daddy wasn't always smooth sailing, but if Mama had ever felt her boat sinking, she never let anyone see how hard she paddled to keep up.

Those were the thoughts holding Amelie together as she slung the strap of her overnight bag across one shoulder and waddled inside her mama's house.

There, she found her grandmother perched on a barstool in the sunlit kitchen reading a thin paperback book. Gauging by her pursed lips and intent focus, she was hard at work studying the pages. *How to Shit in the Woods* stood out in big letters on the cover.

But Miss Ludie's choice of reading material wasn't what struck Amelie as unusual. No, along with oversized Bvlgari sunglasses, her grandmother wore a vestal virgin getup that was impressively weird, even for her.

Amelie briefly considered the psychological subtext staring her in the face and just as quickly decided not to go there.

Like trying to imagine her parents going for a grand time in the backseat of a Volkswagen, some things were simply better left a mystery.

"Hey there, Miss Ludie," Amelie said, chucking her bag in an out-of-the-way corner. "Plannin' a campin' trip?"

"I wanna be ready when the power goes out."

"The power's a problem?"

"Not yet, it ain't."

"Glad to hear it. It's too hot outside to do without air-conditionin', anyway."

Her grandmother nudged the sunglasses down and peered over the dark rim, her rheumy gaze lost in the mists of time. "Who're you again?"

"It's me. Amelie?"

"Are you knocked up?"

"Nope." Amelie patted her pregnant belly. "I'm smuggling watermelons. But I appreciate you noticin'."

"Well, there y'go." Miss Ludie laid her opened book on the table. "I ain't enjoyed watermelon in ages. Think I'll have one with my dinner. Run tell Vonda I'm ready to eat."

"Where is she?"

"Somewheres with those two old ninnies she hangs out with." And she waved a wrinkled hand toward the ceiling.

Identifying the ninnies in question wasn't a stretch, especially since Amelie had grown up with her mama's friends around the house and was well acquainted with her grandmother's opinion of the two women.

"Aunties Tata and Donna Lily?" Amelie cocked her head, listening for any animated voices coming from upstairs. "Y'sure? I didn't see their car."

Neither woman was actually a relative, but that didn't matter. They were close enough. Now that Amelie thought on it, they were closer than some people she *was* related to.

"They've been drinkin'," Miss Ludie said, dropping her voice to a whisper.

"Mama?" Amelie chuckled. "She doesn't drink."

"She does today." Then Miss Ludie made a shooing motion. "Why are you still here? Go on now."

Going in search of, Amelie paused with one foot on the back stair step and sniffed the air.

"Is that paint?"

"Nope." She cackled. "It's your mama's Waterloo."

"Her what?"

"Hurry it up, girlie. I'm hungry."

When Vonda's oldest daughter leaned against the white trim of the laundry room doorjamb, Vonda was busy upending a bottle over the collar of a blouse.

"There you are, Ma," said Amelie. "I've been lookin' for you."

"Been right here, punkin." Vonda smooched her on the cheek. "How ya feelin'?"

"Like two-ton Tilly." Her bottom lip poked out. "And I have cankles today."

Vonda glanced down to assess her daughter's swollen legs. Rather than sporting the nice definition of trim ankle and shapely calf muscle enjoyed by an active woman in her prime, Amelie now walked on stumpy limbs whose ankles and calves had merged into one. Cankles.

"Look on the bright side," Vonda said and scrubbed at the collar. "That won't last much longer. Once the baby comes, your feet'll deflate back to normal. Wait'll you get my age. Cankles become a way of life then. Still don't want to know what you're having?"

"Like I told you, we're doing this the old-fashioned way. No unnecessary tests. No drugs. We'll find out when the baby's born whether it's a boy or a girl."

Vonda upended the bottle on the stain again. "Until then, try to stay off your feet as much as possible."

"Ma?"

"Yes, dear?"

"Is somethin' wrong?"

Guilt, good taste, and parental constraints kept Vonda from ever unloading her troubles on her kids. In this instance, the current unpleasantness lay between husband and wife and didn't involve the girls. Even though Vonda thought Jerome's notion of fidelity had too much elasticity, no matter what else he was, he was still their father.

"What makes you think somethin's wrong, dear?"

"Nothin', except you're using champagne as a stain pretreat." Amelie lifted the bottle out of Vonda's hand and read the label. "Nice choice, too."

Vonda offered a weak grin and said, "I read in the paper that alcohol gets out grease."

"They probably meant rubbin' alcohol, Ma, not drinkin'."

"You think? Well, if the stain doesn't come out, we can always suck on the blouse. Win-win all around." She smiled. Amelie didn't. "Are you sure you're okay, punkin?"

"Sure, I'm sure."

But the dark circles under her daughter's eyes told Vonda a different story. Even if she hadn't read the lie in Amelie's face, her slump-shouldered posture would have given her away. Her whole demeanor made her look like roadkill waiting to happen.

Vonda wasn't one to tease out the truth.

"You and Remy had a fight," she said, more statement than question.

Amelie shook her head. Her eyes misted up and Vonda's heart sank.

"We never fight." Amelie shrugged. "I rant. He listens, adorably clueless, less adorably lubricated. And nothin' changes. Nothin'."

"Oh, sweetheart—"

"We're too opposite, Ma. I like keepin' our bills paid. He likes buyin' drinks for everyone in Malone's. I like us spendin' quiet time at home. He likes goin' out on the boat with the bubbas."

"Fishin' *is* his livelihood, sweetie."

"Not this. He says he's fishin'. What a crock. I can put two and two together and it adds up to him carousin' on the boat. We got us a baby comin', Ma. What am I gonna do with him?"

"You want the truth?"

"No, tell me somethin' that'll make me happy."

"Okay, you look beautiful today."

Amelie kissed Vonda on the cheek.

"Thanks, Ma. Now you can tell me the truth."

"You didn't want my advice before you married him," Vonda said. "Now's a little late to ask, don't you think?"

"Go ahead, say it. It's a match made in hell."

"I wouldn't go that far." Vonda sorely wished she had a few answers, but today, today she was fresh out. So she hugged her daughter instead. "Listen, honey, I know you're scared."

Amelie pulled back from the embrace and scrubbed a knuckle under her nose.

"I wish we could be like you and Daddy."

Before she could stop herself, Vonda spurted out a hollow giggle. "What? United in denial and deception?"

Amelie gave her a watery half-smile.

"Well-to-do and settled," she countered.

Was life really like that? Maybe.

At least, for a while there, Vonda allowed the world to view only that pretty picture of them. In reality, for years Jerome's womanizing was the elephant in the room that neither of them ever wanted to address.

"Enough about us." Vonda wrapped an arm around Amelie's shoulder. "C'mon, let's you and me go find a quiet place and have us a little chat. We haven't done that in quite a while, have we?"

"Not since the weddin'."

"Then we're overdue."

"Vonda!" came a screech from the kitchen. *"Where's my dinner?"*

"Hadn't we better fix Grandma somethin' to eat first?" Amelie said.

Vonda patted Amelie's back gently and then shot down that idea.

"It's high time she learned where the fridge is. Thanks to the deli at Winn-Dixie, there's a plate of collard greens with ham and sweet potato casserole ready to pop in the microwave. I fried her a few pieces of cornbread on the stove early this mornin'."

"Not baked? She won't like that."

"Too bad. It's too hot to fire up the oven."

They were both aware Miss Ludie was a slave to routine. She preferred to eat her big meal at midday, leaving her room for a light supper of leftovers or her favorite standby of baked cornbread crumbled in a thick glass of buttermilk.

For years, Vonda had catered to Miss Ludie according to her schedule, because Jerome expected her to. He reserved the noon meals for schmoozing clients and the evening meals for closing them, and it was simply easier for Vonda to give in than to argue.

On rare occasions, Vonda joined Jerome at the country club or one of the restaurants in town. Most of the time she couldn't. After all, someone had to stay home and make sure Miss Ludie didn't take a notion to donate all their clothes to charity, or burn the house down, or worse, like the time she pledged all their assets to PBS.

And Vonda couldn't count on the girls to step in, either. Between school, work, and their own schedules, they were plenty busy without being saddled with their neurotic grandmother, too.

It had never been Jerome's practice to invite clients home for supper. Vonda had often thought it was to save the embarrassment of subjecting them to his mother's tyranny.

Now Vonda knew differently.

After this morning, she realized Miss Ludie's peculiarities were only the half of it. The other half was that it gave Jerome time to play bachelor and two-step on his wife's head as he was out the door and gone.

"The mess she'll leave that kitchen in will drive you crazy," Amelie said. "Y'know it will."

"No it won't." Vonda's lips formed a tight line. "I won't let it."

"Your nose will grow."

Amelie waited.

"Oh, all right." Vonda tossed the blouse in the direction of the washing machine. "So I'm a wuss. I admit it."

"Don't be too hard on yourself. It was a good try."

"Y'think so?"

"Definitely."

Vonda smooched her daughter on the cheek. Habits were hard to change. She knew the truth in the pit of her stomach: As much as she would like to, she couldn't just ditch Miss Ludie like a bad date.

"Is the downstairs bed clean?" Amelie said.

The question caught Vonda by surprise.

"Why?" she said. "Are you stayin' for a while?"

"How about a few days?"

"A few days?" Vonda echoed, brows furrowing.

"Just until I can sort some things out," Amelie said. "I brought extra clothes."

Vonda guessed her daughter's timing could have been worse. She just wasn't sure how.

"Of course, you can stay," she said with a weak smile. "Stay as long as you like. And as long as you're here, you can help with your grandma."

"Hey, no fair. That's blackmail."

"I know. Isn't it wonderful?"

Amelie grumbled before uttering a clear, "Not really."

"You look tired," Vonda said. "Go on, lie down and rest. I'll tend to your grandma this time. But use the upstairs guest room. I've moved some of your dad's—I mean, some of his junk's in the downstairs bedroom."

"Von-da!" sounded the screech again.

"I swear, one of these days . . . pow! To the moon." Then louder, "Comin', Miss Ludie!"

No sooner had Vonda set a steaming plate of food in front of her mother-in-law than her cell phone started ringing. Miss Ludie squawked something about watermelon, but Vonda wasn't running a restaurant and listened to her complaint with half an ear.

The first call came from her daughter Charlotte, reminding Vonda of a sleepover that had slipped her mind.

"How about cancelin' tonight, sweetheart?" Vonda said. "I was hopin' you and your sisters would have supper here with me."

"Can't y'eat supper with Daddy?"

"Not tonight. You know your father's workin'."

"He's always workin'," Charlotte whined. Then added in a watery voice, "Why y'doin' this t'me? We can eat supper together any old time. Ain't my feelin's important?"

"Aren't. And, of course they are, sweetie. Why are you gettin' upset?"

"There's a skate and everyone'll be there, Mom. Simply everyone. I can't not go." Charlotte's wheedling ended with a direct arrow to Vonda's guilty heart. "You *promised*."

Bull's-eye.

Vonda couldn't recall promising, but brain fog was nothing new anymore.

"If I promised, sweetie, then I guess—"

"Cool. Thanks, Mom." All traces of the waterworks disappeared when Charlotte added, "You're the best. See y'tomorrow. Love ya."

And then she disconnected before Vonda could even say *Love you, too*.

Fast on the heels of Charlotte's call came another from Vonda's youngest daughter, Caroline, the one blessed with a melodramatic flair. She was practically hysterical.

"Where are you, Mom?"

"Italy," Vonda said without hesitating. "Sittin' on the balcony of George Clooney's grand palazzo overlookin' the shores of Lake Como. My, what a beautiful sight. The lake's not bad, either."

"Oh, my God, you're home."

"What gave me away?"

"My life is over, simply over. What are y'doin' home?"

"Well, duh. I'm eating bonbons and watchin' soaps. What else could I possibly have to do but put my feet up and snack on chocolate all day?"

"Y'could do somethin' for the cause," Caroline snapped, "that's what."

Vonda held the receiver away from her ear and stared at the phone as if it had become a snake in her hand. Her first impulse was to give her youngest a dressing-down of epic proportions, but Vonda opted not to face that battle right now, and she decided on diplomacy, instead.

"The cause?" she said, sniffing the air. "Such as?"

Was that smoke she smelled?

"Keep your appointment with Birdlegs. 'Member?"

Appointment?

"You forgot," Caroline said, "didn't you?"

Crap, crap, and double crap.

Vonda bit her lip and responded as any good mother would. She lied.

"No, no, of course not. Appointment with Birdlegs—I mean,

Coach Susan, today. You really shouldn't call her Birdlegs. One of these days we're gonna forget and say it to her face. Now, remind me again why I made this appointment."

"I knew it," Caroline wailed. "I knew you'd forget. I told you all the mothers have t'meet with Birdlegs or we don't go to camp, and you said you'd be there. No camp, no squad."

A mind was a terrible thing to lose. Vonda sucked in a harried breath and kissed good-bye to the mother-of-the-year award.

Was Miss Ludie sneaking a cigarette again?

"Calm down, sweetheart," Vonda said. "I messed up, but not to worry. You'll make it to camp or my name isn't—"

"Whatever, Mom, you're late! And, Mom?"

"Yes, darlin'?"

"Don't even think of takin' Miss Ludie. I caught the weirdo duds she threw on this mornin' and I'm warnin' you, if you take her where anyone I know can see her, I'll die, just die, and I'll never speak t'you again."

"Oh, in that case, I'll make sure you have a nice funeral."

"This ain't funny, Mom!"

"Isn't."

"I mean it! Don't y'dare embarrass me!"

"How about if I just tie your grandmother to the front bumper like roadkill?"

"*Mom—*"

"Okay, okay. I was jokin'. Sheesh. Your sister's here. I'll see if she can help." Slapping her palm over the receiver, Vonda screamed, *"Ame-lie!"*, and then double-timed upstairs to change clothes. "Not to worry. I'm on my way out the door right now."

Five minutes later, dressed in blue Capri pants, a white sleeveless blouse, and white espadrilles, she grabbed her keys and dashed for her car. With her mind on overload, Vonda never stopped to question why none of her immediate family had mentioned her birthday.

6

Life is simpler when you plow around the stumps.
—Old Farmer's Advice

On an ordinary spring day in 1967, Edward Green, Beulah High School's music and art teacher of many years, presented his students with an unintended lesson about life and love.

After instructing his fourth-period class to draw self-portraits, he calmly strolled into the corridor near the white enamel water fountain and the gray metal senior lockers. There, between first and second lunch, he stuck the barrel of a small handgun under his chin.

Then he pulled the trigger.

And missed.

For a man with more degrees than a thermometer, Mr. Green was in bad need of a common-sense fairy to watch over him. But, in short order, he discovered the error in his intentions.

Had he inserted the barrel in his mouth, he would've gotten the deed done and his story would've ended right there. As it was, though, all he accomplished was to blow off his nose, dent his forehead, and give a reason for school to let out early that day.

He also managed to mangle a two-thousand-dollar toupee beyond repair and make himself into a bigger idiot than he already was.

Later, in what was the largest understatement of any journalist's career, the newspaper account stated Green had been upset. For Vonda, *upset* happened when a breezy day ruined a new 'do. Most folks agreed that blowing off a good portion of your own nose qualified as a category-five emotional hurricane.

Gossip attributed Green's purported upset to a failed love affair. That interesting tidbit surprised the stew out of Vonda and his other students, and pretty much anyone else who knew of the man, because no one recalled seeing him dating about town.

So to no one's surprise, except maybe old man Green's, no sooner had he stepped foot out of the hospital than the authorities hustled him off to the state mental facility at Chattahoochee. After all, you had to be nuts to blow your own nose off, right?

The sixties might have been called the decade of free love, but not all love was free, especially in a small Southern town where the Edward Greens of the world weren't embraced or understood. Vonda puzzled this out when it became common knowledge that Edward Green had not only led a secret life, but the reason why he had kept that life a secret.

Truth be told, she hadn't thought of old man Green in eons. But she figured his story popped into her mind now because she had dashed into the high school, panting and all but drooling from the humidity, and run headlong into the person rumor back then had tagged as the object of the lovesick art teacher's affections.

"Oh, hey, Mr. Anthony," Vonda said, skidding to a halt on the same worn beige linoleum floor she'd once trod upon as a mediocre student, back when kerosene trumped whale oil, or so it seemed.

The air inside was still and oppressive, thickened by the aroma of fried chicken. As a cost-saving measure, the school board elected not to run the one-story school's air conditioner in the summer.

Even with the bank of jalousie windows open, the temperature inside the aging brick building was only slightly less warm than it was outside. A body wouldn't know that, though, to see the principal decked out in a dapper brown suit complete with bow tie.

His look and demeanor called to mind an aging thespian: regal bearing, white hair, quiet charm, and passionately reserved.

"It's good to see you, Vonda," Principal Anthony said, extending a liver-spotted hand to steady her. "Everything all right? May I help with something?"

"I'm fine, sir, just headin' over to the gym for a meetin' with Bird—I mean, with Coach Susan—"

He shook his head and said, "Boys' basketball camp is in the gym this week. Cheerleaders meet in the library. I'm glad to see we'll have your Caroline on the squad again this year. A lovely young lady. She brings so much energy and dedication to the team."

"Really? I wish she'd put some of that energy and dedication to helpin' out around the house."

"The bane of being a teenager, and of living with one, I'm afraid."

"Unfortunately. Listen, if I don't make this meetin', she's afraid she may not make the squad."

The principal smiled and said, "She has no worries in that direction. Be sure to tell her."

"Sure thing."

And with a nod of appreciation, Vonda pivoted and headed in the opposite direction.

"Go around by the office," he called. "Repairmen are working the corridor and have it taped off."

Moments later, Vonda had her hand on the double doors leading out to the library building when she was waylaid by a shout.

The owner of the voice turned out to be one of the most durable men in Vonda's life, Terrell Barksdale. Not only was Terrell a reputable architect in one of the largest firms in town, but he was also a childhood friend of Vonda's, which, in the all-men-are-bananas-in-a-bunch factor rendered him bulletproof.

"Well, hey there. What're you up to?" Vonda said, noting his expression cycle from stoically imperious to amused.

"About six-four in my socks," he said.

Vonda rolled her gaze toward the ceiling. "Real cute. Guess I walked right into that one."

"You left yourself wide-open and that's a fact."

With shoulder-length salt-and-pepper hair, an easy tan, and an overdeveloped neck and chest sculpted long ago on the football field, Terrell was imposing-looking and somewhat boyishly handsome. He'd been married once or twice and divorced, no kids, and now had been single for several years. He was also not a slave to fashion, as evidenced by his skintight red golf shirt and wrinkled khaki pants.

He hooked a thumb over his shoulder, in the direction of the office. "I'm just finishing up with some sponsorship details for the firm. Say, isn't today your birthday?"

"No, please," Vonda said, holding up a hand as if warding off evil spirits. "You're not gonna sing, are you? Please tell me you're not."

He laid the palm of his right hand over his heart, poked out his bottom lip, and his expression took on a pained look. "And here I thought you liked my singin'."

"I was bein' polite."

"For thirty years?"

A second's thought and then she nodded. "Pretty much. Yeah."

"You always were a smart-ass," he said, breaking into an earthy chuckle. "Happy birthday, anyway, birthday girl. What are you, thirty-what?"

"It's fifty, and you know it."

He clicked his tongue and said, "Yeah, I thought you were showin' a few signs of wear and tear."

"Gee, thanks."

"No, seriously." He chuckled again. "You make fifty look damned good."

Vonda couldn't help but smile back. Over the last forty-odd years, the relationship between her and Terrell had remained heartfelt and friendly, enough so that Vonda felt a certain easy familiarity and sociability around him.

"You always remember," she said and gave him an affectionate peck on his clean-shaven cheek. He smelled of delicious aftershave and virile man. "You're such a sweetheart, you know that?"

"Is it too soon for this sweetheart to ask you for a date?"

Her smile dimmed.

"I take it back, you're a shithead."

"Hey, I understand," he said, nodding. "You want a minute to think about it. I'm okay with that."

"Try bein' okay with this."

And with righteous ire powered by pride, Vonda moved to leave him eating her dust; except, he sidestepped into her path.

"You mean what I heard this mornin' isn't true?"

"How should I know?" she said. "I'm not a mind reader. I don't know what you heard."

But, doggone, if Vonda couldn't give it a good guess.

"Word is," Terrell said, "you and Jerome had a set-to and split."

Bingo.

"Good lord, now it starts."

Terrell must've read the mortification on her face because he offered a sheepish shrug and added, "Lolo mentioned somethin' to my sister and she happened to tell me when I talked to her this mornin'. I'm sorry, sugar. Y'know how these things go."

"Lolo? Figures. Telegraph, telephone, tell Lolo." Vonda's pride folded like a broken lawn chair and she leaned back against the double doors, endeavoring not to cry buckets. "I was hopin' for a little more time. Are there no secrets around here?"

"Not a one. Gossip flows like sweet tea in this town."

In that brief moment, Vonda felt some of what might have driven old man Green into the nuthouse. She inhaled a calming breath, let it out slowly, and then pushed away from the doors.

"That was rhetorical, Terrell. And for the record, we didn't have a set-to."

"I stand corrected. What was it, then?"

"More a difference in needs, if you must know. I need the horny toad to treat me with respect; he needs to engage in amoral shenanigans with every female who'll let him."

Terrell shook his head. "Makes a body wonder whatever happened to *for better or worse*."

"Nowadays, *better* means a younger version."

"Ouch."

"Is that your professional opinion, or are you speakin' from personal experience?"

"Listen, don't blame me because you got suckered in by a prick with a bad case of the Partridge Family cutes. If you'd married me like I asked, you wouldn't now be—"

"We were six, Terrell. You had your head stuck in your grandmother's banister."

"And don't think your rejection hasn't scarred me for life. I liked to never got my head out, no thanks to you."

"Can I help it if you were born with sugar bowl ears?"

"Watch it, we all had some bad years." His brown eyes were clear and alive. "We're not six now. C'mon, how's about you make it up to me?"

"You've disliked Jerome from the first, haven't you?"

"He's an argument for birth control and that's a fact."

"Seriously, why do you dislike him?"

Terrell dragged in a deep breath, as if deciding how much to reveal.

"Because you're moral and he's not. Never was."

"Is that supposed to make me feel better?"

"You asked. I answered."

"Okay, so I'm gullible."

"In some ways, yes. Now what say we give the prick you're married to some of his own medicine?"

Vonda placed one hand near the base of her throat and batted her eyelashes, giving him her best Scarlett O'Hara.

"Why, sir, are you suggestin' we do somethin' lewd and lascivious?"

"Not me. I wouldn't dream of it."

"Bummer." She dropped the pretense. "Just when I thought I was gonna get lucky."

"At least, not until the second date." Terrell chuckled and added, "Supper's what I had in mind for starters."

"That's all?"

He nodded. "With my crazy schedule, eatin' is hit-and-miss. Anythin' else is a luxury."

Little did Terrell know but Vonda might have considered a torrid affair with him, had he ever asked her.

She grinned and said, "I'm disappointed, but I guess I'll get over it."

"Don't count me out yet, sugar. I may have slowed down, but I haven't thrown in the towel. Start by havin' supper with me tonight? No, never mind. You're probably havin' a party with your family tonight."

Vonda shook her head and said, "Everyone's busy."

"You're kiddin' me."

"They're big kids now, Terrell, not babies. They have their own lives."

"Well, we can't have you celebratin' by yourself, now can we? How about I pick you up at seven? We'll have a leisurely supper, then who knows?"

And he waggled his eyebrows as if he were Groucho Marx.

Vonda laughed and said, "Are you forgettin' your precious schedule?"

"So it'll be a quick supper. I waited years to get Jerome

Thayer's goat, and I'm not about to pass up this chance. After what he's done, you shouldn't, either. Maybe we ought t'go paint the town red. What do you say?"

"Oh, you. Hush up, now." Vonda glanced around with the darting gaze of a middle-aged woman desperate to locate the nearest restroom. "Someone might overhear and think you're serious."

Terrell cocked his head to the side. "But I am serious. As serious as a heart attack." He took her hand in his, holding her fingers lightly and brushing his thumb up and down her knuckles. "Answer my question. What do you say about tonight?"

His fingertips were wonderfully soft to the touch. Vonda studied the planes and contours of his hand, pleasantly aware of his warm regard, of an unacknowledged yearning to feel desirable to a man again, rather than inconsequential, invisible, and excluded.

Terrell's suggestion managed to excite and unnerve Vonda despite her better judgment.

"I don't think that's a good idea," she said, reluctantly freeing her hand from his warm grasp and gesturing toward the library. "I've got to go. There's a meetin' of the cheerleader moms. Good to see you, Terrell."

As she wheeled around to the double doors, she heard him toss out a challenge.

"Chicken."

"Excuse me?"

"You heard me. Bock, bock, bock."

Vonda faced him again full-on.

"Anybody ever tell you," she said, hand on hip, "you can be a pain in the patoot?"

"It's been mentioned a time or two within my hearin'." Then Terrell grinned. "Tell me you've got somethin' better to do, and I'll leave you to it."

Vonda was painfully aware of having nothing better to look forward to than spending her fiftieth birthday and all her birthdays to come catering to Miss Ludie. Damn if she'd admit it to Terrell Barksdale, though. But the words to argue with him stuck in her throat.

"That's what I thought," Terrell said.

"Okay, I admit it—I've always loved your enthusiasm." Vonda crossed her arms over her chest. "If I say yes—and that's a big if—it would be two old friends sharin' a meal and nothin' more."

"Two old friends sharin' a meal," he repeated. "Nothin' could be more innocent."

She had never done anything so foolish in her life. Jerome didn't know that, though. Did he?

Her night out would give him a conniption fit, if for no other reason than he and Vonda coexisted amicably in a well-established rut and now she was changing the rules.

Maybe that's why saying yes felt so good.

"Old is right," she muttered, "and you haven't been innocent in years."

"It's settled then," Terrell said and winked. "Seven o'clock."

Vonda nodded before she lost her nerve.

"But don't come by the house and pick me up," she said. "Let's meet somewhere."

"What? You don't trust me to be a good boy?"

She gave him a helpless shrug.

"Who said you could trust me to be a good girl?"

Move over Edward Green.

7

*Don't interfere with somethin' that ain't
botherin' you none.*
—Old Farmer's Advice

If Amelie were staring at a young woman in a strapless red sequined dress and stiletto heels on her own doorstep, the sight would prompt the question, "What's Remy gone and done this time?"

But a wheezing old man standing on her mama's front verandah in the waning daylight, wearing nothing but an ill-fitting strapless red sequined dress and an oxygen tank, that sight prompted the question, "What fresh hell is this?"

Before the doorbell had rung, Amelie had been in the middle of fixing Miss Ludie a margarita, her favorite evening toddy, because Mama had left several minutes ago to join a friend for dinner. Amelie now licked sticky lime juice off her fingers, fascinated in a morbid sort of way as she took in the gaunt angles standing before her and the nasal cannula stretched across jaundiced cheeks.

His jogging shoes were unlaced, one tongue lolling to the side, the other tongue protruding into the air, as if they were trying to escape his feet. His hands were shaky, with nicotine-stained fingernails. And on his bony chest perched an amazing work of art that captured Amelie's attention: a colorful peacock with the stylized initials LT emblazoned across the center.

He looked at her through tired eyes, watery and red, and pointed to his tattoo.

"You like this?"

"Very much," Amelie said, nodding.

"So did I at the time. I was stinkin' drunk."

She didn't need to ask her visitor's name.

Even though she hadn't seen her grandfather for a couple of years, she recognized the supreme confidence and arrogance borne of age, gender, and sheer crust. Not to mention, except for the ink and his regimen of Botox injections, her father stood in the old coot's reflection.

Nothing but two beat-up suitcases waited beside her grand-father, which struck her as a sad lot to show for a lifetime of living. Had Cletus Thayer been into cross-dressing the last time she saw him?

Amelie thought not. It was the kind of thing she felt certain she would've noticed.

Why now and why here was a tale Amelie instinctively sensed few in her family were prepared to deal with.

"Y'know, there's a pencil-thin line between trashy and

sexy, and I must say, Grandpa, you're trottin' along it like a champ."

"Why, thank you, kindly." He smiled through a phlegmy cough that sounded as if he were hawking up a lung. "Amelie, isn't it?"

"Sure is. I'm flattered you remember. Here, let me help you inside."

"I always remember a pretty lady," he said, waving away her offer, "even when she's filled out some."

Amelie recognized the power of pride and let him have his way, stifling the urge to roll her gaze heavenward. She suspected her grandfather's career as a transvestite probably began and ended right there with the unpleasant surprise on her face.

Compelled to see how big a train wreck his sudden arrival on her mama's doorstep would turn out to be, she threw the door open wider and stepped back, welcoming him into the house.

Beyond his shoulder, she noticed a black-and-white checkered cab waiting at the end of the driveway with its motor running. A nondescript young man in baggy jeans and faded T-shirt leaned his backside against the passenger door, his arms crossed over his chest, his foot tapping a rhythm only he could hear.

Cletus offered no explanation. He simply patted down the sequins, and said, "No pockets, little gal. Can I impose upon you t'gimme a hand with the cabbie?"

"Sure. I—I guess so."

"Much obliged."

"How much you need?"

She reached to her side, for the tin full of silver coins her parents kept on the nearby foyer table for small emergencies, such as student candy bar sales and delivery tips.

"All considered," Cletus said, "oh, about four and a quarter ought t'do it, I reckon."

"No problem. Four dollars?"

"Not quite, darlin'. Four *hundred* dollars."

"Holy cow! Where'd you catch the cab, Gramps, Atlanta?"

But Cletus's mind had raced ahead of her. He was already moving under his own steam, dragging his oxygen tank across the threshold.

"Grab those, will you?" he said, gesturing with his chin toward the suitcases.

Amelie could only gawk, speechless, as he proceeded to take up residence in Casa Jerome.

"Got any beer in the fridge?" he said, his voice growing fainter as he moved deeper down the hall. "Sandwich wouldn't hurt none, neither. If you was to offer, little gal, I could choke down a bite or two . . ."

Fast on the heels of her surprise at such grit, Amelie heard Miss Ludie erupt like Mount Vesuvius, spewing a molten tirade into the air that climaxed in a welter of unflattering, if not inventive, names. Amelie got the distinct impression not much would redeem the old man in his ex-wife's eyes, short of a trip to Lourdes.

She snatched her cell phone out of her pocket and started dialing. Oh, yes, this evening promised to be a doozie.

8

*If you find yourself in a hole, the first thing
to do is stop diggin'.*
—Old Farmer's Advice

Like much of the South, Beulah County was lousy with historical landmarks and buildings.

Among them was the Beulah County Country Club. It was old and established, a place of ritual and restraint, where heat set the pace and humidity set the rhythm of life.

It was also a world all its own, one that honored Southern character and history by marrying tradition with a fondness for cash. Rich mahogany, lush carpeting, snotty waiters in black ties and white coats, and old money were staples.

Inside, chandeliers dripping with Swarovski crystals emphasized the elegance of an overpriced main dining room that was filled with museum-quality gilded mirrors and hand-painted finishes. Tables were topped with starched hunter green linens, antique Rosenthal china, and etched Waterford vases filled daily with fresh-cut flowers coordinated to the season.

A wall of floor-to-ceiling windows led outside to an infinity-edged swimming pool, flanked by flagstone patios and lighted citronella torches that surrounded market umbrellas standing sentinel over teakwood tables. One patio looked out over a well-manicured ornamental garden green, perfect for sneaking a quick puff or an impromptu make-out session, and the other patio overlooked a lighted koi pond with a waterfall and lush vegetation. No fishing allowed.

Beyond it all lay a world without pretension, one with humbler ambitions, where no grass grew, only weeds, natural scrub oak, and pine that jutted out of sandy ground in odd directions. The dense growth around their trunks was a choked jungle of cogangrass, kudzu, thorny vines, and catclaw briars. No sprinkler system ran there, just the unrelenting white-hot sun during the day baking the bark gray and leeching the color from dry leaves.

The blistering sun had set for the day. Twilight rode a soft southerly breeze that ushered in a balmy evening. Easy-listening music played in the background, while bats from nearby conservatories silently swept the air clear of mosquitoes.

Jerome sat inside the air-conditioned dining room, across from a window with its scenic vista, ordering a moneyed matron her third vodka Collins with anchovy-stuffed olives. No pomtini, appletini, or sissytini of any kind for this old gal.

He was employing his best snake-oil approach to close her on a fifteen-hundred-acre horse farm, when the persnickety maître d' leaned down and whispered in his ear. Only the dismal prospect of donning a neon orange jumpsuit for one to five years kept Jerome from strangling the man for lousy timing.

"Will you excuse me?" Jerome said to his client. "A family matter requires my immediate attention. I won't be but a minute." He slid a colored brochure across the tablecloth, underneath which lay a preliminary sales agreement that lacked only a signature. "In the meantime, picture yourself at home."

Then he gave the bleating old sheep his best killer smile, the one that could advertise teeth-whiteners. This was a 3.5-million-dollar deal, and Jerome was taking no prisoners.

Once clear of the table, he dropped the smile. He buttoned his seersucker jacket and waded through the high-end summer renters as he worked the locals crowding the dining room, eventually making his way to where the maître d' had his head together with the sommelier.

"Where the hell is she?" Jerome said, barely containing his impatience.

"The patio, sir."

"Dammit, man, don't play games. Which side?"

Jerome bristled at his own show of asperity. He'd adopted a staid and cultured public persona so long ago, he'd almost made it a reality.

Almost.

"I do beg y'pardon, sir, for failing to be clear. Mrs. Thayer and her guest are seated on the pond side."

Jerome's nostrils flared at the man's intellectual pretension, but that was the least of his worries.

"Guest?" Jerome said. "This guest wouldn't happen to be wearin' a nun's habit, would she, or any other strange outfit?"

"Why, no, sir. Nothing strange in the least."

"That's a lucky break."

"Sir?"

"Nothin'. Never mind."

By way of apology for his earlier curtness, Jerome thrust a folded bill into the man's hand before skirting the dining room to the nearest glass doors.

It wasn't often that Vonda surprised him, but she had surprised the hell out of him today, and the surprises kept coming. Something Jerome wasn't at all sure he liked had gotten into his little wife.

And he had the awful feeling she was about to upset his delicately balanced applecart.

Vonda made her metaphorical leap to freedom when she pulled into the shade of the country club's colonnaded porte cochere scant minutes behind Terrell and left the teen-aged valet to park her four-year-old SUV.

A shapely young thing, looking not much older than Caroline, ushered her to their table, where a waiter was already pouring two glasses of Argentinean Malbec.

"Just in time," Terrell said. "Hope you don't mind the patio?"

Mind? Silly man.

For this small mercy, Vonda sent up a silent thanks to the hot-flash gods.

The table sat in the shadow of the koi pond, which meant the mist from the waterfall cooled the surrounding air several degrees. Let Terrell assume the moisture on her skin came from the overspray, rather than from sweat glands gone haywire for lack of hormones.

"Not at all," she said and smiled. "This is lovely."

And it was. But even if it wasn't, without a reservation, she could hardly complain.

As Vonda was seated, "Fifty Ways to Leave Your Lover" floated out of the patio speakers. She caught a brief reflection of herself in the far window, and a harmless little thrill swept through her.

Who was that brunette in the slinky black dress and what had she done with Vonda?

Not far from where she and Terrell dined, one of the tables displayed all the hallmarks of an engagement fete. She watched the smiling and laughing faces through melancholy eyes and saw her own youth as a young couple raised their glasses, celebrating a dream, a vision of a bright future that Vonda knew was merely illusion.

At another table, a white-haired couple dined alone in quiet contemplation, never taking their eyes off one another.

"Earth to Vonda," Terrell said, sipping his wine.

His voice cut through her mind fog and she dragged her attention back to him.

"Excuse me," she said, fishing her cell phone out of her purse. She wanted to keep it handy should Amelie need her. "I'm sorry. What were you sayin'?"

"You were a million miles away."

"I guess I was."

"How do you feel?"

Vonda reached across the table and placed her hand atop Terrell's.

"You're the first person who's asked, Terrell. The only person, actually."

"We've known each other a lot of years. I care about you. You know that?"

"I do," she said, nodding, "and I appreciate your friendship."

His thumb played with her fingers as he repeated, "So how do you feel?"

She ducked her gaze to the tabletop, thinking about what he was really asking.

"Like I'm not on intimate terms with common sense," she said. "Like my self-esteem is nonexistent. Like I'm a hundred percent moron and then some for wastin' twenty years on Jerome Thayer."

"Only twenty?"

Vonda lifted her wineglass with her free hand and said over the rim, "Give or take a few decent years scattered in there."

"Too few to mention, if you ask me."

She returned her glass to the table. "Are you gonna be obnoxiously judgmental tonight?"

"Perish the thought. I'm never judgmental."

Terrell punctuated that assessment with a large swallow of wine and a signal to a hovering waiter for menus.

"Don't get me wrong," Vonda said. "Jerome didn't get to this point by himself. He had help from me, his mother, from fate."

"Quit makin' excuses for him."

"I'm not makin' excuses. I'm tryin' to be fair."

"Why?"

"Beats me," she said with a shrug. "Habit, I guess. I'm his wife."

Terrell smiled and upended the wine bottle to refill their glasses.

"An accident of timin'," he said. "One easily corrected."

For a moment, Vonda let herself think about the questions running in her mind.

"I wish . . ." she said.

"Yes? Go on."

"I wish there was a magic formula to explain why we fall for the people we do."

"Darlin' girl." Terrell leaned forward, shaking his head. "Daytime television is wholly fueled by poor saps askin' the same question, comin' up with the same answer."

"Which is?"

"Simple. It's the law of averages. Guys are hardwired to say anythin' to make their life easier. Say it enough times to enough women and one is bound to take the bait. Stay the night with me, move in with me, marry me—they all mean the same thing."

"A surefire good time?" she ventured.

"Take care of me," he corrected.

"Really?"

"You think I'm makin' this up?"

"It's just, I figured guys thought about sex every six seconds."

"We do. Sex is part and parcel of *takin' care*. Don't y'see? We're not as complicated as women try to make us. Know what your problem is, Von?"

"I suppose you'll tell me."

"Y'got a good heart, that's your problem. You overlook negatives, never seein' a guy for who he is."

Vonda's mind felt wrapped in a blanket. She hadn't expected such a frank and joyless vivisection of her life.

"Let's drop it, Terrell, okay?" she said. "I'd rather not psychoanalyze my marriage anymore tonight. It's spoilin' the evenin'."

He raised a hand in surrender.

"If that's what you want—"

"It is."

"Fine. Then what should we talk about?"

"Anythin'. You. How are you doin'?" She reluctantly slid her hand from Terrell's and sat back in her chair. "Tell me, why haven't you found a nice girl and settled down?"

"I did, if you recall. Twice."

She accepted the menu board the waiter handed her and began perusing the evening's specials.

"I'm serious," she said.

"So am I. I'm also a sixty-hour-a-week desk jockey."

"But still a good catch."

"Why, thank you, ma'am." He lifted his wineglass in salute. "I may call upon you one day for a recommendation."

"In writin'?"

"In triplicate and notarized. I need all the endorsements I can get."

She dismissed that saying, "There are plenty of women out there who'd jump at the chance for a guy like you."

"Not as many as you'd think are willin' to put up with my long hours." Terrell dipped his chin and added, "Even if I had time for datin', which I don't, it's tough findin' a suitable woman."

Vonda almost choked on her wine.

"Suitable?" she said. "Wow, now that's romantic."

"Romance is overrated."

"I didn't get the memo on suitable. Just what does it entail?"

"Oh, I don't know. A woman who's challengin', vibrant, creative, one who's dedicated to somethin' besides herself, and competent. She must be competent."

"So quirky's out?"

"Definitely. Please." He made a slicing motion with his hand in front of his nose. "I've had it up to here with women who're liberated from all common sense."

"And passion? That's not on your list, either."

"A passionate woman?" He gave a low snort. "In our age bracket, Von, they're an anomaly. Most are filled with misanthropic opportunism."

"Seriously?" She thought about that for a moment. "Is that why older men fall over themselves for younger women?"

"Could be one reason."

"Do you blame them? Older women, I mean? The way I figure it, by the time a woman's gotten some age and maturity to her, she's learned to appreciate honesty and directness. To ask for what she wants."

"Demand is more like it."

"Demandin' doesn't make her a bad person. Listen, if she's demandin', it's probably because she's already horse-traded too many years to a Southern demigod."

As Vonda spoke, she saw Terrell's gaze wander over her head. A flash of anger lit the architect's eyes for half an instant before he vanquished the blaze behind a strong internal code and a lifetime of good manners.

"Jerome's behind me," she said without turning around, "isn't he?"

His gaze still intent beyond her, Terrell nodded and said, "He's headed this way, lookin' like someone pissed in his cereal."

"You're enjoyin' this, aren't you?"

"You betcha, sweetheart. How about I drag him out back to the parkin' lot and bitch slap him a few times?"

"Don't be silly."

"Aw, c'mon. Just a couple."

Knowing it would look to Jerome as if she were engaged in intimate conversation, she leaned in toward Terrell and then whispered to him, "Behave yourself."

Vonda was still posing when she sensed Jerome at her elbow, waiting for her attention. She glanced back over her shoulder and saw flames shooting out of his ears, igniting the night with fireballs.

Okay, so it was an easy mistake to make. The people at the engagement table behind him were yukking it up and marking their happy occasion with flash cameras against the grainy darkness.

Jerome loomed over her table, not a crease on him, filling out his whole suit. Apparently, he found the architect as interesting as a plastic sack but still managed to instill a ring of suspicion in his voice.

"Barksdale," he said.

Terrell dipped his chin in acknowledgment, offering an equally chilly, "Thayer."

Then Jerome turned his predictable and familiar gaze on his wife, sucking her down a black hole and draining every bit of positive energy from her.

This time, though, there was a rankling certainty in the way he said her name. "Vonda . . ."

The sound sent starch up her spine.

"Yes, Jerome?" she said, tilting her head and flashing him her best smile.

"What are you doin' here?" he said.

"Alignin' my chi."

Obviously, he had expected her to gather her purse and head to the house without question. That wasn't happening. His eyes widened and a flush crept up from his neck to his forehead, as if he were embarrassed that his wife had become uncontrollable.

"Your what?"

In her peripheral vision, she caught Terrell gnawing on a heel of fresh bread, probably to keep from laughing.

"Spiritual energy," she said, pleasantly aware of Jerome's discomfort. "I'm renewin' my life force. You should try it sometime. I suppose you're havin' a business supper?"

"Yes. I'm closin' on the old Taylor place."

"That's a lovely farm. I hope your client enjoys livin' there."

"I believe she will. She's inside waitin' on me."

"Then don't let us keep you." Vonda dismissed him with a careless wave. "Run along."

But Jerome stood there.

"This shouldn't take long," he said, "then I'll be headin' to the house."

"Good for you. I'm sure your mother will enjoy spendin' an evenin' with you."

"I'll come back to get you in a few minutes. Be ready."

"No, no. I'm fine. We're just fixin' to enjoy a leisurely supper. Besides, I've got my own car."

Jerome leaned down to her ear and said very softly, very nicely, "May I have a word with you . . . in private? *Now*."

"Vonda?" Terrell said, pushing his chair back and making to rise.

"Keep your seat, Barksdale," Jerome snapped. "This is between husband and wife."

"It's okay, Terrell." Knowing she couldn't put Jerome off any longer, she grabbed her cell phone, afraid she wouldn't notice it vibrate otherwise, and rose from her seat. "Excuse me. I won't be but a minute." And she walked to a secluded corner of the patio, out of earshot of the other diners.

Jerome said, "Just what do you think you're doin'?"

"You tell me," Vonda said. "You're the big-dicked genius here."

"I'm bustin' my hump for you day in and day out, and this is what I get?"

"Want to talk about humpin', lover boy? Fine—"

But the buzzing vibrations of two different cell phones interrupted her. Jerome yanked his cell phone from his coat pocket and scanned the tiny screen.

"Cripes, it's Mother," he said. "I'll call her back later." And he stuffed his phone back in his pocket.

Vonda checked her screen and said, "Amelie here." She glanced up at her husband, her teeth worrying the inside of her lip. "Do you suppose the baby . . . ?"

Miss Ludie and Amelie both trying to reach them could mean only one thing: Something had happened at home.

Something bad had happened.

9

You cannot unsay a cruel word.
—Old Farmer's Advice

Nothing says love to a child like parents going ten rounds in the middle of the living room, especially elderly parents who had a hundred years of crap between them to sling into the fan.

To Vonda's way of thinking, the bout was a long time coming and definitely more fun to anticipate than to witness, which helped to explain why she opted to pitch camp in the den with Amelie soon after parking her SUV and sprinting into the house through the garage door.

Jerome had elected to remain at the country club, leaving Vonda on her own to muck through his dirty work, and she wasn't looking forward to the chore. God forbid anything should throw a wrench into his business deal.

"Don't look at me," he had said to her, gesturing in the

general direction of the table where his horse farm client waited. "I'm fixin' to close this property for a nice chunk of change, and I'll lose a shitload if I don't get back there right now."

"Oh, no y'don't," Vonda said, grabbing his coat sleeve as he made to turn away. "They're your parents; I'm only related by marriage."

"Plenty close enough."

"*What?* I don't think so. Blood is thicker than water, which makes it your turn in the barrel, not mine."

Jerome's face puckered into a scowl. He crossed his arms over his chest and said, "You're ridiculous, you know that? Someone's out here supportin' this family, while someone else is out here putzin' around." He uncrossed his arms and jerked on his lapels to straighten his coat. "You've got it dicked, so quit complainin'."

"I'm not complainin', you are," she snapped, then glanced over her shoulder to see if any of the other diners had overheard her outburst. No one seemed to notice, so she lowered her voice and added between gritted teeth, "And I don't spend my time putzin' around, here or anywhere else."

"Gimme a break," Jerome said. "We've been down this road before: I work, and you do everythin' else." Then, before she could stop him, he had whirled her around toward the door and patted her backside. "Now, there's a good girl. Go handle things at home."

By the time she pivoted on her expensive eel-skin high heel, he had walked off, leaving her either to pitch a hissy fit right there in the middle of everyone's salad course or quietly go home and try to pacify Miss Ludie in her latest meltdown.

Jerome knew damned well Vonda wouldn't make a scene in a public place. Knew it and counted on it.

Vonda fumed.

The sorry truth was that he was right. She didn't know how to do anything other than be a housewife, and she sure wouldn't get much on that lousy paycheck. The yearly salary for playing Betty Crocker couldn't buy a ménage à trois with Juan Valdez and his donkey.

Now, as Vonda hovered in the den, thinking about the exchange between them set her teeth on edge. She told herself she caved for the sake of family harmony, but, in all honesty, she relented out of habit more than anything else.

Amelie lounged on the oxblood-red sofa. A multicolored crocheted afghan lay across her lap as she watched a silly sitcom rerun on the big screen television.

A hunter green brocade footstool propped up her swollen bare feet, and a clear plastic bowl rested on the precious mound that was Vonda's grandchild to be. The mouthwatering aroma of popcorn filled the air.

Next to Amelie, elbow-deep into the popcorn and paying no attention to what was afoot, slouched what looked to Vonda like the crypt-keeper's grandson. His zit-covered face, ill-fitting jeans, and faded T-shirt helped fix the analogy in her mind.

Because she had never clapped eyes on the string-bean kid before, she figured he probably belonged to the checkered cab parked on the street in front of the house.

"Are you okay?" she asked Amelie.

"Fine, Ma, a little tired is all."

Then Vonda hooked her thumb over her shoulder, in the direction of the verbal bombs being lobbed in the living room.

"How long has that been goin' on?"

"Oh, about fifty-eight years, give or take."

"I meant how long right now."

"Since 'fore I called y'all. I thought sure Grandpa was gonna die ugly, but I reckon Miss Ludie's runnin' out of steam now." Amelie shook her head. "To listen to 'em, it's a mystery he ever got a chubby for her in the first place."

"Amelie Thayer Broussard! Is that any way to talk about your grandparents?"

"What?" Amelie's face reflected pure innocence. "I'm just sayin'."

"Well, thank your stars those two did get together, sweetie, or you wouldn't be here."

"You can pick your friends," Amelie said as if quoting scripture, "but you're stuck with your relatives."

Vonda lowered her voice, saying, "He isn't in there with one of his floozies, too, is he?"

Amelie scrunched up her nose and made a singsong noise in her throat.

"Depends on what the meanin' of *is* is."

Bowing her head, Vonda attempted to marshal some patience before marching into the melee.

"You watch entirely too much C-SPAN," she said.

Then an errant thought came to mind and she looked at the crypt-keeper's grandson.

Crap. Was the meter still running?

"Young man," she said. "Are you waitin' to settle on cab fare by any chance?"

The kid dragged his attention away from the teenaged silliness on the television and mumbled, "Cash or check, no credit cards," through a full mouth.

"Okay, give me a minute," Vonda said on a tired breath. "I'll fetch my wallet."

"You wish," Amelie said. She dug into the popcorn, coming up with a fistful. "Fetch your checkbook."

Two-thirty in the morning saw Vonda standing barefoot at the sink in the moonlit kitchen, a gas bubble the size of Texas lurching behind her tonsils. The joy of night sweats was upon her, leaving her restless, wringing-wet in pastel pink shortie pajamas, and chewing antacids like they were Chicklets.

She remained there at the counter—heart-searching, as her late grandmother used to call it—contemplating what could have been, what might have been, wishing she hadn't put so much stock in young love once upon a time, and debating whether depilatory creams or a weed whacker worked better for the witchy white hairs she'd newly discovered sprouting from her chin like an uninvited forest.

Maybe she could lie flat in the lawn and have someone run

her over once a week with the John Deere mower? Sure, why not. The idea had merit, for that would take care of the beard and the hairy legs in one swipe. She was all about multitasking.

Vonda felt the air-conditioning whisper across her over-heated skin; even so, beads of sweat trickled down her jawline. She took a dish towel and mopped her face and neck.

If this was what aging was about, it sucked the big one. And not much in the day's soap opera drama helped to change that opinion.

She hoped not to see a day like this one again anytime soon.

Vonda had always been conservative, not prone to impul-sive decisions or rash actions. She'd always felt comfortable in a traditional role, perhaps somewhat idealistic. Then again, she'd always thought lofty speeches heralded change, too.

Four score and seven years ago . . . Ask not what your country . . . I have a dream . . . Those were the kinds of words that soaked into our ears and enlarged our lives.

But tonight Vonda realized how wrong her thinking was. Sometimes life-altering events arrived on the wings of quiet phrases and simple words. *I do . . . It's a girl . . .*

Grandpa's home.

That was how simply Amelie had stated it on the phone.

Grandpa's come home, Ma, and, from the looks of him, he ain't got anywhere else to go.

Like mother, like daughter. Jerome wasn't going to be happy with Vonda. No, not one bit.

The thought made her smile.

She belched, wishing she could fix life's problems just as easily and with as much welcome relief. But the more she learned about men, the less she understood. One minute they were vowing lasting love and other messy emotions, and the next minute they were planning their escape.

The soft creak of the French door opening behind Vonda interrupted her heartburn-induced melancholy. Immediately following the creak came a soft thud, the abrupt jiggle of a cat toy, and then a squiffy voice mumbling something about tossing a sack into the bayou for the gators.

She knew without turning who was creeping into the house so late.

"No need to skulk, Jerome," she said, her voice dropping like a tin pan into the quiet.

A bloodless gasp sounded, then a rushed, "Holy shit! Woman, you scared the bejeebers out of me. Whatcha doin'? Waitin' up for me?"

He was as lit as a Christmas tree.

"Don't flatter yourself," she said. "I've got a sour stomach. It must've been the sumptuous dinner I didn't get to eat."

She glanced over her shoulder to see her husband's familiar silhouette in the doorway but, apparently, the booze had made him slow on the uptake. His only reaction to her sarcasm was an attempt to scratch the tip of his nose.

"Well, shut the door and c'mon in," she said, taking in his disheveled appearance. His coat was slung over one arm, his tie unknotted and hanging loose around his opened shirt collar. "The coast is clear. They've both gone on to bed."

"*Both?* Together?"

Now there was an image to scare anybody into celibacy.

"Be real, will you?" she said.

Jerome closed the door, not even trying for quiet this time, plopping his shoes on the tile floor next to the braided doorway rug in the process.

"And I wasn't skulkin'," he said, flicking on the overhead light.

"Of course you were. I know skulkin' when I see skulkin'."

Vonda blinked at the sudden glaring brightness and then squinted until her eyes acclimated.

"Was not," he said.

"Were, too." She made a point of staring at his shoeless feet. "What do you call it, then?"

His indolent gaze followed hers to his bare socks.

"Bein' considerate," he said. "People are sleep—no, wait a minute." He snapped his head up. "Did you say *they've* gone to bed?"

"Yep, sure did."

"*They?* Y'mean he's still here?"

"He had nowhere else to go."

"So? That's not my problem. Pack his lazy ass up and send him back to the nursin' home."

"Can't. They kicked him out."

By now, she could see Jerome was red-faced and flustered and wobbling in his socks. He seemed to be catching every third word and scrubbed his fingers from forehead to chin, as if trying to clear the fog. Space-cadet fuzziness Vonda understood only too well.

"Out?" he said.

"Out," she repeated. She nodded and waggled her fingers. "See y'all. Bye-bye. Adios. Don't call us, we'll call you—"

"Why," Jerome said, "for cryin' out loud?"

"For refusin' to go quietly into that good night." Vonda paused for dramatic effect. "Not to mention the smokin', drinkin', and sneakin' in hookers, which seems to be not only a health and safety hazard and a social no-no but against nursin' home policy, too. They invited your daddy not to come back." Then she smacked her forehead with the heel of her palm. "Go figure."

She deemed it way too early in the morning hours to wallow in detail, especially the part about her father-in-law showing up on their doorstep one miniskirt away from being a drag queen. Lord only knew what the owner of the red dress ended up wearing besides a smile and a sunburn.

No way Vonda was inquiring, either.

Jerome mumbled again under his breath, then said, "That son of a . . . he suckered you right in. He's always had nowhere to go. Let him go nowhere somewheres else."

Vonda crossed her arms and threw back her shoulders.

"Are you listenin' to yourself?" she said.

"What about my mother?" Jerome said, and Vonda thought it was high time he got around to asking after her. "How's she dealin'?"

"Not well." Vonda sighed, exasperated. "She's bound and determined to skewer herself on the sword of martyrdom."

Jerome's mouth drooped at the corners and he looked miserable. Not as miserable as he deserved, but enough of a sad sack to melt some of Vonda's annoyance.

Against all sane thought, she felt sorry for him, which was a remarkable feat, considering. No way did Vonda want to feel sorry, but it was happening anyway.

His parents were his cross to bear, and why she should sympathize with his plight was beyond her. But she did.

Her mood evaporated into familiar resignation. She reached into the flatware drawer and removed two sterling silver table-spoons, then bumped the drawer shut with her hip.

"Did you land the deal?" she said, padding to the freezer.

"W-what?"

"The horse farm." She rooted around the freezer contents before teasing a pint of real ice cream out of its hiding place in the back, behind the Weight Watchers boxes, where she'd put it when Jerome's mother wasn't looking. "Did your client buy the acreage?"

Jerome nodded, must have realized Vonda couldn't see him, not with her head stuck in the freezer, so he said louder than he needed to, "Lock, stock, and moldy hay bales."

"Pipe down," she said, turning with one finger to her lips. "You'll wake the whole house."

He patted his shirt pocket and in a forceful whisper said, "I've got a deposit check right here for three hundred thou-sand. Three hundred smackeroos. Yes, sirree."

Vonda had to admit her husband was an excellent salesman if a lousy husband.

"Congratulations," she said and meant it.

"Why, thank you, kind lady. Wait—I know. Let's celebrate. You and me and the bottle of Cristal I've been savin'. How's that sound? It's in the bar—"

Vonda shook her head, saying, "All gone."

"Gone? Y'sure?"

"Oh, yeah. I'm very sure."

That got him shaking his head, and Vonda could guess he was racking his brain to remember for which occasion they'd polished off the champagne. She let the guilty moment pass without volunteering a clue.

"Damn," Jerome finally said. "I must be gettin' old."

"Yeah, I know. Age plays nasty tricks with memory."

About then, his knees came unhinged and he crumpled into the nearest cane-backed chair, muttering English as if he suffered from Tourette's.

Vonda tore a couple of paper towels off the roll, then slid onto a seat opposite him at the breakfast nook and deposited the ice cream and extra spoon in the center of the table.

"Are we celebratin' anyway?" Jerome said.

"Such as it is."

Without waiting for an invitation, he grabbed the spoon and treated himself by bulldozing right into the comfort food.

"I don't like this," he said.

"Since when? It's Chunky Monkey. Your favorite."

"Not *this*." He gestured to the ice cream and frowned. "You know what I mean . . . the old man . . . your date . . ."

Vonda fixed a knowing smile on her face and proceeded to dare the devil to come out to play.

"Tough petunias," she said and licked the soupy remnants of ice cream off her spoon. "You told me to handle things at home, so I did. If you don't like my decision, hubby dearest, then maybe you should've been here to take care of your mother and daddy yourself."

Jerome opened his mouth to argue but took one gander at Vonda's set jaw and saw the door close on further conversation in that area. She leaned across the table so her face was inches from his. He smelled like a gin mill and needed a shave.

"You owe me," she said. "Big time."

He clamped his mouth shut and nodded.

Satisfied, she sat back, adding, "And, for your information, I wasn't on a date."

"Tell Barksdale that."

"Oh, please. Now who's being ridiculous?" She jabbed the air repeatedly with her spoon. "I've known Terrell all my life. Besides, you go out all the time. Why shouldn't I once in a while?"

"Because you're a wife and a mother. Your place is at home."

Vonda became very still. Her face got hot, and her throat tightened up.

"My place?" she said, her voice turning to vinegar. "*My place?* I don't think you wanna go there."

She had the ice cream spoon cocked and aimed again.

A boozy grin spread across Jerome's face then, and he said, "Does this mean a blow job is out of the question?"

Vonda snorted, trying not to laugh. He always did have a knack for throwing her ire off balance.

"Miscreant," she said. "What do you think?"

He looked up at her, relaxed, blue-eyed, and soused. She kneaded her forehead and watched him a moment as he scarfed down more ice cream, ready to gauge his reaction.

"I was at the Grand Motel yesterday morning," she finally said.

"So? I was, too. I didn't see you there."

"I know. But I saw you."

Jerome hesitated a second, then shrugged, saying, "Is that what all this is about? I have to show property to sell property."

Vonda snorted again.

"You don't believe me?" Jerome said, lines overtaking his forehead.

"Oh, I believe . . . I believe you're a lyin' sack of shit." She stated it matter-of-factly, not as an invitation to argue. "Are you ever goin' to grow up?"

"Quit your preachin'," Jerome said. "I'm in no mood."

"When are you ever? I'm tryin' to talk about us here."

"We've been together . . . what? . . . twenty-five, twenty-six years? What's to talk about?"

"Try thirty years come November."

"Whatever." Jerome tossed his spoon into the carton and caught her off guard again when he said, "Okay, talk. Get it off your chest. I'm listenin'."

"Are you?" Vonda leaned forward, almost afraid to hope. "Are you really?"

"Yeah, sure. What else have I got to do at three in the mornin'?"

Elbows on the table, he steepled his fingers, then rested his chin on them, his gaze fixed on her face. It took her a moment to gather her thoughts under such scrutiny and, when she did, her voice came out soft, distant.

"I wanted to say I'm tired of it, Jerome. Of all of it. We need to do something. Does the word 'half' ring a familiar bell?"

"Half?" He wasn't following her. "Half of what?"

Despite his best intentions, his brain turned to Jell-O. His eyes glazed over, his eyelids drooped, his chin slipped off his fingertips, and his hands came unclasped.

"Half of the house, the car, the ice cream," she said into the void, and gave a sweep of her arm. "Everythin'."

Nothing. No reaction. She was babbling to a chair with clothes on.

Only Jerome's head bobbling toward his chest brought him awake. He recovered awareness, grabbed his spoon again, then dove into the ice cream, effectively tuning Vonda out.

"For the love of . . ." she said. "Are you payin' attention here, or am I talkin' to myself?"

"What? Oh. I dunno, are you?"

"Am I what?"

"Talkin' to yourself? I swear it's hard to tell sometimes."

She huffed a dramatic sigh, smacked the tabletop with an open palm, and said, "Sometimes, you're impossible."

"Why are you so upset? Me bein' at the Grand doesn't mean anythin', Von."

"A leopard doesn't change its spots," she said. "Like father, like son."

"Hold up a minute." Jerome halted with his drippy spoon in midair. "I'm *nothin'* like my daddy."

"Oh, right. You stuck around, so that makes it okay?"

"Don't start."

Jerome tossed down his spoon, and it struck the table with a clang. Then he lurched up out of the chair.

"Oh, go on up to bed," she said.

He started to hyperventilate.

"Don't tell me what to do." He poked an index finger toward his heart but missed, hitting in the neighborhood of his belly button, instead. "I'm the king of this castle, the lord of this manor, the emperor—"

"Spare me. I heard you the first time."

His chest puffed up and he said, "As long as you know. Don't ever tell a king what he should do."

"Fine, your majesty. So where're you goin' now?"

His face wrinkled, as if he wrestled with a thorny problem, and he swayed in the breeze.

"Think I'll hit the hay," he said.

Launching into a laundry list of Jerome's faults was wasted energy when he'd been drinking. Vonda deliberately pushed the tirade out of her mind.

"Brilliant idea," she said. "Why didn't I think of that?"

"Because you're not the king."

And then he offered her that effortless grin of his, the one that softened his face and lit up his eyes, the poignant one full of gentle warmth that belonged to the hurt little boy within. The tender one that sent poetry singing through Vonda's blood and convinced her she was the only woman in his world. The one that made her willing to give him her heart to break and kept her believing in love and romance no matter how high life's disappointments piled up.

Who could resist? Her head told her she should, but her heart refused to give up a dream that easily.

Vonda gathered the dirty spoons and the nearly empty ice-cream carton, saying, "There's a pillow and clean sheets on the sofa in your office."

He didn't argue, and the silence between them thickened.

Jerome lumbered to the foot of the stairs, where he paused with his fingers gripping the oak handrail, then said, "Did I see Amelie's car in the driveway?"

"She and Remy aren't gettin' along again," Vonda said, tossing the spoons into the dishwasher.

Jerome bristled at this news.

"You could've told me," he said.

"There wasn't time. I said she could stay here for a few days."

"Sure, okay, as long as she wants. Say, do I need to go on over there and hold services with that Cajun bastard?"

His fatherly concern was impressively asinine, given the hypocrisy of his own bad behavior. Vonda offered him a half-smile, half-amused head shake.

"Leave 'em alone," she said, realizing nothing had changed. She and Jerome were right back where they were, going through the motions. "Let 'em find their stride."

After a thoughtful moment and one foot up on the carpeted stair tread, Jerome sniffed the air and said over his shoulder, "Is that paint I smell?"

Vonda stifled another laugh and cocked her head toward him. "Why, y'know, darlin', I don't smell a thing."

Let him figure it out, she thought. After all, a wife's memory was always selective.

10

Silence is sometimes the best answer.
—Old Farmer's Advice

The polyphonic salsa ring of Vonda's cell phone plowed through her brain as she struggled to come up out of her grave. She groped for the electric clock on the adjacent nightstand, peeling one eyelid open to read the digital face.

Six-thirty? Who was up at that ungodly hour, other than farmers and fussy brats? Neither of which would be phoning her, she felt certain.

She answered, her sleepy vocal cords making her voice sound like a tree frog on crack.

"Von? That you?" came a dusky male voice way too sexy for so early. "Did I wake you?"

Well, fan her with a brick.

"Who—?" she said, thinking she recognized the owner of

the voice but unwilling to speculate in case she was way off base. "Who is this?"

"Terrell."

Bingo.

"I'm sorry to call so early," he said. "I'm on my way to work and I hoped to catch you before things got busy."

"Sure, no problem, I understand," Vonda said, not meaning it in the least. She was not a morning person. "Somethin' wrong?"

"You tell me," he said. "Is everythin' okay over there?"

"Just peachy."

"I wondered is all. You never called back last night to let me know."

Vonda took an embarrassed breath.

"I forgot," she said. "I'm so sorry."

"A late apology is better than none. Don't worry, I can always dab extra shoe polish on the gray hairs I sprouted waitin' to hear."

"Oh, you," she said with an impish smile. "Really, it got crazy around here. My father-in-law moved in."

"Wasn't he in the nursin' home?"

"Not anymore."

"Wow, both in-laws livin' with you—the true litmus test of a marriage." Terrell chuckled, a lazy and delightful sound, like cascading wind chimes. "That's gotta suck to be you."

"Thanks loads," Vonda said with a sleepy-eyed grin. "You realize you still owe me supper?"

"And I'm a man who pays his debts. How about dinner at Jackson's across the street from the office?"

"Please, no green, climate-friendly cafes. I'd rather go somewhere un-PC and eat somethin' sinfully bad for your arteries."

"Hot dogs it is, then."

"Now you're talkin'. With mustard and relish only. No kraut."

"Sounds like a winner. I'll see you around noon at the Pavilion."

"Today?"

"Today. Is there a problem?"

"I—I guess not."

"Good. Don't keep me waitin'."

And he hung up without giving her a chance to argue, not that she intended to. A rush of luscious emotions warmed Vonda to her tingling toes.

Hanging up the phone, she rolled over and peeled open the other eyelid.

The third-floor master suite was drenched in orange sunlight filtered through ruffled white curtains and pooling on the sage green carpet. It took a moment for her mind to register that she'd forgotten to pull down the blackout shades.

Big deal. It wasn't as if Peeping Toms with forty-foot extension ladders were clamoring to catch a gander at her fifty-year-old breasts and cottage cheese thighs anyway.

She shifted the body pillow behind her and sat up, reclining against the headboard. The slats faintly creaked as the feather mattress absorbed her movements.

Her late mother had been born in the ornate four-poster that dominated the bedroom. The hand-carved hardwood headboard, inset with bird's-eye maple caning, rose with arrogant authority over a nearby Chippendale highboy, a reproduction piece Jerome had picked up last year at an estate auction because the furniture came from posher digs and looked . . . What was the word he had used? . . . Oh, yes, *yummy*.

He actually said yummy. What guy thought of that word on his own?

Vonda's eyes hurt, felt gritty.

Her cell rang again. She checked caller ID and was surprised to see the number belonged to Donna Lily. Donna Lily Wagner, the woman who didn't do sunrises, not even on Easter.

"Olga's massage parlor," Vonda answered, letting her head sink back into the down pillow.

"Dish," came Donna Lily's impatient voice.

"About what?"

"Terrell Barksdale. Don't be coy. I want to hear every detail about your date."

"Do you know what time it is?"

"Of course I do. It's time you shared with your oldest and dearest friend. Namely, me. The whole world saw y'all at the country club last night, and I'm the last one to know."

"Like who? Who's the whole world?"

"Tata, for one, and half the Historical Society for another. We had a meetin' last night, remember?"

Vonda gasped, bolted upright, and said, "I plumb forgot."

"No kiddin'."

Memory lapse was becoming a bad habit.

"You covered for me, yes?" Vonda said.

"I mentioned your birthday and you celebratin' with family."

"Oh, no."

"Exactly. How was I supposed to know you weren't? My excuse went over like a lead fart once Tata and a few of the other ladies looked out the window and saw you bigger than life. By the way, congratulations."

"For what?"

"You, my dear, are now the proud head of the Christmas home-tour committee."

"Rats! I'm a better Indian than a chief."

"Now, now, you know the rules . . . She who isn't present at a meetin' gets talked about and volunteered. And, darlin', did you ever get talked about."

Vonda groaned, saying, "Have you heard from Tata already?"

"Why, of course. My phone hasn't quit ringin'."

"For the love of . . ." Vonda said, lying back to stare at the glacier-blue coffered ceiling and watching the five paddles of the ceiling fan go round and round in lazy circles. "Some people need to get a life."

"Tell me about it. It's been too long since I had a date that didn't run on batteries. But you steppin' out with another man so soon after you and Jerome split, well, people take notice of those sort of doin's."

"But we haven't split."

At least, not in a way that was visible to the naked eye.

"Sure you have," Donna Lily said. "Everybody already knows about you catchin' him at the Grand yesterday. Let me ask you this . . . Is the sleazy Svengali sprawled next to you in bed?"

Vonda looked over at the vast expanse of crisp ivory cotton sheeting embroidered with a scallop design that covered the king-sized mattress. At the foot of the bed lay a perfectly folded Matelassé linen coverlet. Both of them were untouched, except for her side.

"Not this mornin', he isn't," she said. "He's on the lumpy foldout in his office, sufferin' a spectacular hangover, I hope."

"Hangovers," Donna Lily said, and Vonda could hear the laughter in her voice, "the gift that keeps on givin'. I rest my case. Once out of the bedroom, it's just a short boot out the front door. Now, about Terrell . . ."

"Really, Donna Lily, there's nothin' to tell. It wasn't a date. I ran into him when I went to the school for the cheerleader meetin'. The country club was all very innocent."

"Is that your story?"

"Yes, and I'm stickin' to it."

"That's certainly not how I heard it."

"I can only imagine. What did you hear?"

"Well . . . that you and Terrell Barksdale enjoyed a romantic tête-à-tête in a secluded corner—"

"Please. We sat at the last table they had available."

"And shared a bottle of wine—"

"One glass—not even, half a glass."

"And candlelight—"

"It was after dark. We were on the patio."

"And holdin' hands."

Vonda had to think about that one a moment. She recalled reaching across the table . . .

"Okay," she said. "You got me there."

"Aha!" Donna Lily giggled. "This is too delicious. Wish I could've been a fly on the wall to see Jerome's face turn fire-engine red."

Vonda had seen his face, had relished the ire creeping up his neck to overtake his staid control. She giggled, too; she couldn't help herself.

"He didn't blow his stack," she said, "but he wasn't a happy camper, that's for sure. When he came over to the table, you could see the tension buildin' behind his eyeballs. I thought for a minute there he'd explode." They both giggled again. "But me and Terrell . . . we're just friends, really."

"Sure, darlin', that's how it always starts."

"Not us. It's not like you think."

"Then tell me what it is like."

Vonda hugged her knees to her chest and rested her forearms across them. For the next few minutes, she recited the short version of the evening's events, including the addition of her new houseguest, ending with, "And so I've gotten maybe three hours' sleep, and I don't see today bein' much better than yesterday."

"Lord 'a mercy," Donna Lily said. "It was bad enough with Miss Ludie to look after. How do they get on together?"

"They'd be right at home in Baghdad."

"You poor thing. What are you gonna do with Grandpa Thayer?"

"I honestly don't know," Vonda said, raking her fingers through her sleep-matted curls. "He needs more help than he lets on."

"Maybe look into assisted livin'," Donna Lily said. "There are several facilities in Tallahassee. You remember Beryl, my second cousin on my mother's side who passed away last year? She met her fourth husband while in a lovely facility. She adored everythin' about the place, said it was like livin' in an upscale hotel and, bless her heart, that girl knew plenty about hotels."

"Y'think Grandpa Thayer would be open to the idea?"

After asking, Vonda cradled the phone between her shoulder and chin, and then took out a pencil and notepad from the nightstand drawer. She jotted down the words *assisted living* to remind herself later.

"Won't know 'til you ask him," Donna Lily was saying. "Beryl had herself a two bedroom with a nice balcony overlookin' a shady duck pond. Of course, Grandpa Thayer wouldn't need anythin' that large or expensive. It's cheaper for a one bedroom or a studio. Any idea how much he can afford?"

"Not much, I'm afraid. That's just it. I doubt he can afford to pay attention."

"My, my, that doesn't leave you much choice, now does it? You can't in good conscience boot the sick old man out on the street, no matter how Jerome feels about him."

"You're right, I can't, no. But if left up to Jerome, his daddy'd be sleepin' under a bridge in a peach crate."

"Tell me you're kiddin'."

"Wish I was."

"I don't know how you do it," Donna Lily said with a honeysuckle drawl.

"I just lie back and think of England."

"Heavens, girl, not *that*. I meant I wouldn't make it two minutes with Jerome Thayer before I'd gladly strangle him and bury his body in the basement."

"Water table's too high in Florida," Vonda said. "No basements."

"Oh, darn," Donna Lily said and laughed. "Standin' trial for murder's not good for my complexion anyway."

"Speakin' of bodies," Vonda said. "I think I hear stirrin' downstairs." She held the phone away from her ear to listen, then heaved a sigh. "Sounds like someone's yelling for me. I better run."

After a promise to call Donna Lily later with an update, Vonda threw back the sheet and headed for a bracing shower. Generations of women before her had coped with extended family, armed with grace and optimism.

She would, too.

And she almost believed it.

The notion took root and blossomed in those few minutes she culled out to shower, dress in sandals, mud-brown Capri pants, and a plain yellow blouse, and open the bedroom door. Then she heard the chaotic voices downstairs coming at her like the wrath of God.

She drooped against the white doorjamb and sucked in a deep, fortifying breath. Somewhere on the road of life, Vonda had definitely fallen into a pothole.

B reakfast turned into a logistical nightmare.

By the time Vonda trotted downstairs, her younger daughters, Charlotte and Caroline, had arrived home from their sleepover to put in some face time before skipping right back out to their summer jobs at the local Tastee Freeze.

Unlike Amelie, who inherited her blond looks from her maternal grandmother's side of the family, Charlotte and Caroline took after their father's side. They both stood reed-thin, with a wash of golden color, long dark hair, and high cheekbones that suggested their Cherokee ancestry.

People often mistook them for twins, although they were eleven months apart, and seeing them today reinforced the notion. Both teenagers wore low-rise faded jean shorts, T-shirts cut to bare midriff, bangle bracelets on both arms, blue nail polish on fingers and toes, pale pink lip gloss, and toe rings.

They had made enough noise coming in the house to wake the dead, all except for their father. He was still sequestered in the office. Not a peep issued from behind the closed door.

Maybe Jerome had decided to take the day off?

Wouldn't that be grand. Then he could deal with his loving and devoted parents himself.

Yeah, right.

No way Vonda would be that lucky.

Last night, after some haranguing on Vonda's part, her in-laws had agreed to be civil, if nothing else, civil for the sake of the children. Whether they would was yet to be tested.

In short order, the girls had landscaped the living room furniture with their overnight backpacks, pillows, and purses. Sandals and skates littered the floor. Wet bathing suits and towels settled wherever they fell for everyone to trip over.

The girls were chatting to each other at the same time they were text messaging most of the free world on their Sidekicks, while Vonda made repeated admonitions from the kitchen for them to clean up their mess. Neither one paid much attention.

Finally Charlotte acknowledged her mother as more of an afterthought than anything else, saying, "Okay, right after I shower," but she never looked up from her screen and her fingers never stopped punching buttons.

Caroline put down her Sidekick, only to hold up a wire hanger sporting a pair of khaki pants.

"Did you fix my button yet, Mom?" she said.

Vonda was putting on a stout pot of Luzianne Coffee & Chicory, figuring everyone would need heavy-duty fortifying to jump-start the day.

"Not yet, sweetie," she said. "Time got clear away from me."

"I need it done now," Caroline said, her voice taking on a nasally tone. "Work's at ten."

"In a minute. Use the upstairs shower, girls," Vonda tossed over her shoulder. "Your grandpa Thayer's in the bedroom down here."

They both groaned.

"Does he have to be here?" Caroline said. "My shampoo and stuff's in there."

"Borrow your sister's for now," Vonda said, which started a gripefest between the girls. "Hey, don't make me come over there and smack you. Quit your bickerin'. This once y'all can share."

"Is he leavin' soon?" Charlotte said.

"That hasn't been decided yet," Vonda said. "But don't be rude. I expect y'all to be nice to him for however long he stays. Y'hear me?"

Neither girl answered, letting Vonda's question become rhetorical.

"My coffee ready?" came Miss Ludie's voice down the stairway.

"Comin'," Vonda called back.

"Make sure it's hot this time, dammit!"

"Ask, and ye shall receive," Vonda muttered. Then she wrapped a pot holder around a mug of coffee the temperature of lava and shoved it in the nearest daughter's hand. "Run this up to your grandmother, please."

"It's Charlotte's turn," Caroline said, all but stomping her foot. "Why do I always hafta do drudge work?"

Vonda offered an indulgent smile, saying, "Because there's an ebb and flow to life, and today, you're in the ebb. Now, run along. There's my good girl."

A second later, Miss Ludie called down again, "My oatmeal comin' along?"

"Almost," Vonda called up to her, shooing Caroline on her

way, and then hunted in the dishwasher for the pan she usually used.

Well, crap. Vonda had forgotten to turn on the dishwasher last night, too. She started washing the saucepan by hand.

"You want to eat up there?" she called to her mother-in-law.

"Hold your horses a goddamned minute and I'll be down!"

"Fine," Vonda muttered to herself. "Whatever."

Charlotte stuck a wallet-sized picture of a young man under Vonda's nose, one of those black-and-white photo booth candid shots, her voice turning all light and dreamy when she said, "He's startin' Auburn in the fall. What do you think, Mom?"

Vonda focused on the grainy mug shot, zeroing in on the spiked hair and nose ring, and said, "What do I think?"

"Yeah."

"I think there's a little kid somewhere sayin', 'That's the man, officer.' "

Charlotte huffed and smacked the photo on Vonda's arm, saying, "I take it back. Tell me somethin' that'll make me happy."

Vonda smiled and then lied through her teeth. "He looks drool-worthy."

Charlotte hugged the picture to her chest, did a little pirouette in the middle of the kitchen floor, and said, "I know."

In no time, Caroline bounded back down the stairs, sliding into an ear-grating whine.

"Mom! What about my pants?"

"Geez, Louise," Vonda said, flinging soap bubbles into the air as she pointed toward the table. "Lay them over a chair. I said I'll get to them, and I will. After I fix breakfast."

"Waffles for me, Mom," Charlotte said, singing her favorite song and dancing with the photo of her college-bound friend. "No syrup, just apple butter."

Caroline answered her cell but paused long enough to call out, "Bacon and two eggs over easy for me. Don't make 'em too runny, either. Do we have wheat toast?"

Grandpa Thayer shuffled in from his bedroom about then, looking as pasty-faced as he had last evening, but today he was sans the red prom dress, thank goodness. Instead, he'd chosen a deadheader's tie-dye T-shirt over navy cargo shorts that made his legs look like dangling strings.

"Mornin', Grandpa," Vonda said, wiping her hands off on a dish towel. "Sleep well?"

"Like a baby," he said, sounding anything but, as he coughed and dragged his oxygen tank behind him. A deaf person could hear emphysema bebopping on both lungs every time he breathed. "Is that coffee I smell?"

"Fresh brewed. How do you like it?"

"Just like my women—full of booze."

Vonda manufactured a smile for that moldy saying and poured him a cup.

"C'mon in and sit wherever you're comfortable," she said, tamping down the urge to drop everything and help him make it the few feet to the table. "Breakfast'll be ready in a jiffy. You remember Charlotte and Caroline?"

"It's been a dog's age. Grown some, I see."

"Girls?" Vonda said. "Set the table, please."

Grandpa and the girls exchanged pleasantries. At first, they were reserved but friendly. When one of them commented on his vintage T-shirt and they learned their grandpa had actually jammed once with Jerry Garcia, well, that was all it took for them to welcome the old geezer into the fold.

Vonda pondered whether he was telling the truth, then decided it didn't matter. The girls' attention was occupied, and he was soaking up their rush of curiosity like a contented sponge. It worked for her.

The noise level increased when Amelie joined them with a sour expression overtaking her face.

"Feelin' okay?" Grandpa Thayer asked her.

"Aggravated," Amelie said, shaking her head. "My husband, Remy . . . Remy Broussard . . . he's not answerin' the house or cell phone."

Grandpa hesitated a moment, his forehead crinkled in thought, and said, "I know that name. Say—not the fishin' pro in the paper?"

"The same. We got married last year."

"Cripes, little gal, don't worry none 'bout him. More 'n likely he's out in a swamp up to his ass in gators."

"I hope you're right." Amelie turned to her mother and said, "Has he called?"

"Not this mornin'."

"Oh. I thought I heard your phone ring."

"You did." Unacknowledged guilt sapped the moisture from

Vonda's mouth and she flushed with a hot and reckless feeling. "Donna Lily called."

Jerome stumbled barefoot into the kitchen, looking like a rat that had just crawled out from under the house. Dark circles ringed his eyes, deep furrows bordered his sunken mouth, and his wet hair stuck out in every direction, which was a step up from him cruising the house in an old T-shirt and boxers, with his balls hanging out like twin tailpipes on an old Chevy.

He'd showered, tussled with a razor, and thrown on a Tommy Bahama black silk shirt over brown suit trousers. Shoes and socks dangled from two fingers.

"What the hell did the old bat want?" he said, continuing his freefall from grace.

"To talk to me," Vonda said, unwilling to share more. "Appreciate you askin' so nicely, though."

A brief shadow crossed his face and was gone as quickly as it appeared. If Vonda had to guess, she'd say her husband had noticed she had begun to change the rules of their well-established marriage.

On his way past her to the counter, Jerome shook a hornet's nest by adding, "We'll talk later about the paint."

Well, the shaking worked.

"I don't think so," Vonda said, adopting a voice that reminded him he owed her. "The color's nice. I like it. So it's stayin'. Lord knows the office smells one hundred percent better."

Her stiff tone must've made him feel guilty, because rather than argue with her, Jerome looked askance at his father.

"Don't go gettin' too comfy, old man," he said. "This arrangement is my wife's idea, not mine. It's only temporary. Least 'til I can figure somethin' else."

Grandpa Thayer nodded.

"Hello to you, too, son. Long time no see. You look like shit. What's your secret?"

"Blow me," Jerome said.

A nanosecond later all three girls erupted into peals of laughter. Grandpa Thayer joined them, braying so hard he strangled on his own spit and suffered a coughing fit.

Vonda simply rolled her gaze heavenward and gestured to Jerome with the pot.

"Coffee?" she said.

"Alka-Seltzer," he corrected, slumping on a barstool at the eat-in counter.

She plopped a cup in front of him anyway and poured it full so the strong aroma of chicory went straight up his nostrils. She might as well have been chewing Skoal and spitting in a cup.

"How about a slice of greasy cold pizza?" she said nice and easy, low enough for his ears alone. "Or a big slab of Jimmy Dean pork sausage?"

And then she tilted her chin and smiled.

Jerome shook his head, the same dead-fish look as last night spreading over his face. He swallowed, swallowed, swallowed again, lost the battle with his pitching stomach and then bolted off the barstool toward the nearest bathroom.

Sometimes the best lessons came in the ugliest packages.

"Is he okay?" Caroline said, watching him beat a four-second sprint down the hallway.

Vonda replaced the coffee carafe on the heating element and said, "Who? Your dad? Oh, paint fumes got to him, I expect. He'll be fine."

A few minutes later, his skin more bleached of color than when he left, Jerome staggered back to the kitchen to don his socks and shoes. Miss Ludie joined the family for breakfast about the same time. Her bearing was tight, and she wore a fretful countenance.

One look and the family froze in posture and released a collective gasp of awe, even Jerome. All eyes watched her proceed to the table.

She'd ditched the nun getup in favor of a virginal white gauzy oversized tunic-and-pants set, complete with white sandals.

And were her toenails painted a creamy white, too?

To Vonda's surprise, Miss Ludie had taken pains with her 'do this morning. A halo of short silver hair framed her face and softened the lines of bitterness around her mouth.

And was that the barest touch of pink lip tint?

Holy crap. The only things she lacked were white feathery wings growing out of her shoulder blades.

A sinking feeling attacked the pit of Vonda's stomach. What was the old bat up to this time that was going to interfere with Vonda's day?

"Mornin', Miss Ludie," Vonda said. "What's the occasion?"

Miss Ludie's eyes opened wide and she spoke slowly, as if relaying common knowledge to the mentally challenged.

"Grand openin'," she said, and then spoke each word deliberately, "Rayburn's . . . the new crematory?"

Vonda felt the beginning throb of a sleep-deprived headache come on.

"Is that really necessary?" she said.

"I'm not young anymore."

"You never were," Grandpa Thayer muttered.

"My time's runnin' short," Miss Ludie declared, ignoring him. "I intend to be ready when I'm called to my glory." Then she really sugarcoated it. "And I wanna get over to the grand openin' early, before all those goddamned old folks come in from the nursin' home and eat up all the finger sandwiches."

"Of course you do." Vonda turned a pointed stare on Jerome, a scowl wrinkling her forehead. "And how do you plan to get there, Miss Ludie?"

Jerome correctly read the intent in his wife's eyes, saying, "I don't do errands. I have—"

"To work," Vonda finished for him and nodded her head. "I know that song by heart."

"Look, someone has to—"

"Support this family," she finished for him again. "I know the chorus, too. How about we make a tape recordin' and play it on cue so you can save your breath. Will that work for you?"

"Har dee har har," he said and slid off the stool. "Say what you will. It's still true."

And, hungover or not, Jerome headed toward the front door.

"Where're you goin'?" Vonda said.

"To chuck the hamster back on the wheel," he threw over his shoulder. "Where else?"

"At least say good-bye, Jerome."

Without halting a step, he gave a backhanded salute over his head and echoed, "Good-bye, Jerome."

A chorus of "so longs," "byes," and "have a good day at work" followed him out of the house.

Before Miss Ludie could interject a further word about her mission for the day, Amelie said, "I can run her over to Rayburn's, Ma." She swiveled her attention to Grandpa Thayer. "You, too, Gramps, if you want."

Her oldest daughter's sudden helpfulness surprised Vonda, but she suspected the offer of assistance wasn't so much out of altruism as it was to satisfy a nagging urge to check up on a wandering husband: Her trailer park was on the way to Rayburn's Funeral Home. But Vonda wasn't going to look a gift horse in the mouth and kept her suspicions behind her teeth.

"Thanks, hon," she said and sent her an air smooch.

"They servin' beer?" Miss Ludie said.

"I don't know," Amelie said, blowing the steam off her coffee. "Probably not."

"Forget it." Miss Ludie gestured in the direction of her ex. "The cantankerous old flint over there ain't gonna go nowhere he can't suck down a few beers."

Grandpa Thayer snapped his chin up.

"The hell you say, woman. I'll go anywhere I damned well

please and do what I damned well please." He pointed to Amelie. "Count me in, little gal."

"That junk heap you drive got A/C?" Miss Ludie said.

Vonda piped up then, afraid the chance to get rid of them might slip away.

"My air conditioner works," she said. "Use my car."

The Pavilion wasn't that far. Vonda could stroll over to meet Terrell in under an hour.

Coffee mug in hand, Miss Ludie parked herself opposite her ex-husband at the kitchen table, doing her best to deny his existence. She failed.

His very proximity was an insult.

"Can't a body get cleaned up," she said, "without you makin' a goddamned fuss?"

"Did I open my mouth?" Grandpa Thayer said, hands up in surrender. "Crazy old woman."

"You were thinkin' it, though. Weren't you?"

"Cripes, what're you now? Miz Cleo the mind reader?"

"Psychic, numb-nuts. Get it right. Miz Cleo was a psychic."

Quick, fast, and in a hurry, Vonda turned from the counter with a steaming bowl in each hand. She placed one in front of Miss Ludie and changed the subject.

"What can I get you to go with your oatmeal?"

Vonda was thinking along the lines of milk or sugar, maybe juice. Miss Ludie pointed to her ex.

"His head on a platter," she said, and then sipped from her mug. "Good coffee this mornin'."

"Thank you, Mother Teresa," Vonda said, leaning closer to

her mother-in-law and whispering, "You agreed to be civil. Remember?"

"Hell's bells," returned Miss Ludie with a sardonic hand wave. "It's not as if I said the goddamned lying sonovabitch was a goddamned lying sonovabitch."

Vonda straightened, figuring there was no winning that argument.

"Point taken," she said and glanced at the oven clock. "Girls? Showers, or you'll be late for work."

"What about breakfast?" they said in unison.

"This isn't a restaurant," Vonda said, rubbing her temple. "Eat oatmeal, or eat when you get to work. You pick."

The teenagers bolted upstairs with unbridled enthusiasm and without any of the stuff they dragged in the door from the night before. Miss Ludie spooned into her breakfast as Vonda walked around the table and set the second bowl in front of Grandpa Thayer.

He thanked her and politely asked her to tell Miss Ludie to shut the hell up.

Vonda refused to answer that ringing bell, too.

She was saved from having to when her big sister Lolo sallied forth ahead of the blistering heat and Tata MacKnutt. For a house that usually didn't get much foot traffic, they were doing a bang-up business this morning.

After exchanging greetings, Tata gestured with the antique wooden racket in her hand and said, "Tennis, anyone?"

Her voice was all smiles.

Clearly, she'd gone off her meds. Tata appeared on the

tennis court with the same frequency that Halley's Comet appeared in the sky.

"What're y'all doin'?" Vonda said, planting her hands on her hips.

"Headin' to the club," Tata said. "I'm playin' a set, and gettin' a massage after."

Vonda glanced at Lolo's empty hands and said, "Massage, too, I suppose?"

Lolo shook her head.

"I'm old school," she said. "Somebody says take your clothes off, I want to see a weddin' ring first."

Both of them remained in the doorway, Tata looking like a Billie Jean King wannabe in a spanking white tennis skirt and sleeveless top, her face flushed with excitement, as though she had a secret she was busting to impart; and Lolo looking like freeway flotsam in a print blouse over green floral polyester walking shorts, her expression annoyed.

Terrell Barksdale. That was who they were itching to rake Vonda over the coals about.

She could read it in their faces without having to ask. Vonda sighed to herself.

And all she could do was smile.

11

If you wallow with pigs, you can expect to get dirty.
—Old Farmer's Advice

A terminally ill retired Navy dive instructor had owned and operated the local watering hole, Down the Hatch, back in the 1980s when former Marine Sergeant Major Patrick Riley Malone bought the failing bar off him.

Paddy Malone was a pit bull of a man with thinning white hair, a gut like a welder's apron hanging over his belt, and an attitude rooted in Boston poverty. He first fell in love with the Sunshine State in his younger days when he spent a stint as a hotshot instructor at Pensacola Naval Air Station.

He was buff back then, a shit-kicker who routinely bench-pressed four hundred, chiseled, six-pack abs hard as granite, even boxed Golden Gloves for a time. The ladies creamed their pants when he strutted into a room. No doubt about it, Paddy Malone was The Man.

And he wasn't ready yet to surrender that image to reality. Hope sprang eternal in the flabby breast. The hope of recapturing that golden time, of nurturing that happiness, of marinating in his memories fueled Paddy's decision to retire and settle down in the last frontier that was northwest Florida.

Renaming the bar Malone's was both a tribute to his late mother, who had died on her knees scrubbing other people's toilets, and to appeal to more than just a few aging veteran barflies. He left the brass dive helmets, naval diving and salvage emblems, and assorted shipwreck and submarine pictures that littered the walls, mainly because he deemed it too much trouble to remove them.

Instead, Paddy spruced up the mix with pictures of the Blue Angels and other memorabilia from his own thirty-year career in and around aviation. After that, new tables and chairs, a coat of paint slapped on, and a good cleaning from bottom to top gave a much needed face-lift to the tired honky-tonk.

Providing a noontime burger and sandwich menu helped to draw in the middle-aged locals, and adding live music nightly appealed to the dance-loving younger crowd. All that work enticed the paying customers through the door, but Paddy learned from his early days trolling the Combat Zone in Boston that peddling booze wasn't where the profits were.

The real rake came from the sports book . . . football . . . baseball . . . hockey . . . horse racing . . . boxing.

For the house, bookmaking was fast money. The beauty was that it could involve any event that lacked certainty, no matter how ridiculous the event.

The advantage of a bookie to the bettor was simple: extended credit, better payoffs, and no income tax. None. Nada. Zip.

No one talked about Paddy's bookmaking activity. Bookmaking was illegal in Florida. But, somehow, every man around town knew where to go if he wanted a piece of the action, especially if he wanted to buy in on local betting pools.

One such betting pool occurred around the winter holidays when the sinners crawled out of the community woodwork to bet whether it would snow. That and how many pounds of horse apples would be shoveled in the Fourth of July parade were the two most popular pools.

The house take then was usually slim to nil, but Paddy tolerated, encouraged, and even patronized such informal pools to keep his customers happy, because happy customers spent money. And lots of it.

Not to mention the Paddy Malone old-age fund was always amenable to new and eager donors.

So it was that, twenty-four hours after Amelie Broussard drove out of the trailer park in her Volkswagen and headed for her mama's house, Paddy sent over two former pro wrestlers who worked odd jobs for him to roust Remy Broussard. They were to coax him back to Malone's for a sit-down about his recent losses.

Gossip had spread like oil on a driveway about Remy's in-laws and outlaws all living under one roof. Paddy was no fool. He listened to the gossip and knew opportunity when it knocked. As he saw it, the shot at making a buck had landed in his lap as easily as big mouth bass landed in Remy's boat.

See, Paddy knew Jerome Thayer. Knew him as all hat and no cattle. Knew he was less than the urbane gentleman he pretended. Knew he wouldn't have the money now to make Solomon blush if not for the business that became his those many years ago when the brown-nosing little snot had his lips tattooed to his father-in-law's ass. Nor would he have the social acceptance if not for the good fortune to slide a ring on Vonda Thayer's finger.

Paddy liked Vonda. She possessed erotic brown eyes, plenty of meat on her bones to keep a man warm, and long legs that aroused his interest.

The explosive situation at the Thayer household was too juicy not to make book on.

Chances were good Vonda Thayer wouldn't last until Labor Day before sending someone packing. The sixty-four-thousand-dollar question was, which someone? For that answer, Paddy needed a snitch to give him a steady supply of inside dirt.

And he figured Remy Broussard could act as that snitch.

Besides, Remy owed him.

When Remy sailed through the double doors of Malone's under the steam of his human bookends, to say his mood was enthusiastic was to stretch the truth.

He fully expected something unpleasant. Something like being dragged deep into the bowels of the dimly lit bar, where he'd be put to work blowing hairy-assed sailors for five bucks a pop to pay off the five-grand gambling debt he owed Paddy Malone. Maybe after a couple of years, he could look forward to getting Sundays and the occasional holiday off.

If Remy was lucky, that was all that would happen. If he wasn't lucky, he'd be in a position to witness the apocalypse firsthand.

His short black hair clung to his scalp, plastered down by heat and nervous sweat. The familiar fumes of stale booze and cigarettes greeted him, while the sublime lilting blues of Corinne Bailey Rae sighed out of overhead speakers and teased his ears with feel-good music.

A furtive glance around revealed no rescue help at hand: A couple with one foot in the grave sopped up martinis tucked away in a quiet booth, a sallow-faced hard-hat type hunched over a nearly empty pitcher of beer at a table, and three blistered tourists at the other end of the bar looked to have spent the afternoon promoting Captain Morgan to an admiral.

Paddy appeared out of nowhere and startled Remy by clapping him on the shoulder from behind. Remy swiveled his gaze around to find Paddy grinning through pale gray eyes that lurked behind silver-rimmed glasses.

"Remy," he said.

"Paddy."

"Glad you made it, boyo. The fellas had their doubts 'bout you coming round to pay us a visit, but not me."

"Hey, no problem." Remy returned the grin. He shot a quick glance at the bouncer holding him under his left arm, and then to the bouncer holding him under his right. "For you, Paddy, anytime. My pleasure."

His cordiality might have been more convincing if he hadn't been sandwiched between the thick-skinned bruisers. A barely perceptible nod from Paddy dismissed the two and, when they let go of Remy, his dangling feet hit the floor with a squeaky *flump*.

To his surprise, hands like cantaloupes enveloped his in the kind of warm greeting usually reserved for long-lost cousins.

"Good to see ya," Paddy said and gestured to a backless wooden stool at the end of the mahogany bar nearest them, the stool sitting under a sign that read NO DAMNED CUSSING AL-LOWED. "Take a load off."

Remy knew an order when he heard one. He sat.

"Wanna burger?" Paddy said in his usual *rat-ta-tat-tat* burp gun speed. "Fries? Howz about a beer? Family doing okay?" Without waiting for an answer, Paddy hollered over his shoulder to a bartender who was making love to his own reflection in the mirror. "Yo, Challie? Bring us a lunch special."

"Too late," the bartender yelled back. "Lunch is over, boss."

"It's over when I say it's over. Quit gawking at your ugly mug and do what I pay ya for."

Remy shook his head, saying by way of apology, "Paddy, I'm a little light this week. We're savin', what with the baby comin' and all—"

"Boy or girl?"

"Don't know."

"Ain't they got tests nowadays to tell?"

"That's the way the little woman wants it." Remy shrugged. "M'wife reads a lot, and got a notion in her head to do everythin' natural. No drugs, no nothin'."

"She feeling all right?"

"Fair to middlin' most of the time."

"Good, good."

"Course, she's at her mama's right now, visitin' for a few days."

Paddy nodded, saying, "I hear women take to nesting when their time's near."

Remy chuckled, relaxing, feeling quite the sage on the subject of pregnant women since he was an old married man and Paddy was still a clueless bachelor.

"Y'don't have to tell me. I said, 'Sugarplum, now you just go on off and let your mama fuss over you awhile. It'll do her good.' My Amelie, she didn't want to be away from me for long, and I'm here to tell you it took some doin' to talk her into goin'."

"Well, then, she's lucky to have a good husband, Remy."

He blushed and dipped his chin.

"It does my heart proud just to make her happy," he added, feeling virtuous.

About then the bartender delivered a cheeseburger basket with the same care and finesse a disgruntled postal worker gives a fragile package. The basket hit the bar so hard the top of the bun and the fixings slid into the fries and buried the kosher pickle spear. Paddy shot a glare to the bartender's back, and then pushed the basket closer to Remy, brushing off his protests.

"On the house," he said and smiled. "Salt? Ketchup?"

Remy shook his head no, saying, "Tabasco sauce, if you've got it. And sliced jalapeños? The hotter, the better."

Paddy then called the order over his shoulder to the bartender and added, "Bring the man a frosty amber bock while you're at it, and be quick 'bout it."

"Why not hand over the bar and be done?" came the sullen reply.

"Keep y'fucking trap shut," Paddy told him and seemed satisfied to see the bartender finally snap to. "I'll deal with y'later."

Encouraged by the unexpected hospitality and fatherly concern, Remy spread his hands atop the bar, speaking low, "Listen, Pad, I'm gonna get ya the five grand—"

"Z'at mean ya ain't here to settle up then?"

Remy thought Paddy might be joking, so he tried to follow his emotional lead.

"Hey, y'know me, Pad, I'm good for it . . ."

"And if my aunt had balls, she'd be my uncle."

". . . just not today."

Paddy leaned in close until Remy could smell the lingering vapors of the spicy sausage the man had eaten for breakfast.

"A bet's a bet," Paddy said. "Y'ain't thinking of welching on me, are ya? 'Cos I don't mind telling ya . . . I *hate* welchers."

Although Paddy smiled amiably and his voice was calm, a note in his tone made it clear the remedy for his displeasure involved a lot of pain. And none of it his own.

"Me, welch?" Remy said and chuckled again. "Never. I'd never do that, Paddy. You and me, we're buds."

"Yeah, sure y'wouldn't, boyo." Paddy gave a couple of rough pats to Remy's freshly shaved cheek. "I believe ya."

About then a beer mug with a full head came sliding toward their end of the bar. Paddy easily palmed the mug without spilling a drop and shoved it handle first in front of Remy.

"Much obliged," Remy said.

He upended the proffered mug, almost finishing off the dark beer in three large swallows, and felt his courage find its second wind. A redheaded barmaid sauntered by, wearing laced-up sneakers, a short tight skirt, and a tongue ring, and he nodded his appreciation.

Paddy waited until Remy wiped the foam off his upper lip and then said, "Getcha another?"

"Don't mind if I do."

The second beer followed the first in short order when Paddy eyed him with a mysterious twinkle and said, "But there is something you can help me with, if it's not too much trouble."

Remy felt something in the air change, felt they were forging a new and advantageous friendship. His voice all but broke with excitement.

"Sure thing, Paddy. Whatever I can do. Whatcha need?"

"A few of the fellas and me were tossing around the idea of starting a new pool." Paddy scratched the graying bristles on his chin. "We were thinking maybe . . . you'd like in on it? For a nice percentage, of course."

Remy perked up and leaned his forearms on the bar.

"How *nice?*" he said.

Paddy smiled, wrapped an arm around Remy's shoulder, and said, "Let's you and me talk."

"I'm all ears," Remy said.

12

*Good judgment comes from experience, and a lotta that
comes from bad judgment.*
—Old Farmer's Advice

Mama's late-model SUV had running boards and three rows
of seats: captain chairs front and middle, and a rear bench
seat followed by a generous cargo area.

Loading the three of them into her car was as simple and
painless as digging out of prison with a fork.

Amelie, pregnant out to there, assisted Miss Ludie into
the front passenger seat with a little boost to her rump. That
done, she rounded the car and spotted for Grandpa Thayer as
he launched himself onto the seat behind the driver. Once he
was settled, she forked over his portable oxygen tank to rest in
what little lap he possessed.

By the time Amelie hoisted herself behind the steering
wheel, she was sweating like a marathon runner and breath-

ing hard from the oppressive heat in the airless garage. The engine roared to life as she made sure seat belts were fastened, pointed out the air conditioner vents and controls, and told the older couple to fix the dials however they wanted to be comfortable.

It was going to be a long morning.

"We're gonna take a little detour," Amelie said when she pulled out of the driveway.

Grandpa Thayer shrugged and sank deeper against the leather seat's armrest, saying, "I ain't in a hurry, little gal. Drive where you want."

Miss Ludie was far less accommodating.

"Speak for yourself, you old goat," she snapped, then turned her attention back to the front. "Are we gonna be late? How do you turn on the radio? Is your seat belt on, girlie? Step on the gas, I wanna be back in time to see my program. Watch the squirrel . . ."

She chattered so much Amelie surrendered any hope of finishing a coherent thought. Grandpa Thayer, Amelie noticed, didn't seem to mind his ex trumpeting whatever crossed her mind. Bless his heart, the old man must be going deaf and couldn't hear her that well.

Amelie waited until Miss Ludie paused for breath, then jumped in with, "We're good on time. Trust me. I'll get you to Rayburn's, and I promise you won't miss your soap. Sit back and relax."

"Relax?" Miss Ludie said. "Are you old enough to drive? You look too young to me . . ."

Instead of heading straight out to the main highway, they passed several quiet streets lined with stately old oak trees hanging with Spanish moss. Manicured lawns fronted one-story brick homes. A Baptist church stood sentinel on every other corner.

As tranquil as the scenery was, the ride took longer than usual.

The baby was tap-dancing on Amelie's kidneys today, and she had to stop to waddle to the restroom at every fast food place along the way. At least it felt that often. Not to be out-done, Grandpa Thayer's iffy bladder had him checking out the john at a convenience store on the route.

Minutes after the last stop, Amelie cruised into the entrance of the mobile home park where she and Remy had rented a double-wide for the past year. Trailers were angled like match-sticks into narrow lots on each side of the street, with an over-grown vacant lot scattered here and there.

Wood fencing or chain-link separated the yards. No one was outside, most of her neighbors either being at work or smart enough to stay inside enjoying the air-conditioning.

"Where the hell are we?" Miss Ludie said, her gaze swivel-ing left and right. "Not another potty break?"

"We're good this time," Amelie said, patting her mound of growing baby.

Miss Ludie tapped Amelie on the elbow, saying, "Are you lost? Do we need to send up a flare?"

"Just drivin' by," Amelie said. "I wanna make sure things are okay at home."

"Which trailer is yours?" Grandpa Thayer said.

Amelie eyed him in the rearview mirror.

"Third from the end of the street," she said. "The gray one with a dogwood in the front yard and hummingbird feeders hangin' from the carport."

"And a litter of cats on the stoop?" he said.

Amelie chuckled, saying, "None of 'em are mine. I don't know how they find me."

"Animals are smart," Grandpa Thayer said. "They can spot a meal ticket right off."

So can some people, Amelie thought, but kept the uncharitable observation to herself.

She slowed the car to sightseeing pace, mindful of the speed bumps crisscrossing the street at regular intervals. Without being obvious, she glanced out the tinted window to see if Remy's black truck was parked on the backside of their trailer.

She was in luck.

Not only was his pickup there, but Remy was there, too, with his back to the street, apparently plagued by a wedgie, because he looked to be digging underwear out of his ass.

He stood on the concrete parking apron next to the neglected yard, one knee bent in a reflexive stance, his shoulder propped against one of the carport's aluminum braces. A navy blue baseball cap covered his head, and he wore a white muscle shirt, black swim shorts, and sandals.

But he wasn't alone.

Miss Ludie pointed out the obvious first, saying, "I declare, will you looka there at that redhead. Her skirt's too tight for her rear end. And I haven't seen hair that color since Little Orphan Annie."

"The shithead she's yappin' to doesn't seem to mind," Grandpa Thayer said.

"No, he doesn't," Amelie said, checking out the gum-chewing bimbo with the skid row style and flair about her, "does he?"

As far as Amelie could tell the two of them were simply talking, but Lord only knew what transpired between them before she happened upon the conversation. Judging by their proximity to one another, it was plain to Amelie the bubble-gum bimbo had captured more than Remy's casual notice. For that reason, the bimbo needed to go to her own home.

And she needed to go *now*.

On the bright side, at least Remy wasn't out gambling somewhere.

Amelie kept her cool, mindful that her grandparents were both one brick shy of a load and would make sorry character witnesses.

Your honor, the defense would like to call the potty-mouthed nun and the geezer in the prom dress.

Oh, yeah, Amelie could imagine that scene going over big-time.

So she decided to dump her grandparents off at the funeral home and come back to let Remy know in no uncertain terms that she wasn't a woman to be messed with.

For a split second, it crossed Amelie's mind that she could be jumping to the wrong conclusion. There could be a perfectly innocent explanation why nothing except daylight stood between Remy and sweet sin.

But, then again, sometimes things were exactly what they appeared.

"Hang on," she said more animated than she felt, "we're turnin' around. Next stop, Rayburn's."

She sped up and swung a three-point turn at the end of the street that Mario Andretti would envy. When she checked behind her in the rearview mirror, she caught Grandpa Thayer shaking his head.

"The shithead's your Remy?" Grandpa Thayer said.

"Gee, Gramps, what makes you say that?"

Oblivious to the drop in temperature inside the SUV, Miss Ludie added, "Somebody really needs to tell your neighbor it's okay to take her Christmas lights down."

Amelie reached for words as if they hovered in the air, saying, "Oh, her? She's . . . she's not our neighbor."

Grandpa Thayer leaned forward, poking his face between the driver and passenger seats.

"Ain'tcha gonna stop at home, little gal?"

"Later, Gramps. Not right now."

"Better stop," he said.

"Y'gotta use the john?"

"Now that you mention it . . ."

But something about the way he spoke rang false.

"What're you thinkin'?" Amelie said.

"Me? Nothin'."

"Why don't I believe that?"

Her bullshit detector working overtime, Amelie pulled to the side of the street and stopped under a shady live oak that dominated a snaky-looking vacant lot. She let the engine idle in park to keep the air-conditioning circulating and turned in her seat to face her grandfather.

"Yes?" she said.

"Help me out," Grandpa Thayer said.

"Not until you tell me—"

"Is he the father of that youngin' you're carryin'? Yes or no?"

"Yes, sir."

"Then quit arguin'. Climb back here and help me get the damned seat belt off. This button contraption won't cooperate."

Miss Ludie threw a vacant glance her way and shrugged. So Amelie cut the engine and did as her grandfather asked.

"Want me to go with you?" she said.

"Stay put," Grandpa Thayer said. "I've managed near eighty years without your help, reckon I can manage a few minutes more."

He left her waiting by the driver's door while he moseyed the short distance up her driveway. She cupped her hands to shade her eyes against the sun's glare off the concrete and watched him, chuckling to herself.

Her grandpa was a crackerjack, that was for sure.

She didn't believe for one moment he had to use the facilities. So what in the world did the old man think he was up to?

Prodded by skyrocketing curiosity, she inched forward,

watching as Grandpa Thayer stopped a few feet shy of the couple who still hadn't paid any attention to anything except each other. Then he calmly grabbed his oxygen tank with both hands by its neck valve and hefted the two-foot cylinder out of its small trolley as if it weighed nothing.

In the next instant, he raised the cylinder above his shoulder, clearly intending to wield it like a club. When he checked for swinging room over his shoulder, Amelie caught the determination on his face.

The old man actually looked ready to rumble.

She thought she might throw up. She all but dry-heaved in disbelief.

He wouldn't, would he?

Her answer came in the next heartbeat: Hell, yes, he would. He was old and sick, had nothing to lose, and he was one satin dress this side of the loony bin.

Amelie's choices were simple, act or do nothing. In the blink of an eye, she decided.

Remy Broussard was her husband, her problem to deal with for better or worse, 'til death do them part. It was the *death* part she was contemplating. She wasn't about to let her grandpa fight her battles or touch a hair on Remy's sweaty head.

No, sirree, Bob!

If anyone was going to murder the no-good, lazy, cheating coon ass, Amelie was.

13

*The biggest troublemaker you'll ever have to deal with
watches you from the mirror every mornin'.*
—Old Farmer's Advice

L olo and Tata stayed at Vonda's for coffee after everyone
had left. Vonda figured they would. They were dying to
hear the dirt straight from the horse's mouth, no matter what
con job they tried to sell her.

Well, they weren't getting anything out of her, because
there wasn't anything to tell. And she wasn't sure if there ever
would be anything.

She'd been married to Jerome almost as long as she'd been
friends with Terrell. And, right now, Vonda wasn't sure in what
direction she wanted either relationship to go.

She recited the same story to Lolo and Tata that she'd given
Donna Lily earlier, including the part about her father-in-law
moving in with them for an undetermined stay. After sidestep-

ping their questions, Vonda shooed the two women out the door as quickly as possible without confessing she was meeting Terrell at noon.

No telling what they'd do with that tidbit.

Once the house was empty, Vonda jumped on her chores and got them out of the way in record time: dishes, beds, laundry, bills, and general straightening up before going upstairs and changing into ankle socks and sensible walking shoes. She remembered to slather sunscreen on exposed skin, mainly hands, arms, and neck, and grab her gardening hat—the straw one with the wide, floppy brim that shaded her entire face.

She dug a fanny pack out of the drawer and filled it with her driver's license and social security card, so paramedics could identify the body if she should happen to get flattened like roadkill while out walking. Then she tossed in her house keys, some cash, a credit card, facial tissues—you just never knew—a lozenge or two, a couple of blister Band-Aids, a tube of Carmex, and her cell phone. Oh, what the hay . . . She chucked in a small tube of sunscreen, too. Satisfied, she fastened the bulging pack around her waist.

On the way out of the bedroom, she gave herself a cursory glance in the full-length mirror attached to the door . . . and stopped cold.

Who was that?

Vonda twisted around to check behind her to make sure she wasn't seeing someone else's reflection. Nope, that dumpy house Frau stood in her shoes.

How pathetic can you get?

She examined her reflection, really studying the unflattering choices she'd unconsciously made, and shook her head. Beauty rarely came one-size-fits-all, but what was she thinking?

Where was the charm? The allure? The romance?

The ragbag?

To her dismay, Vonda realized all the woman in the mirror needed was blue hair, an I-love-Liberace bumper sticker stapled to her butt, and a bus ticket to Branson in her hand to complete the frumpy senior citizen look.

Maybe she'd be there one day, but that day wasn't today.

Today, Vonda didn't feel old and, by golly, she wasn't going to dress old, either.

She ripped off the gardening hat, tossed off the sensible but dull shoes, stripped off her housework clothes, and dove into her closet. When she emerged several minutes later, her bearing screamed confidence, style, and fun.

She'd donned a pink and gray sporty sleeveless jersey over gray knee-length shorts, pulled her hair through a pink ball cap, and slipped her feet into white athletic shoes. Because there was a difference between being practical and being paranoid, she dumped out the contents of the fanny pack and took nothing with her but the essentials.

In the left pocket of her shorts, she stuck her cell phone, her ID, and a few dollars. In the right pocket, she slipped in the key to the back door and her lipstick. She dumped the fanny pack back in the drawer.

That was it. Anything else was superfluous.

She slathered more sunscreen on the newly exposed skin, tossed the tube on the dresser, and she was ready to go.

Downstairs in the kitchen, she jotted a note to Amelie and left it stuck to the butcher-block cutting board where she'd be sure to find it: *Grilled chicken salad in the fridge.*

Then Vonda marched out the door and down the sidewalk toward the Pavilion and Terrell.

The Pavilion, where she and Terrell were to meet, was the name locals gave to a central park area on the lake's perimeter that sat adjacent to the public boat ramp. It was an easy three-quarter-mile scenic walk to the opposite side of the lakeyard from Vonda's house.

In the park were an outdoor amphitheater with tiered concrete seats, a picnic area with several barbeque grills and covered tables, and a children's playground, all nestled beneath the cooler shade of a stand of towering slash pines. During the spring and summer, the amphitheater was a gathering place for concerts, theatrical performances, and art shows. In the fall and winter, it was the scene of the Great Pumpkin Patch and Hometown Christmas.

The Pavilion also boasted the most accessible cuisine in town: The Best of the Wurst hot dog stand, which was a restaurant on wheels. The menu included hot dogs, sausage dogs, Polish dogs, and bratwurst with all the fixings, plus a variety of cold drinks and ice cream.

The sky was a cloudless blue, the combination of heat, haze, and humidity softening the world's hard edges. The aromas of Confederate Jasmine and honeysuckle sweetened the air. Dragonflies flitted about, riding a warm breeze out of the south and gorging themselves fat on mosquitoes. High among the magnolias that lined the path, squirrels chattered to each other and mockingbirds squawked because they could.

Vonda circled the lakeyard, an extra spring in her step and a ready smile on her face. A few other souls ignored the temperature to walk, jog, or bike on the path as well.

Underneath her pleasant exterior, Vonda was burbling with excitement.

The seconds after Grandpa Thayer hefted his oxygen tank over his shoulder were surreal to Amelie. Time and events seemed to spill over in slow motion.

Maybe it was the heat. Maybe it was her brain working through an electrical hiccup. Maybe it was stress shooting her blood pressure to the moon.

Whatever the origin, a more rational person might have questioned the sensation of swimming in molasses.

Not a pregnant woman. She'd never think twice, just embrace the floaty feeling as par for the course and keep on keeping on until the feeling evaporated.

Amelie pushed away from the car door and hollered. Like looking through water, she watched Remy angle her way. He moved so slowly. Then she tripped on a tree root and saw nothing but weeds.

"Sir?" she heard Remy say, then Grandpa Thayer's voice followed, only their words sounded like trains going by.

"That little gal yonder about to have your youngin' is my granddaughter. Don't make me come over there and beat you like a government mule."

Amelie recovered her balance without falling and raised her gaze as images cascaded before her like dominoes. Grandpa Thayer lost his grip on the green cylinder, the cylinder grazed Remy's ball cap, Remy cursed in two languages, the cylinder clanged to the concrete and rolled to a wobbly . . . wobbly . . . wobbly . . . halt.

Good Lord, he nailed him.

Amelie thought she'd died and gone to hell.

She sucked in a deep breath through her nose and blew it out through her mouth, and repeated the action, which was as close to Zen as she could expect at the moment. The fresh air helped, for the thick and floaty sense faded away. Then as fast as her cankles would let her go, she waddled up the driveway.

The bimbo blew a quick bubble, slapped her bare thigh, and said, "Man, are we being Punk'd? Where's the camera . . . ?"

"This is an intervention," Miss Ludie said.

Amelie started, hadn't even noticed her grandmother hopping out of the car. The old woman watched too much television, but a body wouldn't know that to see the bimbo's face. She nodded at Miss Ludie as if her announcement made complete sense.

"Cool," the skank said and pointed to Miss Ludie's outfit. "Y'know, you look like an angel. Can I help?"

Grandpa Thayer was bent over, swearing worse than a longshoreman and punctuating each word with a phlegmy cough. He was having a time retrieving his oxygen tank, what with the hose attached to his cannula wrapped in knots on the valve.

Remy danced around, his hands and arms covering his head, saying, "What the hell, man? What the hell? Y'gave me a concussion."

"Cripes, it's a little bump," Grandpa Thayer said. "Quit bein' a baby. Rub some dirt on it and shake it off. Where's a chair? I gotta sit down. I'm all tuckered out."

Amelie came up behind Remy and cuffed him on the shoulder.

"It was an accident," she said. "But it serves you right, you two-timing—"

"Bend over," Miss Ludie told him, "and put your head between your knees. I saw this on *Oprah*."

"Hey, lemme go," Remy griped.

The bimbo joined Miss Ludie in pushing him almost doubled over. Amelie didn't think the advice sounded quite right, but if the position made his head hurt more, she was all for it.

"Shut up, will ya?" he said, trying to shrug the bimbo and Miss Ludie off of him.

The bimbo popped a bubble, planted both hands on her hips, and immediately copped an attitude.

"Don't y'tell me to shut up, Kevin. I'll—"

Kevin?

Amelie had raised her hand to cuff him again and now halted with her arm in midair.

"Who the hell is Kevin?" she said.

She and Grandpa Thayer exchanged puzzled looks, then Amelie unceremoniously yanked the navy blue ball cap off to verify up close who was really underneath.

"Oh, for the love of Mike," she said.

The man staring back at her through angry eyes had the same body size and dark hair, but that was where the resemblance faded. He was a good ten years older, had a boxer's flat nose, bushy eyebrows, and thin lips.

"Little gal?" Grandpa Thayer said.

Miss Ludie perched next to him on the porch steps, fanning herself with her hand.

"Wrong shithead, Gramps," Amelie said. "He isn't my Remy."

The bimbo pointed back toward the trailer, saying, "Y'all lookin' for the dude who lives here? Check inside. A bad cheeseburger got him and got him good. Man, it wasn't pretty. Oh, if you're wondering, me and Kev drove him home. Well, Kev drove. I sat in the middle and hung on to the dude's shirt while he puked his guts out the window." She pulled a face, adding, "Y'may wanna run his truck through a car wash."

"Forget the truck," Kevin whined. "What about my head? Who's gonna take care of it?"

Amelie couldn't decide whether to laugh, cry, or retain a high-priced lawyer to handle the lawsuit that would be coming at the speed of light from this mistaken identity.

She opted for nonchalance and a bluff.

"Don't worry, I'm a nurse," she said, eyeing the goose egg on the front of his noggin. "The swelling'll go down in a day or so. Put your hat back on and nobody'll notice. Where'd you say Remy ate the burger?"

"Malone's," the bimbo said and smiled, the gum pushed to one cheek. "Y'know the place?"

"I've heard the name mentioned," Amelie said, not returning the beam.

"I been waitin' tables there all summer," the bimbo added. "Can you believe? Me, waitin' tables?" And she chuckled at a joke only she knew the punch line to.

"Who'd a guessed?" Amelie said under her breath.

A four-door sedan pulled up in front of the trailer and they all turned at the honk. The bimbo waved to the driver, saying to the others, "Our ride's here. C'mon, Kev." She waved and tossed over her shoulder, "Y'all come on down to Malone's sometime. I work days. Take care."

Only after the car sped off did Amelie realize she never asked the bimbo's name. Oh, well. Amelie knew where she worked.

She glanced back at the trailer. For a minute there, she had started to feel sorry for Remy. Now she wanted to murder him again.

No wonder he hadn't answered the phone. He was too busy pissing away their money at a bar. And, if he was at Malone's, that meant betting good money after bad.

It served him right to be sick. Without a backward glance, she hustled her grandparents to the car.

Miss Ludie hooked her thumb in the direction of Kevin What'shisname, saying, "He's the father of your baby? I thought the other young man was your husband."

Amelie groaned and pulled out into traffic, headed for the crematory grand opening. Grandpa Thayer rested in the seat behind her, his face glistening with sweat, his eyes closed.

"The other guy *is* my husband," she said.

Leaning in closer to her, Miss Ludie tsk-tsked and said, "Does your husband know you've been screwin' around?"

"I haven't been—" Amelie ran out of steam then and simply finished by saying, "No, ma'am. No, he doesn't."

Miss Ludie made a zipping motion with her fingers over her lips.

"To my grave," she said and winked.

14

Every path has a few puddles.
—Old Farmer's Advice

Vonda and Terrell picnicked at one of the wooden tables under the pine trees. He paid for their three-course meal of dogs, bottled water, and Nutty Buddies, refusing to go dutch, even though she had insisted.

"Nada," he said in a tone that made her feel dopey for assuming otherwise. "The guy *always* pays."

He made it hard to argue and win. While he devoured three hot dogs suffocated in kraut and chili, she enjoyed a sausage dog and watching him.

But not necessarily in that order.

Terrell was easy company, a good listener, and had a ready smile that revealed a lone dimple gaining prominence as he grew older. Around him, Vonda never felt pressured to be someone other than who she was.

She was hot and sticky from her walk. He looked cool and relaxed in a white T-shirt and khaki Dockers. Only the hint of dark wet hair clinging to his neck gave him away. Every so often Terrell swatted at the no-see-ums swarming by or at fruit flies trying to freeload off dropped crumbs.

Midday was a beehive of activity around the park.

Business types in ties and starched shirts were lined up to buy dogs or were brown-bagging it on the park benches scattered among the trees. Several couples shared Terrell and Vonda's idea of an early fall picnic and spread blankets on the grass.

A few families were grilling chicken and burgers, sending a fog of tantalizing aromas into the air to mix with the squeals and laughter exploding from the nearby playground. The boat ramp area was organized chaos with empty trailers parked every which way and with what seemed like a constant stream of canoers or kayakers taking advantage of the sunny day to use the launch.

Across the street, painters spruced up the exterior of the Episcopal church, the high whine of their sanders adding to the rumble of lawn mowers and weed whackers farther off. Vonda could feel, rather than hear, the *lub-dub-lub-dub* vibes of somebody's boom box.

A handful of elementary school–aged kids were throwing food pellets to mallard ducks that swam in and out of the reeds off the shoreline. Mama mallard was in the lead, quacking at six babies to keep up, ahead of two mallard drakes that lagged behind the family.

Vonda smiled, her senses sucking up the scenery and the pure contentment of the moment and the company.

"This is fabulous," she said. "I love it here, don't you?"

"October's my favorite time," Terrell said, smacking his palm on the table and sending a brown bug to its final picnic. "The temperature's comfortable and the rug rats are usually in school."

"Y'ever notice hot dogs taste better when someone else cooks them? I wonder why that is?"

Terrell wiped the remnants of chili off his mouth with a paper napkin.

"It's not who cooks them," he said. "It's what's in them that makes them taste good."

"What do you think . . . beef? Pork? Turkey? Maybe they're kosher?"

She took another big bite, savoring the smoky flavor.

He shook his head, saying, "Try lips and snouts and fat that'll raise your cholesterol four hundred points."

"Geez, Louise." She chuckled. "Tell me it ain't so."

"Wanna hear Dr. Barksdale's diet theory?"

"Knock yourself out."

He popped an errant bit of kraut in his mouth.

"If it tastes good, it's bad for you. If it tastes like cardboard, help yourself to more."

"I don't know about that," Vonda said. "Okra's not bad for you. I love okra with stewed tomatoes."

Terrell screwed up his face, obviously disagreeing with her assessment.

"We all know you have a warped sense of taste," he said,

and Vonda wasn't at all sure he referred only to food. "Fried okra, I can handle. Boiled okra has the consistency of snot."

Surprised, Vonda burst out laughing and almost choked.

"Thank you for that graphic," she said. "It'll be a good long while before I eat gumbo again."

Finished with her dog, she swiveled around and sat with her back to the table. She reclined on her elbows, her legs crossed at the ankles and stretched out with her heels sunk into the pine needles in front of her.

There was a time when she could sit like that and her breasts would've torpedoed her jersey with no help from Maidenform. Vonda glanced down at the effects of aging on her body. Boy, were those days ever gone.

"How's life in Peyton Place treatin' you today?" Terrell said, biting into his ice-cream cone.

"What? Your ears haven't been burnin' all mornin'?"

"Maybe a little. People kinda expected us to get together years ago."

"One more thing I forgot," she said, shaking her head. "My mind's become a sieve lately. Besides the garden club, we are now the topic of conversation for the Historical Society."

The unsurprising news garnered a dismissive wave.

"Figures," Terrell said. "The same people are in both clubs. Forget 'em. They produce gossip by the truckload."

Out of the corner of her eye, Vonda caught Terrell staring at her again and knew the draw wasn't her boobs. She could sense him turning something over in his mind.

Finally, he leaned forward, resting his forearms on top of the picnic table, and said, "Why didn't we ever get married?"

She lolled her head toward him. He was working on the last bites of his cone.

"Because you never asked," she said, passing him her untouched ice cream.

"Would you marry me now?"

"No."

"Why?"

"Because I'm already married."

"How about if you weren't?"

Vonda saw reflected in his eyes the God-given glory of an undeniable attraction . . . and something else . . . a fearful longing, a man afraid he was about to fall into the crosshairs. A weighty silence passed between them, and then Vonda grinned.

"The answer would still be no," she said.

"Why is that?"

She pushed off the table and gained her feet.

"Because you don't really mean it," she said.

There was that smile of his again. He checked his watch. Vonda took the gesture as the signal their picnic was over.

"I gotta get back to the grindstone," he said.

"Me, too." She gathered up their trash. "I imagine Amelie and her grandparents are home by now, wondering if I've dropped dead."

"You didn't tell them where you were goin'?"

Vonda shook her head.

"No, I didn't think it was a good idea," she said. "They wouldn't understand."

"How about Jerome?"

"What about him?"

"You stayin' or leavin'? Or have you decided?"

"I don't know," she said, stepping over to the trash barrel. "I'm still thinkin' on it."

"What's to think about? He deceived you; you caught him. Can you live with that?"

"Livin' with it's the easy part," she said. "I don't have to pretend to have a happy life anymore." She shrugged. "Everyone knows. Oddly enough, it's a relief."

"I don't understand you," Terrell said, polishing off the second ice-cream cone.

Vonda fixed a knowing smile on her face.

"That makes two of us," she said.

"Listen, if you ever wanna talk, you know where I am."

"That I do. Thanks."

"I enjoyed today," he said, skimming his fingers down her arm to clasp her hand in his. "Let's do this again."

"Sure," Vonda said.

Delicious tension mounted in her core, and her heart beat a little faster.

"Promise?" he said.

"Just give me a holler." She stepped into his embrace, curled one arm around his neck, and kissed his rough cheek, inhaling the sensual fragrance of his skin and feeling his erection rise against her thigh. "See y'later, Terrell."

And then she walked away.

"Love ya, Von," he called after her.

She smiled, but kept walking, letting Terrell's words hang in the air, not touching them, much as she wanted to.

Instead of taking the path the way she'd come, Vonda crossed the street to follow the winding sidewalk home. The route took longer, which was what she wanted. It gave her more thinking time.

Up ahead, a waist-high gardenia hedge marked the property boundary of the Episcopal church. The hedge was green, the blooms dried up and gone, the remnants littering the ground.

Movement in the branches caught her attention. She figured it was either little kids playing hide-and-seek, or maybe a bird with a nest.

She tiptoed closer to catch a glimpse. The very human sneeze sounding from the hedge convinced her it must be the former. She stretched on her toes to peer over the bushes, and what she saw trying to crouch out of sight made her annoyed and somewhat perplexed.

"Tata? Lolo?" she said. "What are y'all doin' hidin' in the bushes? Are y'all spyin' on me?"

Lolo squealed and grabbed for her chest. Tata broke out in nervous giggles and leaped up first, saying, "Spyin'?" She shook her head as she reached down to help a struggling Lolo to her feet. "No, not us. Whatever gave you such an idea?"

"The leaves and grass stains on your knees," Vonda said.

"There's a perfectly good explanation," Tata said, breaking into another nervous giggle.

"Such as¿"

"Give me a minute to think up one."

"Come off it," Vonda said and turned to continue a humorless walk toward home.

Lolo skipped to catch up, her hands fluttering as she tried to find her voice. Vonda halted and pivoted on her heel.

"Is this gonna be a good story¿" she said. "Or a bad story¿"

"Oh, all right," Lolo said in a rush. "We were spyin'. I admit it. But it was for your own good."

Vonda crossed her arms over her chest, saying, "Keep goin'. I'm listenin'."

"I'm here to save you from yourself," Lolo said in a fierce whisper. "I'll have you know you and What'shisname are makin' a spectacle of yourselves."

Vonda glanced around. Not a soul in the Pavilion paid them any attention, but the painters on the scaffold at the church were nudging each other and staring in their direction.

"Let me get this straight," she said. "Two grown women are in the churchyard pretendin' to be gardenias, yet I'm the spectacle¿ You're such a dork." She swung her attention to Tata. "And I'm surprised at you. What were you thinkin'¿"

"That the hedge was a pretty good plan¿" Tata said and shrugged. "Obviously, I was mistaken. I'm your best friend, Von. I've been where you are—twice, if you count the cute Italian, the one with the big blue eyes. I told you about him, didn't I¿ When we went—¿"

"A-hem," Vonda said, clearing her throat. "In this lifetime."

"Oh . . . yes . . . anyway, as I was sayin'," Tata added, "I just want to see you don't do somethin' you'll regret later on."

"Sorry to disappoint you," Vonda said. "Nothin's happened. We talked, we ate. We ate, we talked. That's my great affair in a nutshell, which is no affair at all."

Lolo said, "Even if you lust in your heart—"

"Don't!" Vonda held up her index finger. "Don't you dare quote Jimmy Carter to me. I never voted for him, and I don't have to agree with anybody whose brother had a beer named after him."

But Lolo wasn't about to leave well enough alone.

"How does Jerome feel about you meetin' other men?" she said.

"There are no other men, Lolo. It's Terrell." Vonda raised her arm in an expansive gesture toward the Pavilion. "You saw for yourself."

Out of self-preservation, Vonda deliberately left out mention of the pup tent in Terrell's pants.

"But if you're so all-fired anxious to know," she added, "why not ask Jerome yourself?"

"Don't you give a hoot what your husband thinks?"

"Not really. I give all the time. For years I've given, and he seldom gives back. I'm tired of playin' second fiddle to the Peter Pan of local real estate."

"You seem to forget," Lolo said, "he's the jackass you chose."

"I know. I know." Vonda studied the leather tops of her walking shoes. "Don't rub it in."

But Lolo continued to chase that philosophy like a hound on a fresh scent.

"There's not a thing in the world you can do," she said, "but stick it out."

"Like you, y'mean?"

Lolo's face blanched. Her eyes widened as if she'd been slapped, and Vonda wished with all her heart she could recall the ugly words.

"At least I try," Lolo said, her back stiff. "When I make a commitment, I stick with it. That's what Mother and Daddy taught us."

Vonda inhaled a deep breath and said, "I'm sorry. I didn't mean that the way it came out. What I meant was I'm not you, Lolo. You're my sister . . . I love you and I appreciate your concern."

"Do you really want to be the first divorce in our family? Do you?"

"Let me figure this out on my own. Please? Now, excuse me. I need to ease on home. It's not fair to saddle Amelie with Miss Ludie and Grandpa Thayer for so long."

Vonda started to move around them again when Tata said, "This thing . . . whatever you wanna call it between you and Terrell . . . do you see it movin' toward marriage, Von?"

For a second, Vonda debated whether to play it safe and lie, or tell the truth and face their reactions. The truth won out.

"Not at all, Tata."

"So what's the point? What do you get out of it?"

Vonda shrugged.

"Companionship," she said. "The chance to expand my horizons. Enrich my intimate life." And then she flashed a wicked smile and added, "And maybe get laid like Georgia carpet."

15

The best sermons are lived, not preached.
—Old Farmer's Advice

Cletus's daughter-in-law refused to allow him to smoke in the house.

Cripes. Nothing got past the woman; she had eyes in the back of her head.

Not only was her edict damned inconvenient, but it forced Cletus to sneak outdoors to the patio. Sneaking, he didn't mind. He'd spent half a lifetime perfecting the ability.

It was putting up with the clunky oxygen gear in the sweltering humidity that chapped his hide. Of course, he could always quit smoking, but as far as he was concerned that was unthinkable.

At his age, a good stogie was as much a part of him as the color of his eyes. Cletus believed in living life, and he intended to do so as much as he could, right up to the moment death called his name.

He claimed squatter's rights in the La-Z-Boy recliner that sat in front of a twenty-inch plasma television out on the covered lanai, self-medicating his way through Jerome's liquor cabinet. The boy kept some high-end hooch on hand—not as good as a fruit jar of shine, but pert near.

The oscillating fan on the corner was set on arctic blast and was pointed right at Cletus. He loved his comfort and felt down-home easy in Jerome and Vonda's house.

And why not.

Cletus had his own nicely decorated room, his own toilet, access to a full bar and fridge, and cable television with six— count them—*six* adult channels. A man's golden years didn't get any better than this.

Taking command of the remote control, he whipped through the programs, stopping for thirty seconds or so if something caught his attention. That's why he paused on the Weather Channel, where a cute young blonde gestured at colored maps and cloud formations and a host of other graphics.

" . . . *a hurricane's a vertical heat engine that's driven by warm ocean water . . .*"

Amelie stepped outside, a sweating glass of iced tea in her hand, and settled into a painted aluminum lounge chair beside him.

"Hey, Gramps," she said, putting her swollen feet up. "Watchin' anythin' good?"

"Not yet," Cletus said. "I can't find where the rednecks are playin' poker."

"Temperatures in the tropical Atlantic are running well above normal . . ."

"Try ESPN?"

"Nothin' there but baseball," he said, "and neither team was the Braves, so I ain't innerstead."

The camera shot cut to a group of the regular meteorologists who were gathered around a desk.

"See the guy on the right?" Amelie said and sipped her tea. "Remember his face. Jim Cantore's his name. If you get on a plane and see him sittin' there, just turn right around and get back off."

"How come?"

" 'Cause wherever he's goin', the weather's gonna get ugly and you don't wanna go there. They're all the time sendin' that poor man to the backside of beyond. It's a wonder if he can get health insurance."

Cletus shifted the remote into four-wheel drive and zoomed through more channels, finally halting to watch a pride of lions intent on thinning a wildebeest herd. The silence between him and Amelie was companionable, not strained.

Amelie inhaled her tea. After a few minutes of clinking her teeth while sucking on the remaining ice cubes, she pointed to his cigar and said what was on her mind, said what Cletus figured had brought her out to the patio in the first place.

"Those aren't good for you."

"I know." Cletus blew a coil of blue smoke, watched it disappear, and suffered a racking cough for his trouble.

"Listen to you. Maybe you should think about quittin'."

"Ain't no tragedy in an old man dyin', little gal."

"There is if he goes before his time," she countered.

Cletus shook his head, saying, "Nobody dies before his time. Young, old, or in-between, we all go at the exact minute we're supposed to. Remember that."

He puffed more on his stogie, waiting for her to lecture him further about his bad habits. When she stayed quiet, he figured he'd gotten off easy.

"Where's your grandma?" he said.

"Upstairs, in her room."

"She still upset?"

"I'll give you three guesses and the first two don't count."

Cletus shrugged, saying, "She never could take a joke."

"Well, duh," Amelie said. "Let's explore that, shall we? Miss Ludie says she wants to be put into her favorite blue sweater when she dies. Do you leave it alone? No. You have to go and tell her a sweater's too hot for where she's headin'."

"I call 'em as I see 'em."

"And yet you wonder if she's upset. Hell-lo?"

Cletus merely slanted his granddaughter a lopsided grin.

Which was why Miss Ludie had stormed off to her bedroom in high dudgeon right after they'd returned from Rayburn's, and was holed up there still, babbling incessantly about things that didn't matter. Well, that, and because she'd missed an episode of her damned soap opera.

Cletus figured her self-imposed exile wouldn't last long, not once she reckoned it was more of a trial to her than to anyone else. He thumbed the remote, accidentally hitting the back button, and the weather people appeared on the screen again.

"Shoot," he said, tossing the remote down on the side table. "Nine hundred channels and nothin' to watch."

" . . . the 100 Fathom Curve marks where the continental shelf drops into the abyssal descent . . ."

"Fishermen work the curve for blue marlin," Cletus said, "don't they?"

Amelie shrugged, saying, "Remy doesn't fish for marlin."

"Listen, speakin' of him . . ." Cletus studied the cigar stub he rolled in his fingers. "I'm sorry 'bout jumpin' the gun earlier. It wasn't my intent to make trouble for you, and that's the God's honest truth."

"You old fraud," Amelie said, patting his bony hand and smiling. "You just beat me to it is all. I'll check with the waitress and see how her friend Kev is doin' and play it by ear from there."

About then Caroline stuck her head out the French door, screamed, "Supper's on. Mom says c'mon get it while it's hot!" and slammed the door shut again.

"About time," Cletus said, hoisting himself out of the recliner.

His stomach growled. As the weather people droned on in the background and the ice cubes settled in the glass on the table and the fan whirred away, he and Amelie shuffled inside to join the rest of the Thayers for a good old-fashioned evening meal.

Nothing could top this.

"... *it draws closer to the Florida Panhandle than any other spot on the Gulf of Mexico* ..."

16

Once you teach a bear to dance, you gotta dance
as long as the bear wants.
—Old Farmer's Advice

Say hello to Stella.

The tropical storm roared to life in the warm waters
of the southeastern Caribbean, and four days later aimed for
the Florida Panhandle. The beach had *target* written all over it.
Three hundred miles across, Stella graduated from a category-
one hurricane to a category four in sixteen hours.

Vonda was taking clothes out of the dryer when Charlotte
yelled from the den, "Guess what, Ma! Your favorite weather-
man's reportin' from the beach!"

"Not Cantore?" Vonda yelled back. "Are you sure?"

"I'm lookin' at him on channel three right now!"

Here we go. Vonda dumped the clothes in the laundry basket and snapped up her purse on the fly with the dexterity of someone running with the bulls at Pamplona.

"Girls," she hollered on the way to the garage, "grab your car keys and meet me at Winn-Dixie. Amelie? Stay and watch your grandparents. Put a move on, girls! We need to beat the crowd."

Forty-eight hours from landfall, Stella hit category five, the highest level on the Saffir-Simpson Scale. Her sustained winds were one hundred sixty miles per hour, gusting to one hundred eighty, and she was riding in on ten-foot seas, with a tidal surge expected to reach thirty feet.

Vonda agreed with the comedian Lewis Black when he said on a television program they should forget cutesy names and label such storms Hurricane "Holy-fucking-Moses."

Once word of the impending strike spread, customers stampeded Lowe's and Home Depot like they were hitting the beaches at Normandy. They liberated supplies left and right. Donald Trump wannabes worked the parking lots, hustling out of the backs of U-Haul trucks, where they hawked coolers, wood screws, batteries, kerosene lamps, and gas generators at crack cocaine prices.

A black market for plywood sprang up overnight. Shoppers emptied grocery store shelves of candles, canned goods, bottled water, and ice faster than sale day in Macy's Basement.

The cost of crude oil doubled per barrel in anticipation of offshore rigs taking a hit. Cars clogged gas stations to top off tanks, in long lines reminiscent of the gas shortages in the '70s.

The governor called for evacuations of low-lying areas, which Vonda always found a bit of a misnomer, considering the highest point in the whole state lay up the road a piece and measured out at a skosh over three hundred feet above sea level. Meanwhile, the sheriff's department issued a county-wide warning: Bridges would be closed when sustained winds reached forty-five miles per hour. This emergency order cut off all access to help until the storm had passed, for anyone remaining on the barrier islands.

The halcyon days of hurricane parties had pretty much ended back in the late 1960s when Camille nailed the Mississippi Gulf Coast. After Katrina hit the same area with twice as much vengeance thirtysome years later, no one in their right mind from Gulfport to Apalachicola waited to be told twice. People heeded emergency management warnings and acted quickly in their preparations so they could get the hell out of Dodge.

At the lake house, Vonda decided against waiting for Jerome to come home from work. The more she prepared now the less she'd have to worry over later. She jumped into action, issuing orders like a general to an army.

This wasn't her first hurricane, but it was the first one the girls were old enough to remember and the first one where Vonda had to allow for two immature teenagers, two elderly parents, and a very pregnant daughter, as well. The house sat twenty miles inland as the crow flies, so she knew storm surge was no problem for them.

But the devastating winds and rain were.

Jerome finally called, in a rush to say he had to secure the office and several properties for absentee owners before he could head out.

"When do you think you'll get home?" Vonda asked.

Outside the kitchen window, cloud banks raced by and the sky darkened from blue to angry gray. She was feeling more anxious and alone as the mantle of obligation weighed heavier and heavier on her shoulders.

"Don't start," Jerome snapped. "How many times do I have to tell you I've got a job to do? Can't you appreciate that I've got a responsibility to our clients to care for their property and safeguard their capital?"

She plunged ahead, even though his unexpected broadside made her feel guilty for asking.

"Yes, yes, of course," she said. "I understand the numerous responsibilities you have. But what about the responsibility to your family? Don't we count in there somewhere?"

"That's where you pick up the slack. We're partners, aren't we?"

"I don't know. You tell me. It feels like an awfully one-sided partnership to me."

"For the love of—Quit bein' a baby, Von. How can I keep a roof over our heads if I don't work?"

"Accordin' to the Weather Channel, that roof you're so fond of is about to blow to kingdom come."

"Now you're bein' melodramatic . . ."

"Maybe so, but I feel justified. Whenever I need help, you're never around."

"That's not fair. How about givin' me credit where credit's due? I do plenty. I'm a good father and a damned good provider."

"I never said you weren't."

Although Vonda was no stranger to rejection, she tired of her life constantly taking a backseat to her husband's wants, desires, and overbearing pride. He lived and moved in a world that excluded her and once, just once, she wished Jerome would pick her first.

That wasn't happening, and she felt another idealized expectation, another youthful dream dashed by time.

"The roof's tied in to the foundation," Jerome was saying, completely oblivious to her cry in the dark. "It's not goin' anywhere, so relax."

Vonda rubbed her forehead and blew out a tired breath, wasting no further energy dwelling on hopeless wishes. She'd made her bed years ago and, as Lolo was so partial to reminding her, now she had to lie in it.

"Are you comin' home or not?" Vonda said.

"Where're the girls? Can't they pitch in?"

"Should I take that as a *not*?"

A loud *whoosh* followed by the sharp crack of glass breaking echoed from the phone and drowned out whatever Jerome said next. Suddenly, the sound muffled, and then the line went quiet, as if he had slapped his palm over the receiver, but not before Vonda heard a distinctly female voice giggle and say, "Oopsy daisy, sugar—"

Then a nanosecond later Jerome came back on the line and practically growled, "Gotta go."

"Who's there with you?" Vonda said. "Is that a woman's voice I heard? It was, wasn't it?"

"Now, Von, you're lettin' your imagination run wild."

"Cut the weasel words, Casanova," she said. "I'm not a whack job yet. I know what I heard."

"Okay, then you know it doesn't mean anythin', Von."

She stared at her cell phone in disbelief. The bastard didn't even have the courtesy to sound remorseful.

"What I know," she snapped, "is we're fixin' to be washed away by a cat five, and you're playin' hide the sausage with some bimbo. Go ahead, deny it."

She expected to hear him either try to sweet-talk his way out or to argue.

Instead, he changed his tone and said, "Can we discuss this later?"

"Sure . . . in divorce court. Y'better watch your step, Jerome, I might stop carin'."

He chuckled and said, "Do what y'all need to at the house, sweetheart, and I'll finish up when I get there. Bye, now."

And then he abruptly hung up, without addressing his wife's assertion and without a word regarding the welfare of his parents.

Figured. He took it for granted Vonda would play nice and forgive him whenever his ego outstripped his age and maturity. Took it for granted she would batten down the house, as well as ensure they had enough food and supplies on hand to feed Sherman's Army.

Oh, hell. And why shouldn't he?

Why would Jerome bother to change his ego trip for two when Vonda always did what needed doing? And as usual, she'd have to manage Miss Ludie without him.

No big whopping surprise there.

Whatever shenanigans Jerome was really up to, it was obvious to Vonda he wasn't making mischief all by his lonesome. She hadn't heard enough of the woman's voice to recognize who it belonged to, but this was a small town.

Secrets didn't stay secrets for long.

For now, Vonda would no longer worry about what Jerome did.

She put him out of her mind for the time being and joined the girls to continue sweeping the outside of the house clear of any items that could become missiles. The chore was a good learning experience for them and kept Vonda from thinking too much.

"Grab the garbage cans," she said.

"And put 'em where?" Caroline asked.

Vonda pointed toward the garage, saying, "The workshop. Wherever they'll fit."

"Plants, too?" Charlotte said, pointing to the pots.

"No, they'll die for sure. Haul them into the house."

Doormats, chair cushions, and the like followed the garbage cans and were stuffed into the overflowing garage workshop.

"Mom?" Caroline yelled from the backyard. "What 'bout the patio furniture?"

Vonda cast about for a place with enough room to accommodate the three bulky lounge chairs, one dining table, six dining chairs, two side tables, and a market umbrella.

"Stick the umbrella behind the sofa in the den," she said. "Chuck the rest of the furniture to the bottom of the pool."

"The pool?" Charlotte said. "You sure?"

"It can't fly," Vonda said, "if it's under six feet of water. Now hop to."

Grandpa Thayer and Miss Ludie had temporarily suspended hostilities so were recruited to fill lanterns with oil and replace old radio and flashlight batteries with fresh. The white wicker chairs and hanging plants were removed from the front verandahs and scattered throughout the den, living room, and upstairs hallway.

When Vonda checked the lanai later, she pulled up short.

"Charlotte?" she called as her daughter rounded the corner with another clay pot of red geraniums in her arms. "What's your daddy's recliner, fan, and TV doin' in the pool?"

"The backstroke?" Charlotte said and grinned. "Gotcha! You walked right into that one."

She joined Vonda at the edge of the swimming pool. Vonda rolled her gaze heavenward, and then pointed to the now-ruined furniture.

"We are not amused," she said. "For future reference, electrical appliances won't work right, if they work at all, once they've been submerged. And chlorine really does a number on leather."

"Then why'd you say toss 'em in the pool?"

A deep, calming breath later, Vonda said, "Never mind."

Caroline came over then, and mother and daughters enjoyed a bonding moment, standing there on the coping and staring into the azure water of the very crowded pool, their heads bobbing like Katharine Hepburn's as a stiff wind whipped across their faces.

"Y'want us to pull 'em back out?" Caroline said, clawing hair out of her eyes.

"The recliner's waterlogged." Vonda shook her head, her gaze fixed on the water but her mind already on the next problem. "Probably weighs the same as a baby hippo by now. It'll take more than the three of us to lift it out." She raised her hands in surrender. "Leave them. The damage is done, and we don't have anywhere to put them, anyway."

"Maybe Daddy won't notice," Charlotte said.

Caroline snorted at her sister's hopeful tone and said, "Oh, he'll notice. One baby blue eyeball gazing at the blank space where his TV used to sit and we are so busted."

"Accidents happen," Vonda said and shrugged, not concerned in the least if Jerome popped a blood vessel or two or three.

Next, she lowered the metal hurricane shutters on the windows and across all but one side door. The shutters were electric. The trick to opening them would come when the storm passed and the electricity was gone with it.

At this point, wind damage was no longer Vonda's chief concern.

Rising lake water was.

Hurricane Stella's first rain bands moved onshore around noon, pushed sideways by winds gusting to sixty miles per hour that bowed pine trees nearly in half and had the lake water black and churning with angry white caps.

As unnerving as the weather was, it was a beautiful sight to see the rough, wild, uncontained fury of Mother Nature. Such storms were her way of reminding humans who was really boss.

Vonda stood on the front verandah, leeward of the blustery wind, and stared at the sidewalk that circled the shore of the lakeyard. Or rather, that used to circle the shore.

Right now, the rainfall exceeded one inch an hour, and the sidewalk was disappearing beneath the encroaching water. She glanced to the sullen sky, and then again to the lake.

And then it registered.

When the hurricane moved onshore and the torrential rains came—not *if* they would, but when—nothing would stop the black water from advancing. It was coming fast now, much faster than she'd ever seen it or even imagined it could.

Crap.

There was no way to fight a flash flood that she knew of. At least, not and win.

She quickly gauged the shortening distance between the water and the house.

Crap. Crap. And *double crap.*

They had to hit the road soon or risk being trapped for who knew how long in the upper floors of the house. She'd been there, done that, burned the T-shirt when she was younger. She was too old to live through that mess on purpose again, not when she had alternatives.

Jogging to the side door, the only one not yet shuttered, she darted inside, hollering upstairs for everyone to pack a bag. Then she swept through the first and second floors, gathering the personal photos and knickknacks she hated to lose and depositing them on the third floor, just in case.

Next, she headed to the kitchen to box and sack the supplies. When her cell phone rang, it was Terrell, and part of her was relieved.

"Are you watchin' the lake, Von?"

"We're loadin' the cars now."

"Good. I was gonna come over there and push you out of the house myself if you were stayin'."

"I'll admit I thought about it for half a second. Ever tried to clean the smell out of carpet and Sheetrock that's been soakin' in swamp water for three days?"

"It's just stuff, Von. We can replace stuff. We can't replace people."

"Don't worry, I'm not ready to drink the Kool-Aid yet. As I was about to say, we stayed durin' the hurricane twenty years ago, and I thought then I'd never get that nasty smell out of my sinuses. I said never again."

"Is Jerome goin' with you?"

"No clue. He's not here yet. But he can do what he wants."

"I'm fixin' to leave for my sister's," Terrell said. "If you need any help, I can run over."

"I appreciate the offer, but, no, we're fine. You go on. Tell your sis hey for me, and y'all keep yourselves dry."

"Will do. Are you headed out to your daddy's cabin?"

"Sure am. It's built like a fortress. I figured that was the best place to hunker down."

Years ago, Vonda's daddy had built a sturdy hunting cabin on a quarter section of what was once an old cotton plantation. The plantation sat on higher ground in a rural area about ten miles this side of the Alabama line.

The cabin—built of pine logs, fully furnished, two full bathrooms, fully equipped kitchen and laundry—slept twelve with room for more if they camped out on the floor.

An old farmer and his wife looked after the property, which was an easy gig because the cabin rarely saw use during the summer months, except for the occasional smoker Jerome would host for preferred clients. The main work came October through February. That was when a mix of clients and hunting buddies showed up every weekend, mainly to swap lies and thump their chests while drinking voluminous amounts of beer.

"No tellin' how long the phone lines'll stay up out there," Vonda said, "but I'll have my cell with me. With luck, the towers'll last longer."

"I'll stay in touch, then," Terrell said. "To check y'all are all right. In case Miss Ludie or Grandpa Thayer need anythin'. Oh, y'know what I mean."

"And I'm glad for you to," Vonda said.

That was one of the admirable traits about Terrell—he

always seemed to sense a person's mood. He knew when to tease and when to nurture.

"It's good somebody besides Lolo knows where we are," she added.

"She goin' to the cabin, too?"

"Not this time. The school gym. They've designated it as a Red Cross shelter. I talked to Lolo a bit ago, and she said her husband, Marcel, wants to ride out the storm there because the buildin's made of brick. Like brick didn't get blown to hell and back in Katrina."

"I'll huff, and I'll puff, and I'll blow—?"

"Yeah, somethin' like that." Vonda chuckled. "He's got a few issues to work through. Anyway, I won't keep you. Thanks so much for callin', Terrell."

"You don't have to thank me, Von. I'm happy to help, you know that. Take care. Remember . . . if you need anythin' . . ."

"You're the bomb. I'll remember."

"Bye."

She nodded, even though he couldn't see her, closed her phone, and sent up a silent thank-you for Terrell Barksdale. The man was a living testament to the fluidity of friendship.

Whatever she'd done to deserve him in her life, please, please, please let her keep on doing it. For reasons she could only guess at, he understood her train wreck of feelings and intentions better than she did, and he continued to endure her pitiful existence in his life anyway.

Lord love a duck, what would she do without Terrell? If nothing else, he raised a good question in Vonda's mind, one she'd have to ponder on for an answer: When the helper needed help, who did she turn to? Who threw her the lifesaving ring and kept her from drowning in good intentions, anger, and frustration?

By rights, that helper should be Jerome. Shouldn't it?

Maybe in another life, but the role wasn't a good fit in this one.

Then again, maybe the answer was simpler than she imagined—someone more like Terrell, that's who. Someone perceptive enough to recognize her insecurities.

Terrell would've dropped everything and come to help her this afternoon, Vonda harbored no doubt about it. She didn't need him to as it turned out, but it was, oh, so nice knowing he would.

By the same token, it was humiliating and a downright bubble buster to allow that was more than she could count on from her own husband. Hell's bells, thirty years ago her heart had told her brain to shut up about having her very own bad boy, and look where it had gotten her . . .

She would think twice before listening to her heart again.

Vonda felt God tapping on her shoulder when she accepted that she hadn't been able to count on Jerome for quite a while.

But even acknowledging that wasn't enough to prod her into investing her energies elsewhere. And why not? The reason was a tough thing to admit to herself, let alone to the world, but she couldn't avoid the truth any longer.

Bottom line, Vonda was a chickenhearted wimp.

Like so many young girls of her generation, she'd gone from her father's house to her husband's, ignorant of what marriage really meant. And, in fifty years on this earth, the only jobs she'd ever held were those of wife, mother, and, eventually, caregiver.

Simply put, she was afraid to go it alone, afraid to be stranded both emotionally and financially.

The grass wasn't always greener on the other side. And there were no guarantees she'd find a better life down the road than the one she already had.

There. The ugly fact was out in the open and hovering about her in the ether like her own private black cloud: Having a sorry husband was better than having no husband at all. Jerome was one hundred percent rounder and then some, no question about it, but he was a predictable and familiar rounder.

Lolo's I-told-you-so echoed in Vonda's head.

Just then Charlotte startled Vonda with a shout from the living room, asking if they should move the pricier pieces from the first floor to the upper floors.

"That'll take too long," Vonda called back, her thumb caressing the smooth texture of her phone's screen where Terrell's number still shone. "Leave it all where it is. It's stuff anyway . . . just stuff. If it's gone, it's gone. There's nothin' we can't replace."

She shoved her cell phone into her pocket on the fleeting thought that self-enlightenment came at the most inopportune times. A hurricane waited practically at her doorstep, and that storm was what she needed to concentrate on right now.

Time to get down and busy.

Jettisoning her morose thoughts, Vonda propped the laundry basket of clothes on an ample hip with one hand and grabbed as many plastic sacks of groceries as she could carry in the other hand. Outside, the girls loaded the cars through a steady rainfall.

Vonda would get through this storm all right, just like everything else that came down the pike. If nothing else, after thirty years of marriage, she was adept at dancing between the raindrops.

17

Timing has a lot to do with the outcome of a rain dance.
—Old Farmer's Advice

Amelie's landlord was a retired paper mill worker aptly called Shorty by most everyone. Shorty's paratrooper son Junior actually owned the trailer Remy and Amelie rented, but seeing as how Junior was sucking down camel hump kebobs somewhere in beautiful downtown Afghanistan, he'd left Shorty to look out for things until the Army saw fit to transfer him stateside again.

Other than the occasional repair call, Shorty made a habit of leaving his tenants alone and of butting out of their lives. He came around so seldom it was a surprise for Amelie when she drove up to the side of the trailer and saw him in the blustery wind, tiptoed on the top rung of a tall wooden step ladder that looked to have been ancient in Noah's time.

As Stella's rain bands continued to move onshore, a steady

drizzle fell in between the intermittent downpours and ran in rivulets off the bill of Shorty's ball cap. He was soaked through his T-shirt and shorts to the skin and busy pounding a nail into the last sheet of plywood with a wooden-handled hammer almost as thin as he was.

Under a fabric-lined taupe raincoat, Amelie wore the last dress she fit into, a yellow baby-doll confection with an empire waist, spaghetti straps, and pearlescent shell buttons down the front that ended in a delicate scalloped hem. No telling how the trailer would fare in high winds, so she meant to grab more clothes and personal items while there was still time.

"Hey, Shorty," she yelled, climbing out of her VW as best she could.

"Hey there, your own self, Missy. How y'all doin'?"

"C'mon and hop down from there before you break your neck."

"No need to fret, it's jest a mite breezy is all."

"Yeah, sure, like it's only a mite humid out, too," Amelie said, and then pointed to the plywood. "We should be doin' that."

Not that Amelie could have lifted the first piece of wood or hammered the first nail in, but Shorty caught the drift of her concern.

He chuckled and called down to her, "I ain't too feeble yet for a day's work. 'Sides, Remy done most of 'em. That man of yours is a good worker when he puts his mind to it."

"Where is he then?"

"Gone for more board." Shorty motioned with the hammer, and her gaze followed. "We lack but two pieces yonder on the kitchen side."

Shorty started back down the rungs, so Amelie grabbed one side of the drenched ladder out of habit to steady it, gaining a splinter in her palm for her trouble.

"Where on earth did he come by plywood?" she said. "The television reported the stores were sold out early this afternoon."

"Beats me." Shorty hopped the last rung to the soggy grass and set about folding up the ladder. "I done figured that boy's got an in with the right folks."

Malone immediately sprang to Amelie's mind.

A master capitalist, if anyone could put bribery and influence to work during a natural disaster, he darn sure could. She'd bet her eyeteeth on it.

"Can't never tell what a storm'll do," Shorty added, eyeing his handiwork. "Y'done gone through inside and picked up what y'don't want ruint, ain'tcha?"

"Not yet. S'why I'm here." Amelie wiped raindrops off her face. "I been busy at Mama's."

"I wouldn't wait, if'n I was you, Missy. That sky yonder to the south's lookin' awful mean." For someone so slight, Shorty hefted the unwieldy ladder with ease and headed toward the kitchen windows. "Holler when yore ready and I'll tote for you."

"It's not that much," Amelie said. "Really."

"Never you mind. Don't go totin' nuthin' to y'car. Lemme do that, y'hear?"

"Yes, sir." Amelie nodded, and Shorty seemed appeased.

He hefted the ladder a smidge for better purchase, saying, "Y'mama and them doin' all right?"

"Fine, thank you."

"Be sure to tell 'em I said hey."

"I will." Amelie started for the front door, and then angled back. "What about the cats? What'll we do with them?"

Shorty halted, leaned his weight on the ladder, and smiled, saying, "Don't fret y'self none. They fend for they own selves. Cats is like chil'run—they hightail it quick as spit, an' then come a runnin' back soon's they need sumpin'."

"I hope you're right," she said.

"Y'know, Missy, it ain't none of my business, but I was wonderin' . . ."

He was as subtle as a chain saw. Amelie knew what was coming and finished his thought for him.

"But you're wonderin' why Remy's here by himself," she said, "is that it?"

Shorty ducked his chin and came back up wearing a very wet gap-toothed grin.

"It's just," he said, "y'all are good tenants, and good tenants are hard to come by. I sure do hate to see you young folks not gettin' on together . . ."

He kept talking, unaware the subject fired on an open nerve and chipped away at Amelie's pride. Obviously, either a neighbor or Remy himself spilled his guts to Shorty about their spat, but Amelie had no clue who squealed or what was said exactly.

She was saved from asking when a county squad car sped past with sirens wailing. The emergency vehicle's aural urgency was a reminder that she needed to hurry and grab her few things and get gone, or continue trusting the testy voltage regulator on her VW to hold up under the uncertain mercies of blowing rain.

"I appreciate your thoughts, Shorty," she said, "and I'm sure Remy does, too. But . . . . well, sometimes, there's no accountin' for it, things just don't work out."

More than likely, Shorty was fishing for assurances of their continued rental, but Amelie was unwilling to speculate about what the future might hold for them. She needed a cookie and a hug.

Sighing to herself, she mounted the steps to her front door. Now was as good a time as any for her fairy godmother to show her face, and if the old broad could sprinkle a suggestion or two about what Amelie should do, even better.

The satellite dish at the cabin still received a signal, so Vonda settled her bickering in-laws into the matching blue corduroy recliners that sat front and center of the living room's portable television.

No telling what gentle prelude opened their latest disagreement. Vonda wasn't interested enough to ask, either.

But her druthers didn't matter. She found out whether she wanted to or not.

Miss Ludie flung her arm out, gesturing toward her ex, and

said to Vonda, "Tell this know-it-all the soap in the bathroom is not Ivory. It's called Irish Spring."

"Am I wearin' a blue uniform," Vonda said, pointing to herself, "with U-M-P stamped on my forehead?"

"Call it *Winter in Rio* if you want," Grandpa Thayer interjected, "you crazy dame. All I know is the damned soap *floats*."

On that note, Vonda wisely kept the hysterical cackles behind her gums as she parked a maple-colored TV tray table beside each chair. Their constant squabbling was driving her nuts, and it was proving a short journey.

She served Miss Ludie and Grandpa Thayer both a deviled egg, a tuna sandwich, and a very stiff screwdriver to swallow the food down with, in hopes the snack would mellow them out until she could fix a proper meal.

Vonda planned an early supper for them all this evening. She wanted as much of her day finished as possible before the power left them in the hot and humid dark.

The television remote lay on the end table between the recliners. Vonda left it there, figuring Miss Ludie and Grandpa Thayer could battle it out to see who would command their viewing. Vonda's money was on Miss Ludie to win.

Aside from taking potshots at each other, Vonda's in-laws had been cooperative toward her, or as cooperative as they were capable of being. She was too grateful to question why and sent a silent thanks to the powers that be for the peace offering, however unintended it probably was.

Leaving the pair to monitor weather reports, Vonda hoofed

it back out to the double carport to finish helping the girls un-load the cars. A hard gust caught the mudroom screen door just as she crossed into the open breezeway and almost blew the screen off its hinges before Vonda could slam it closed behind her.

When her daddy had built the cabin, he'd situated it in the middle of a sleepy five-acre Bahia grass pasture that was sur-rounded by oak bottoms, wetlands, and thick deer woods. The locale was usually a placid and undisturbed place, one far from the glare of town lights and insulated from the noise of inter-state traffic.

As a child, Vonda had spent many a summer afternoon in a rocker on the back porch, watching thunderclouds come out of the south, driving rain across the pasture grass. No one had to tell her—she just knew someone in heaven had turned on a giant sprinkler.

Now, the wind howling in mournful surges through the tops of the outlying pine trees sounded anything but heavenly. She caught sight of another band of rain beating a running path across the pasture toward the cabin.

On the tin roof overhead, drizzle soon increased to show-ers that came down in sheets, drumming in eerie waves. Water flooded the aluminum gutters in a noisy rush so that Vonda smelled the earthy perfume of wet grass, moldy leaves, and ripe dirt above the sweet acidity of rain.

Not a bird was in sight. Not a squirrel, a rabbit, or a white-tail deer. Even the banana spiders seemed to have taken refuge somewhere, sensing the impending storm.

Vonda sent up another silent thanks, this time for their part-time man who had cleared the porches and boarded up windows before she and the rest of the family had arrived. That little bit of help was a welcomed relief.

"Twenty-eight rolls of toilet paper," Caroline said, kicking the passenger door closed with the toe of her sandal. "Miss Ludie brought a pallet of TP, Ma. Does she know somethin' we don't?"

"Hemorrhoids, maybe?" Vonda said and shrugged.

Caroline scrunched her nose and made a face, saying, "That's disgustin'."

"Come back in twenty years and talk to me about it," Vonda said. "For now, go ahead and divide the rolls between the two bathrooms, please." She pivoted on her heel to double-check that everything was out of her SUV. "There should be room under the sinks. Anyone seen Amelie?"

"Not me." Caroline shifted the unwieldy load of TP in her arms and gestured with her chin. "Why don'tcha ask lazybones over there."

Charlotte popped her dark head out of her trunk to say, "Watch it, douche bag. I'm helpin' as much as you. More, even."

"Girls!"

"She started it," Charlotte said, pointing. "Make her give back my pink tank."

"Not now." Vonda's warning gaze swiveled between the two. "We've got too much to do, so quit your squabblin'."

"Like, what else do we afta do?" Caroline said.

"Why?" Vonda said. "Do you have a hot date?"

"Me and Bev are 'posed to practice our routine."

"Not tonight. I don't think so."

"She's expectin' me over. Birdlegs said—"

"No one's goin' anywhere in this weather," Vonda said, incredulous eyes wide. "Not you, not Bev. Birdlegs will under—I mean, Coach Susan will understand. Y'all really have to stop callin' the poor woman that name. It isn't at all nice." Then Vonda counted off on her fingers, adding, "We have to set out flashlights and candles and matches in every room, unless you want to stumble around in the dark and hunt for them. There's laundry—"

"Can't laundry wait 'til after the hurricane?" Caroline said. Her whine was grating on Vonda's nerves.

"Only if you beat it on a rock," she said, "and hang it over a bush."

Both girls shared a confused glance, and Charlotte said, "Somethin' wrong with the washer and dryer?"

"Yeah," Vonda said. "They're two-twenty, not one-ten. They pull too much juice for the generator. We're gonna live like pioneers for a while, girls. It'll be fun."

The scowls on their faces suggested otherwise.

"Okay, then, let's not get ahead of ourselves," Vonda said. "First we clean and fill the tubs, the sinks, every jug and pitcher we can find . . ."

As the list grew, both girls emitted obnoxious sighs.

"That's *so* not fair," Caroline muttered, all but stomping into the cabin with her armload of supplies. "Doesn't anybody care that child labor is against the law?"

Vonda ignored her complaint and asked again, "Charlotte, do y'know where Amelie got off to?"

"Her house, I reckon. No—wait, here she comes."

A few moments later, Amelie's VW whipped into the driveway right behind Vonda's SUV. The engine sang an anthem for the dying with a baleful mixture of clanks, clunks, and chug-a-booms.

"Good Lord," Vonda said. "It's a wonder that junk heap made it. It sounds like the drum solo from In-A-Gadda-Da-Vida."

"Inna who?" Charlotte said.

"Iron Butterfly?" Vonda said. "Y'know, like Wipe Out but different?" Still receiving a blank stare, she waved the notion away. "Never mind. Before your time. Add it to your iPod wish list."

A gray tabby stared through the rain-soaked windshield, clinging to the dashboard with the determination of a lion clutching a tasty gazelle. His gaze locked onto the back-and-forth motion of the wipers until Amelie cut the engine and the wipers stopped in midslap.

"Hope you brought a box and litter for that," Vonda called to her, pointing to the cat. "Because I don't have either one here."

Amelie waddled through the downpour, ducking under the overflowing waterfall from the gutters, and into the shelter of the carport. Water dripped off her and puddled on the concrete flooring.

"I couldn't run him out of the car, Ma." She cast off the hood of her raincoat. "I opened the door to toss in some clothes and baby stuff and he made himself to home." She shrugged. "We'll figure somethin'. He'll be okay."

The terrified look on the cat's face indicated that maybe Amelie was being overly optimistic. Vonda eyed her eldest daughter, thinking the youthful glow of pregnancy Amelie usually wore seemed to have faded from her cheeks today. She appeared more vulnerable, more wan.

"You see that husband of yours?" Vonda said.

Amelie shook her head and said, "Remy didn't make it back before I left. Shorty said he'd gone to get more plywood, and I imagine he had to see about his boat, too. He didn't call me or nothin', Ma."

Vonda automatically started to offer a weak argument in Remy's defense, a white lie to make her baby happy, but the words crumbled to dust in her mouth.

"I'm sorry, punkin," she said instead and grinned. "I'll always love you."

"I know, Ma." Amelie ducked her chin. "It's just not the same, that's all."

"C'mon." Vonda wrapped an arm around Amelie's shoulder and gave her a light squeeze. "Let's get you inside and into some dry clothes. You're soaked. I'll bet you're tired, too. Charlotte? You and Caroline come back out and get the cat and the rest of Amelie's stuff from her car, please."

As a concession to her big sister's delicate condition, Charlotte nodded without complaint but, in the next instant, managed to quell any notion that she internalized what she was thinking. She opened the screen door for her mom and sister and screamed over their heads for Caroline to get her happy ass outside to help.

On the way past Charlotte, Vonda nonchalantly popped the teenager in the back of her noggin.

"Watch your mouth," she said, "and quit gettin' uppity."

"Hey, ow!" Charlotte said, leaning against the opened screen and rubbing her head. "That's child abuse, y'know."

"And it's my cross to bear," Vonda tossed over her shoulder, not a bit contrite.

The three-bedroom hunting cabin featured predictable masculine furnishings. Trophy mounts littered the walls, braided rugs covered the slate floor, and a great room sported traditionally styled heirloom wood tables and relaxed leather sofas.

It was a split plan: two bedrooms and a bath at one end of the cabin, furnished with two sets of pine bunk beds each; while the sprawling master suite occupied the other end and boasted two queen beds.

Since there was no way Miss Ludie and Grandpa Thayer liked sharing the same universe, let alone sharing the same room, Vonda assigned them each a bunk room to themselves. That left her and the girls to divvy up the master bedroom. Charlotte and Caroline claimed one bed, leaving Amelie and Vonda the other.

"Where's Daddy gonna sleep?" Caroline said.

"Air mattress on the floor or the livin' room sofa," Vonda said, a sour edge to her voice. "He can have his pick."

That is, she silently added, *if he bothers to show up at all.*

She'd phoned him once today, only to get kicked in the

teeth. She wasn't phoning him again to find out how he planned to ride out the hurricane.

Over the years, she and Jerome had drifted apart while sharing the same house. Now they had three kids and the best that could be said about their relationship was they disliked each other.

In all honesty, his sneaking around never hurt less. It just hurt less and less often. They hadn't yet sunk as low as openly living in separate bedrooms with the doors locked, but that day wasn't long in coming.

No two ways about it, something had to change if the grumpy bastard expected to remain part of this family. He'd have to pull the plug on his phony excuses and come clean about his outside activities.

That is, *if* he expected to remain part of this family. If? The thought gave her pause.

Maybe he had different expectations?

Until this moment, Vonda hadn't considered that possibility. It was a notion worth pondering further.

But speak of the devil and he appears. Exactly four hours later, Jerome and his son-in-law were bunking with Grandpa Thayer.

18

Quit counting the chickens you might have,
and count the chickens you do have.
—Old Farmer's Advice

During the summer, daylight in the Florida Panhandle usually stretched into the evening until well past eight o'clock or so. Today was an exception.

Grim skies, together with the plywood, hemmed in the windows and doors and acted as a blackout so time appeared later inside than the moose clock over the cold fireplace indicated.

The clock had been bestowed, years before, on Vonda's late daddy, presented to him by a drinking buddy who knew far more about gag gifts and mixology than he did about which animal species were indigenous to Florida. McMoose, as the children and cousins affectionately dubbed the molting timepiece, had been a part of the décor for so long and was such a conversation starter, the idea of retiring him to the toolshed never occurred to anyone.

McMoose now looked down his considerable nose at a great room that was ablaze with table and floor lamps. Between the air conditioner and the ceiling fans, each room stayed cool and comfy despite the high humidity.

Vonda had the television tuned to the local weather report, but with the sound lowered since the national updates occurred only on the hour. Local reporters focused on school and road closings and on shelter availability, information not pertinent to the Thayer household or of interest to them at the moment.

Outside, rain thundered down nonstop. Insistent wind battered the rainfall against the backside of the cabin, and raced down the chimney chase in an eerie, screaming whistle.

Vonda had worked up a sweat cooking pork and greens with cornbread for supper and was washing the last dish when Remy and Jerome scurried through the door, dripping water on the gray slate with every step. She stared at them like a confused carp and almost choked.

Somewhere along his day, Jerome had changed from his usual Southern planter suit into a Baltic blue-and-white vertical-striped piqué knit shirt and British tan twill shorts with alligator belt. Luxury and style were key to his façade. How like him not to let anything, even a hurricane, interfere with his delusion.

"Lookee what the cat drug in," Jerome said, smiling wide, as if he were a politician on the stump.

He hooked his thumb over his shoulder. A sun-weathered Remy trudged in behind him, clad in a well-worn white Guy

Harvey T-shirt over faded brown cargo shorts. From his boat shoes to the white lines where his sunglasses usually sat, he looked exactly like what he was: a fisherman. In his arms, he lugged two cases of bottled water and had three flashlights and a portable handheld television resting on top.

"Hey, y'all," he said, shaking his drenched head like a dog. "Think it'll rain?"

Charlotte and Caroline squealed and jumped up from the dining table where they were beating Amelie at a game of Uno. First, they gave their dad a quick peck on the cheek, then they relieved Remy of the cases.

"Where do you want these, Mom?" Caroline said.

Vonda found her voice and said, "On top of the dryer is fine. They'll be easy to get to."

"Hey there, sugarplum," Remy said to Amelie, who still sat at the table. "Is that pot roast I smell?"

With his mussed hair black as night and his lazy grin, he looked like the carefree rascal he was. That, and the earthy, lustful look heating his gaze seemed to Vonda to have stolen her eldest daughter's wits. Amelie was smiling a silly smile back at him and nodding her head.

Obviously, she hadn't reached any definite conclusions yet about what she wanted to do.

She had improvised a litter box out of potting soil and a boot tray, and the stowaway cat seemed tolerant of, if not entirely contented with, its new digs. Remy stepped forward into the great room and promptly stumbled over Amelie's cat, which was torturing a cricket underfoot.

"What the he—?"

"Watch for kitty!" Charlotte cried and scurried to catch up the alarmed feline before it turned ugly and retaliated for the intrusion.

Executing a graceless hop-skip two-step was all that kept Remy from planting his kisser on the sharp corner of the coffee table.

"Are you all right, hon?" Amelie said.

"Fine." Remy held up a hand. "I'm okay. Nothin' six weeks of chiropractor visits won't cure. Damned cat blends right in with the slate. I couldn't see him."

The cat decided to abandon the cricket and not stick around to view the damage. It scampered toward the opened door of the master bedroom, none the worse for wear, with Charlotte hot on its trail.

"Come, Remy," Vonda said. "Sit down and I'll fix you a plate. You eat pork, don't you?"

He regained his footing, pushed away from the table corner, and managed to say, "Pork? Sure. Greens, too?"

"Natch."

"Pepper sauce?"

"Comin' right up," Vonda said.

"How about me?" Jerome peeled off his soggy shoes and socks and slung them in the direction of the coatrack nearest the sofa. "I could eat the crotch out of a sawhorse."

Amelie accepted the buss on the cheek from her husband and said, "You didn't call."

"Sorry, sugar. I had me some things to sort out."

"Me, too."

"You feelin' poorly⸮"

"Tired is all . . ."

Vonda witnessed the private look that passed between Amelie and Remy, and realized they needed breathing room. She crooked her finger at Jerome.

"Help me in the kitchen," she said to him.

His frown would have been comical if not for him pointing to the dining table and saying, "Can't I eat—⸮"

"Yes, dear, you can." She gestured with her eyes, snapping her gaze between Amelie and Jerome until it had to appear she'd developed a demented tic. "In the kitchen. *Now, please.*"

Vonda could almost see the lightbulb go off over Jerome's head when he finally caught her silent message. He cut his glance to the two young people canoodling at the table and his frown cleared.

"Oh," he said. "Yeah, sure, let me lend you a hand."

Vonda's irritated sigh followed him.

"Showers, girls," she called. "Get a move on before the power goes off if you want to wash your hair."

Jerome leaned his backside against the edge of the butcher-block Formica countertop, close to the stainless steel double sink. He reeked of cigar smoke. Folding his arms across his chest, he stretched his legs out in front of him and then crossed his bare feet at the ankles.

"Where's Mother and the old man⸮" he said.

"Gone to meet their maker."

A half second later, Jerome let loose a bloodless gasp, an

inspiration so quick and so deep he nearly sucked all the air out of the kitchen. Vonda crooked a smile at him, one she hoped made him worry a bit.

Then she let him off the hook, saying, "Just kiddin'."

With a long, audible sigh, Jerome said, "Not nice, Von. Don't go gettin' my hopes up like that."

"Spoken like the good son you are."

She reached into the overhead cabinet for two more plates and went about filling them with the leftovers she took out of the fridge. Vonda really was in no mood for her husband's superficial charm.

"Your parents are lyin' down," she said. "It's been a stressful day, to say the least."

"It's too early for bed. Did you give 'em a sleepin' pill or what?"

"Heavens, no. What do you take me for, a drug dealer? I pickled them in Stoli all afternoon."

·"That'll work," Jerome said and chuckled. "They're passed out cold, y'mean?"

She shrugged, and then placed the plate in the microwave oven. While the food warmed, she grabbed a paper towel and wiped beads of moisture off her nose and mouth. Her entire body was dank beneath her black Capri pants and white v-neck T-shirt. Face and neck both had broken out in a cold sweat.

Of all the times for her internal thermometer to go haywire again, why now? Her skin felt clammy, but her innards felt as hot as two hundred hells.

Her body wasn't sure if it wanted to freeze or melt, so it did both at the same time.

"You okay?" Jerome said. "You're red in the face."

"Power surge."

He nodded. "Ain't menopause grand?"

"It's not for wimps, which is probably why God didn't saddle men with it."

Vonda could feel her face baking in her own rising steam every time she leaned down or bent over. And putting up with it was getting damned frustrating.

She wanted a cold bath and a colder beer. She wanted to rip off the underwear sticking to her like a cheap date. She wanted to throw her head back and howl at the hot-flash gods to leave her the hell alone.

But as she'd discovered over the years, wanting and getting were two different things.

Jerome offered a har-de-har-har roll of the eyeballs, scrubbed a palm down his chin, and said, "Seriously, I don't know what I'm gonna do with my parents. They okay? I mean, other than bein' soused?"

Vonda raised her eyebrows and planted a hand on her hip.

"Since when do you care?" she said.

"I don't." His lips went tight and defensive. "But since neither one of 'em bothered to plan for much of any kind of future, includin' their own old age, I'm stuck havin' to deal with it."

I'm stuck? I'm . . . stuck? Vonda snorted. She couldn't help herself. Her pride stung.

Listen to that son of a gun. Did he truly believe what he said? He certainly showed no qualms about taking credit and giving Vonda's contribution short shrift.

"Don't be solicitin' votes for sainthood just yet, Ghandi," she said, passing him the plate from the microwave.

"Oh, y'know what I mean, sweet pea." He shoved off the counter's edge and took the plate from her.

"Not really." She shook her head. "No, if memory serves, I'm the one stuck dealin' with your parents' old age. Not you, *sugar dumplin'*."

Vonda wanted to believe it was the heat of the kitchen that proved too much for her, wanted to believe it was the girls constantly yapping at each other, or the storm, or hormones, or the television reporters droning on about potential catastrophes. Whatever the cause driving the primal scream bubbling up from her toes, try as she might, she couldn't swallow back what came exploding out of her mouth next.

"And it's been no damned picnic," she said, "believe you me. This weather's got 'em both stove up. They're achy as all get out and short-tempered. And where is their son, their only child? Not here, puttin' up with their bullshit, that's for damned sure. You and your middle-aged tally whacker are out God knows where havin' a ball, but, hey, ain't actin' the old fool grand?"

On that sour note, she stopped for breath. Lord love a duck, the diatribe felt good to get off her chest.

Jerome's mouth twitched and his eyes narrowed, emotions that defied description crisscrossing his features. When he opened his lips and no sound came out, Vonda knew she was treading on quicksand.

She'd painted an unflattering picture. Trampled his pride. Hit his vanity below the belt. Maybe he recognized the truth in her words? Then again, maybe not.

For a worrisome second, Vonda wondered if her husband was considering hurling the plate of food at her.

Only one thought sprang to mind and that was, *So what if he did?* As far as Vonda was concerned, their relationship had finally hit the rocks.

"Go ahead." She glanced down at the plate and back up to his face. "If you think it'll make you feel better about yourself, go ahead. But when you're done, I promise you, you're gonna clean it up."

They stared at each other, and Vonda realized if he was going to toss the plate, he would've done it already. He was all bluster.

He stood there, debating with himself, probably waiting for her to say some social nicety that would let him save face. So she held off saying anything.

Instead, Amelie made the decision for him when she chose that moment to toddle in after her husband's supper.

"This for Remy?" she said, reaching for the plate Jerome held out. "Daddy?" Her attention swiveled between her parents and she canted her head. "Everythin' all right, you two?"

Reluctantly, Jerome tore his gaze from Vonda and resurrected his plastic smile.

"Yeah, babe, you bet. I was just bringin' this out to you. Here y'go."

He nodded and passed off the plate to Amelie, along with a fork and paper napkin.

Once she was out of earshot, Jerome said, "You're weirdin' me out, Von. What's gotten into you lately?"

"Funny you should ask," she said.

He held a finger to his lips, staving off any protest, and saying, "Hold it down. Y'want the girls to hear? Try to stay calm and rational for once, will you?"

Rational? she wanted to scream. *Don't you realize I'm closer to sixty than to thirty . . . realize I wasted my skinny years on you . . . realize life isn't a do-over?*

"I'll give you calm and rational," she said in a fierce whisper, punctuating each word by slinging a spoonful of greens onto another plate. "Am I the one tryin' to be Casanova reincarnated? The one sneakin' around on the sly? Leadin' the planet in deflowerin' virgins like nobody's business—?"

"Okay, okay, if it makes *you* feel better, I admit I'm the villain here, I guess."

"You guess? I'd smack you upside the head here and now, 'cept I think you'd enjoy it."

Then Vonda shoved the second loaded plate none too gently at him, and he popped it in the microwave to warm. He sighed, exasperated and somewhat bemused.

"Deflowerin' virgins?" he said. "Where did that come from? You may find the idea titillatin', but it sure sounds like a lot of work to me."

Vonda hardened her tone, wiping any trace of humor from it, when she said, "Go ahead. Laugh all you want. Frankly, I've had enough. E-n-u-f-f. We need to talk, Jerome, and we need to talk now."

"Now? This very minute."

"Now."

"You're serious, aren't you?"

"Very."

"All right." He nodded. "But, cripes, Von, could you pick a better time? We're in the middle of a hurricane. First things first. Let's get through this storm, do what we have to do, then you and I'll sit and talk. Okay? How's that sound?"

"I'm not kiddin', Jerome." She shook the serving spoon at him. "This has gone on too long. We need to make some changes; *you* need to make some changes."

"I know, and we will."

"You say that, but you don't mean it."

"I do. I do mean it."

"Promise?"

He laid his hand over his heart, saying, "I promise."

She watched that effortless grin of his appear, but this time he looked different. No, on second thought, he looked the same. She was the one viewing him from a different perspective.

Nothing softened his face for her or lit up his eyes as she once thought they used to do. This time there was no gentle warmth reaching out to prick her sympathy, or tenderness to tug at her heartstrings.

Instead, his smarmy grin made her want to knock out his whole grille.

Vonda searched his eyes, hoping to see a grain of truth to back up the words he uttered. The two of them were heading toward a legal reckoning, whether she wanted it or not. She saw that clearly and distinctly now.

Maybe she had always known it and had preferred to wear blinders. Well, now the blinders were off.

"Fine, then," she said, yanking the plate out of the microwave. Without giving Jerome a chance to change his mind, she jutted her chin in the direction of their son-in-law. "Where'd you find lover boy?"

His smile drooping, Jerome grabbed a fork from the drain board and shoveled into his supper.

"Tryin' to head to the lake," he said. "His truck had stalled out."

"Risin' water?"

"Yep. Looked like the storm sewer couldn't handle the load and was floodin' the road. The county's gotta do somethin' about the drainage there."

"They've been needin' to for years."

"I tried callin' here," Jerome said, reaching over the stove for the salt-and-pepper shakers.

"Sure, you did."

"I did." He shrugged, showing his indifference more than anything else. "I couldn't get a signal."

"If you say so."

Turning to find space for the leftovers in the fridge, Vonda opted to leave off mention of having received two calls from Terrell during the afternoon. He had called to check on their welfare, just as he'd said he would.

"Don't be that way," Jerome said.

"What way? All I'm saying is no signal problem here. The girls have been textin' all afternoon."

Vonda gave a sidelong glance to measure Jerome's reaction. He seemed more interested in feeding his face than in salvaging the truth or her feelings.

"So how'd you know where we were?" she added, closing the fridge door and turning back to the counter.

"I have my sources."

"No, really. How'd you know?"

"Easy." Jerome waved his empty fork in the air in front of him, a gesture that encompassed the world at large. "You don't have anyplace else to go."

And that, Vonda thought, explained her life in one very sorry nutshell.

She tossed the dirty flatware into the soapy dishwater in the sink and opened her mouth to sputter out a retort. No words passed her lips though, because, suddenly, everything happened at once.

19

Every man thinks his goose is a swan.
—Old Farmer's Advice

An ungodly, loud, splintering *crack!* and *boom!* outside shook the dishes on the kitchen shelves. The sudden sound startled the bejeebers out of everyone.

All at once, the girls screeched from the master bathroom. Amelie yelped. Vonda flinched, and Jerome set to cursing.

"There goes the transformer," Remy hollered.

Vonda had been trying to outrun the power outage all afternoon, yet when it finally overtook her and plunged the cabin into total darkness, it still caught her off guard.

Without waiting to be told, Remy struck a match and lit the first of two fat hurricane lamps that sat on the dining table. The flare of yellow light piercing the blackness prodded Vonda into action.

She grabbed the nearest two flashlights off the counter,

pushing one into Jerome's hands and saying, "Check that your folks are all right. I'll see what the girls are wailing about."

The turbulent wind built into a demanding howl, and the rain attacked the plywood on the windows, sounding as if a horde of golfers was using their trusty three-woods to drive golf balls from six feet away. A violent splitting was followed by something heavy slamming into the back deck.

"Reckon that was the chimney cap?" Jerome yelled.

"Sounded like the whole chase," Remy said.

Vonda stepped into the noisy and pitch-black master bath, correctly figuring the girls couldn't locate the switch on the battery-powered Coleman camping lantern that she'd placed in the center of the double vanity earlier.

"Pipe down, girls." She paused in the doorway and aimed the flashlight under her chin, which outlined her face in eerie shadow. "I . . . see . . . dead . . . people."

"Mom!" Charlotte said. "Not funny."

"You're such a killjoy."

"You had the wrong movie, anyway."

"How did I end up with kids with no sense of humor?" Then Vonda aimed the flashlight at the lantern. "See the switch there? Flip it."

A moment later, fluorescent light filled the bathroom, giving Vonda a chance to take a gander at her daughter. Charlotte lounged in a skimpy blue tank top and a lacy thong, her hair held back by a wide headband and secured in a severe ponytail, her face hidden under a thick, white, fruity-smelling facial mask.

"Lookin' good," Vonda said and chuckled. "Shall I bring the camera in now for the Christmas card pictures?"

"No water," Charlotte said by way of explanation for the lemon meringue puss, "and Caroline's got shampoo in her eyes. When's the water comin' back?"

"A week, maybe less," Vonda said, shutting off her flashlight.

"A week?" came a screech from the shower.

"Maybe more, just depends."

Caroline started crying and stumbled out from behind the shower door, wrapped tight as a mummy in a sage green bath sheet. Her tangled hair was foamy white.

"Call somebody!" she said.

"And who would you like me to call?" Vonda leaned against the vanity. "The pump works on electricity. The electricity is out, so no pump. They won't begin to send crews until after the storm, and even then, I imagine they'll start repairs in the heavily populated areas first."

Charlotte growled and said, "That's so not fair." Then she leaned her head out of the doorway and yelled, "Daddy! Crank up the generator, please!"

Vonda might as well have been wearing a hair suit the way she felt like squirming. Her girls loved their father, shared a profound faith he could fix anything.

Could she really pop that bubble by unloading on them with the news the man was not only human but a serial shithead, as well?

A second later, Jerome called back, "It's a gasoline genera-tor, sweetie. Daddy can't fetch it until the storm passes."

Caroline reverted to wailing. "How am I gonna get the soap out with no water?"

"Where there's a will, there's a way," Vonda said, holding up her index finger. "I'll be right back."

She returned shortly with two mixing bowls, a jug of white vinegar, and two bottles of water. To that, she added a wash-rag she snatched from the pile of towels stacked in the cabinet under the sink.

"Listen up, now. We're gonna go back to nature. Think your pioneer ancestors used conditioners and mousse and blow-dryers and straighteners and all that must-have junk they ad-vertise on TV?"

"Nope," Charlotte said, "which explains why our family re-unions look like the bar scene from *Star Wars*."

"That's on the Thayer side," Vonda whispered. Then louder, "My side was much more photogenic."

One cultured marble sink was filled with water, the other was not. As they talked, Vonda set one bowl in the empty sink and placed the other bowl on the vanity top, where she filled it with equal amounts of bottled water and vinegar.

Pointing to the bowl in the sink, she said, "Lean over, Caro-line. Here, cover your eyes with the washrag. Charlotte? Give us a hand."

Charlotte started clapping.

"Don't make me come over there and smack you. I want

you to keep pourin' this over your sister's head until her hair isn't sticky."

"Ick," Caroline said around the washrag. "I'll smell like a salad."

Shrugging, Vonda said, "And your other choices are what? Oh, yeah, there are no other choices." She gestured to Charlotte's goopy face with the second bottle of water. "Use sparingly. Save some for brushin' your teeth."

"Ma?" Amelie waddled out from the toilet area. "Potty won't flush."

With a single voice, her sisters said, "No water."

"Pump works on electricity," Vonda repeated and pointed toward the bathtub that was filled with water. "Grab the pitcher on the side of the tub. Fill it up and dump it in the toilet."

"Like this?"

Amelie did as she was told, reached back to the old country, and let 'er rip. Water blasted into the porcelain bowl and immediately half of it splashed back out, splatting all over the wall and floor.

"All righty, then," Vonda said, eyeing the mess. "Not quite that hard."

Seconds later, a slurping-glug-glug issued from the toilet, and gravity emptied the bowl.

"Voila!" Amelie laughed. "We don't need no stinkin' man. I am woman; hear me roar. Least now I know what fillin' tubs and such was all about."

"You know all my secrets now," Vonda said, less impressed than her daughter. "I can die a happy woman."

Charlotte dried her freshly rinsed face and said, "Livin' like a pioneer ain't so bad."

"Isn't," Vonda said.

"Isn't so bad. We can do this. Oh, yeah." Charlotte grooved across the bathroom tiles then, and Caroline joined in, wrapping a towel around her wet hair like a turban, and then pumping her arms as if she held pom-poms in her hands. "Easy-peasy, yes, Louisey . . ."

Vonda laughed at their antics. In the back of her mind, she wondered how many days it would take before the novelty of living without creature comforts wore off for the girls, or for all of them, for that matter.

Three? Maybe four days?

As it turned out, Vonda seriously overshot her estimate.

20

Never try to corner something meaner than you.
—Old Farmer's Advice

By two o'clock in the morning, tempers inside the cabin hovered around the boiling point.

The storm raged outside, while the heat and humidity blossomed inside. It was especially hard for Vonda's coddled babies, who had only imagined they were roughing it by existing without curling irons, blow-dryers, cell chargers, or running water.

As time crawled by, they discovered what hell on earth was, namely no air-conditioning. No ceiling fans, either. With so many bodies sucking up the oxygen, the inside of the cabin felt as muggy as a steam room.

Caroline stretched out like a cadaver on the cool floor tile between the dining table and the living room sofa and fanned herself with a teen magazine, whining, "I'm positively meltin', people. Can we please open the door? Pretty please?"

"Not on your life," Vonda said, and Jerome echoed her sentiment. That was probably one of the few times they had agreed upon anything in years. "You get to sit here with us and sweat like pigs. Now, don't ask again."

Even though the mudroom door was protected by the breezeway that ran between the carport and the cabin, opening the door for fresh-air relief was foolhardy until the eye of the hurricane passed over and the monster winds shifted direction.

"But we're hot," Charlotte said.

"And who isn't?" Vonda said. "We're in the same boat, sweet cheeks, so will y'all quit gettin' on my last nerve? Please?"

In their current unhappy state, little did the girls consider that the oppressive heat and suffocating humidity of summer would return with a vengeance once the hurricane was merely a colorful memory.

Oh, yes, Vonda looked forward to the coming days with the same eager anticipation she felt for a root canal without Novocain.

One small blessing . . . Miss Ludie had slept through the evening despite everything. Vonda figured her mother-in-law managed to log some z's regardless of the airless discomfort due to her practice of wearing a vintage nun's habit. Either that, or there were advantages to being piss-ass drunk.

Every time Vonda had checked to make sure the old gal was still breathing, she found her on the bottom bunk, as peaceful as the grave and engaged in Olympic-class snoring. It was then Vonda made a mental note to stock the lake house with several cases of Stolichnaya.

As for Grandpa Thayer . . . no more onions or pickled eggs for him. He was up and down to the bathroom all evening, gifting them with a crotchety disposition and an uneasy stomach, and passing gas in audible blasts that eventually drove Vonda and the girls to seek relief for their abused noses behind the closed doors of the master bedroom.

Remy messed with the portable radio, but gave up when only static came in. Then he fiddled with the antenna of the four-inch handheld black-and-white television.

Finally, one of the three local channels appeared on the tiny screen. The video was mostly snow, but the audio was clear, so Remy elected to tough it out in the living room and monitor the storm's progress.

At least, that was his story. Jerome wasn't so tactful.

Restless and unable to sleep—due to the ugly perfume that dominated the bunkroom, he griped—Jerome dragged a mattress off one of the top bunks and camped out in the living room with his son-in-law. Vonda could hear the murmur of their voices through the wall, although their exact words were lost.

She and the girls had removed the comforters from the queen beds and had settled down on the crisp top sheets. In what felt like no time at all, the coolness of the Egyptian cotton died out and the sheets wilted right along with Vonda and her daughters.

Finally giving in to fatigue, Vonda lay fully clothed in a comfortable but holey white nylon T-shirt and faded blue running shorts, listening to the wind and rain, her mind active although her body was tired. She wasn't in as much misery as Caroline and Charlotte, who sprawled with arms and legs every which way on the other bed.

They finally slept after tossing and turning like puppies that had hunted up just the right spot. In between them lazed Amelie's cat, dry, comfortable, well fed, and totally unconcerned with any human discomfort.

Vonda could see their silhouettes against the moody light spilling from a low-voltage portable lamp in the bathroom. The lamp was in case any of them needed to navigate to the potty in the dark.

"Ma?" Amelie whispered, nudging her in the kidney with an elbow. "You awake?"

On her left side, her back to Amelie, Vonda whispered back, "I am now. What's up, punkin? The baby botherin' you?"

"Not the baby. The heat."

"Is it hot?" Once again, Vonda was all but drowning in her own sweat. "Here I thought it was me."

"I wish it was just you."

"Why, thank you. I'm always happy to take one for the team. Now don't talk so loud. If you wake your sisters, I'm cutting your name out of the will."

"How can they stand it?"

"They're pretending to lie out at the beach, I think."

"Ma?"

"Yeah, babe?"

"Can I ask you a question?"

"You just did."

"*Ma*, I'm havin' issues here. I need my mommy."

Amelie's cranky tone, combined with her feet doing a mild stomp against the mattress, prodded Vonda to roll over and face her.

She propped her head on her bent arm and imitated Elmer Fudd as she used to do when Amelie was small and feeling needy, saying, "Mommy's wight here, my widdle snookums."

"That's better."

"So what'd you wanna ask me?"

"When you were carryin' me, did you want a boy or a girl?"

Vonda waited for her to continue and, when she realized that was all that was coming, said, "That's it? That's your big issue?"

"Can I help it if I'm curious?"

Worried. Scared. And probably too uncomfortable to rest was more like it. Vonda kept silent on that guess, though, because there was little comfort she could offer other than empty platitudes.

"I dunno." Vonda shrugged. "I figured maybe you wanted somebody whacked. Or bail money. Maybe an annulment . . . Y'know, the usual."

"An annulment? On what grounds?"

"That the marriage wasn't consummated, of course."

Amelie stifled a snorting giggle behind her hand, muttering, "Stop that. You're gonna make me pee my pants."

"Too hard to sell?" Vonda said.

Still trying to muffle her giggles, Amelie nodded in agreement.

"Guess you're right." Then Vonda relaxed and squeezed her daughter's hand. "To answer you, I wanted a sweet-tempered little angel who looked like a China doll and had manners to die for." Vonda smiled with the memory and sighed. "Instead, the stork dumped you on the front porch and the rest, as they say, is history."

Amelie smacked Vonda on the arm, saying, "Not nice. You take that back. Take that back right now."

"I'm kiddin'." Vonda threw her an air smooch. "You know I'm kiddin'."

"Boy or girl?" Amelie pressed.

"Let's see. If I recall, two of your great-aunts worked in a Carter's mill and had mailed me a big box of baby clothes. Some new. Some not. All were seconds, but I didn't care. They were just too cute for a boy, so I predicted you would be a girl. And I was right."

"Did Daddy have a preference? Do you remember?"

"As far as I know, he's only ever had one preference."

"Which is?"

"A voluptuous eighteen-year-old with collapsible teeth who can suck the chrome off the ball of a trailer hitch."

A few seconds of stunned silence, then, "He doesn't."

"Would I lie?" Vonda said. "That's been his fantasy for the last thirty years or more. Ask him. He'll tell you."

"Speakin' of Daddy . . . are you two okay? As a couple, I mean? I thought I felt a . . . a . . ."

"A disturbance in the Force?"

"Somethin' like that, especially earlier, in the kitchen."

Vonda flipped to her back, her weary head sinking into the down-filled pillow and her hand still entwined with Amelie's hand, which she placed across her stomach. She stared into the comforting dark, glad she couldn't see the disappointment in Amelie's eyes.

"How much did you hear?" Vonda finally said.

"Enough."

"I'm so sorry, that wasn't supposed to happen."

"Ma? If I tell you somethin', you promise not to get mad?"

"Put that way," Vonda said, "this couldn't be good."

Were Amelie and Remy splitting for good? She'd need a place to live and help raising the baby. Is that what she was trying to say?

Hello, diapers. So long, golden years.

Vonda inhaled a cleansing lungful of air, at the same time steeling herself to take in stride whatever came next.

"I promise," she said. "Go ahead. You can tell me anythin'."

"I think . . . oh, God, I don't know how to say this."

"If it's that tough, straight out is usually best. Spit it out and get it over with."

"Okay . . . I think . . . I think Daddy might have a girlfriend."

Having spewed that out in a rush, Amelie lay there in apparent misery, while her words tried to penetrate Vonda's harried brain. It took a moment for them to register.

Once they did, Vonda sucked in a surprised, and somewhat relieved, breath.

"He's got a flavor of the month, y'mean," she said.

"You already knew?"

"Yeah, but how did you¿"

"A friend saw them together."

"Have you¿ Seen them, I mean¿"

"Not yet."

"I guess it won't be long before . . ." The ugly thought struck and Vonda made a mewling noise in the back of her throat. "Do the girls know—¿"

"Probably not. They ain't said anythin' to me, and I think they would. Ma¿ Are you and Daddy gonna call it quits¿"

Amelie was after answers, but it went against Vonda's nature to bad-mouth Jerome to his children.

"I don't know, punkin. Why don't you try to go on to sleep¿ You need your rest. We can talk later. Just remember your dad and I love you, and that it'll never change."

"Please, don't. I'm a big girl. I deserve better than a pat on the head and a kiss-off answer."

Vonda slowly smiled while her throat tightened. No matter how old Amelie was, Vonda wasn't really ready for her baby to grow up.

If only she could stop the clock.

"Maybe you're right," she said. "Where has the time gone¿ While I wasn't lookin', you became a mature woman, and I reckon you do deserve more." She took another deep breath and let it out. "Nothin's settled, and that's the God's honest truth. Neither one of us is happy, and we haven't been for quite a while, but I suspect you and the girls can see that much for yourselves. What your daddy and I'll do 'bout it, and when we'll do it, is still up in the air."

"No one in your family has ever gotten a divorce."

"So your auntie Lolo keeps harpin' at me in a dozen different ways. She's been on my case big-time about the respect I owe to old family values. I've lived life on someone else's terms for so long, punkin, it's scary to contemplate livin' life on my own terms."

"Y'know what they say about old dogs and new tricks."

Vonda leaned over, until their heads touched.

"I don't mind gettin' older," she said. "Really I don't. What I mind is *bein'* old."

"There's a difference?"

"A big difference. I don't wanna find myself a dried-up and bitter old woman one day, sittin' on the porch in my rocker with nothin' to talk 'bout 'cept my aches and pains and regrets. And I'm comin' to believe if I do nothin', that's what's gonna happen for sure."

"Sorta like Miss Ludie?"

"Too much like Miss Ludie. Your grandmother is the way she is partly because of personality, but mostly because of the poor choices she's made along the way. I don't care to repeat her mistakes."

"I don't know this side of you, Ma." Vonda could hear the smile in Amelie's voice. "But I like it. I love you."

"I love you more." Vonda sighed again, in relief this time, and patted Amelie's hand.

"Ma? Whatever you decide . . . whatever you and Daddy decide, I want you to know it's okay with me. I want y'all to be happy, even if you can't be happy together."

"That means a lot, punkin." Vonda kissed her on the temple. "Thanks for bein' you. Now enough 'bout me. What about you? You talked seriously with Remy yet?"

"I dunno . . . What do you think? Should I?"

"It's not for me to say. I wondered is all. Your heart seemed set on it a few days ago."

"Maybe I'll wait awhile," Amelie said. "I hate to spoil his mood."

"Which mood is that?"

"He has a quiet, gentle sweetness about him tonight. Hadn't you noticed?"

"Sweetness? No, I hadn't noticed. Wonder what he's up to? Any idea?" Rather than waiting for a response, Vonda answered her own question. "Probably wants out of the doghouse."

"Which proves he loves me, right?"

"From what I see, he has a love for life and a lust for you. Well, that, and he seems to spend a good deal of his time nursin' hangovers, but who's countin' those?"

"Oh, I know he can be difficult. But, Ma, he can be priceless at the same time. Does that make any sense?"

"Unfortunately, it does. You forget I'm married to your father."

They drifted into a companionable silence then, each lost in her own thoughts, surrounded by the cozy darkness and listening to the rhythmic pounding of the rain.

Vonda turned her head on the pillow and said, "How come you asked if I had wanted a boy or a girl? Are you regrettin' your decision not to know your baby's gender until it's born?"

"Maybe a little. I was tryin' to picture our son or daughter . . ."

As Vonda listened to Amelie talk quietly about the coming baby, an uneasy feeling stole over her. The hairs on her neck prickled. It took a bit longer to pinpoint why, until she picked out a change in the feel and timbre of the wind.

It felt as if the very air around them was being vacuumed out.

"Hush a minute," Vonda said, raising up to a sitting position and listening intently. "Hear that?"

She leaned over and grabbed the six-cell Kel-Lite off the adjacent nightstand.

"Sounds like a train comin' right at us." Amelie pushed herself upright on the bed, confusion evident in her voice, because the nearest train tracks were a good seven miles away. "Ma, what—?"

In the next hair-raising moment, the cabin walls shuddered violently. Pictures crashed to the floor, and the outside racket built to a mind-numbing roar.

Spiraling wind battered the cabin from all sides. Spurred to action by a sound she'd heard only once before in her life, Vonda jumped off the bed, hauling Amelie to her feet with her.

"C'mon, Toto," she shouted. "We ain't in Kansas anymore. Head for the bathroom!"

Adrenaline pumping, Vonda launched Amelie toward the only interior room without windows. Then she turned her attention to the girls. The escalating shrieking had awakened them, and they bolted upright at their mother's shout.

"Huddle in the bathroom," Vonda screamed. "On the floor and stay there!"

Bursting from somewhere on the other side of the confusion, Vonda thought she heard Grandpa Thayer. He barked like he was in a rice paddy outside Hanoi, *"Incomin'!"*

Vonda sprinted for the bunk rooms, unsure she wanted to know what the geezer thought to do next but feeling morally obligated to find out. She met Miss Ludie heading in her direction.

Remy and Jerome had each clamped a hand under one of the groggy-eyed old gal's elbows and they were hustling her toward the safety of the master bath. Her bare feet dangled in the air.

Sidestepping out of their way, Vonda hollered, "I'll see to Grandpa." And received a silent nod from Jerome.

By flashlight she found the other bunk room empty. A quick pass around the adjoining bathroom revealed nothing there, either.

Just as she was about to panic, she checked the kitchen. There, she found Grandpa Thayer on his belly, flat to the floor. Her eyes widened and her heart dropped to her toes.

"Omigod," she said more to herself than anyone. "He's dead. Old man, how could you pull this stunt now? And on my watch, too?"

21

Don't build a new fence out of old wood.
—Old Farmer's Advice

Dressed only in baggy-butt white drawers, Grandpa Thayer gripped a cordless spotlight in one bony hand, its 120-watt halogen beam cutting the dark at ankle height. In the other hand, he secured a white-knuckled grip on two unopened cans of beer.

The undignified death pose galvanized Vonda into action. She reached to yank the beer cans away, and that was when Grandpa Thayer moved, tightening his grasp on the beers.

Hell's bells!

Damned old goat. He'd scared Vonda out of a good ten years at least.

As the cabin walls shook, cabinet doors flew open and glass crashed onto the counter and shattered in the sink, shards flying in all directions.

Grandpa Thayer traveled on alcohol and grit. His exit strategy seemed to be to scoot across the humidity-slickened floor using his forearms, dragging his tipped-over oxygen trolley behind him.

The thundering wind drowned out most other sounds now; he wouldn't be able to hear his own thoughts let alone Vonda's voice. She recovered her wits, dropped to the floor next to him, and yelled in his ear, "Need help?"

"Damn straight," he said, holding the beers aloft. "Church key's lost. Gotta find me another 'un."

She solved his problem by turning one can over in his palm and saying, "They're pop-tops."

He stared for half a second, then shouted, "I knew that."

Not allowing her rattled nerves to get the best of her, Vonda set aside her fear and gained her feet. Then she reached down to scrape her father-in-law off the tile.

But that's as far as she got.

In the next moment, a good portion of the kitchen roof sheared off.

Vonda screamed, startled and angry, more than scared this time. Grandpa Thayer flattened himself back down to the floor, hauling Vonda with him, and covered his head. He dropped the spotlight, but she noticed he managed to hang tight to the two beers.

Shredded pieces of Sheetrock and pink insulation rained down on them. Water poured in, beating a tattoo on the stainless-steel appliances. Rain spattered the cabinets, the countertop, and soaked the floor.

Wind howled down the newly made hole in the ceiling.

Magazines, newspapers, playing cards, napkins—almost anything not nailed down—swirled in an eddy around them. Rolls of toilet paper flew through the air like kite streamers.

Window blinds flapped and banged against the panes, threatening to break the windows. McMoose lost an ear and an antler when a kamikaze wood duck mount nose-dived into him. The antler clobbered the portable television sitting directly below and knocked it off its stand.

Vonda and Grandpa Thayer were drenched in less time than it took to cuss a cat. Her T-shirt and shorts were clinging to her like a second skin.

Hearing Jerome shout, she looked up and was immediately blinded by the flashlight he wielded like a light saber.

"All right already," she screamed, signaling with a wave of her arm before shading her eyes.

He finally got the message and lowered the light. She could see he carried one of the bunk bed mattresses over his shoulders and back.

Who said chivalry was dead?

Surely he wasn't hiking up Mount Ego, looking to carry out some kind of Viagra-induced equivalent of the Mile High Club. Was he?

"You can't be serious," she shrieked.

"Are you hurt, Von?" He, too, screamed to be heard. "Can you get up?"

Not as quick as you can.

"We're fine," she said, nodding, miffed at herself for misunderstanding his intentions.

Although she couldn't fault her logic, she could lay the blame squarely at his feet, or a bit higher actually, for jumping to the erroneous conclusion about engaging in a little rumpy-pumpy. Even if she wanted to knock boots with her husband, no way was she interested or adventurous enough to explore the horizontal joys during a hurricane.

"Hurry up," Jerome said. "Let's go." He shifted the unwieldy mattress, watching the two of them scramble to their feet. "Over here, in the middle, old man. Cripes, use both hands to steady yourself. Drop the beer already, y'lazy bastard."

"Blow me."

"Von, grab the other end of this mattress!"

Nodding again, she dug her nails into the fabric and passed the wet bed across their backs and heads as if it were crowd-surfing a mosh pit. She and Jerome sandwiched Grandpa Thayer between them, using the mattress as a shield against flying debris, and all three trooped toward the master bathroom.

She leaned in to her father-in-law and said, "You okay?"

"Hell no," Grandpa yelled. "My oxygen. Hold up!"

"Can you do without it?" Jerome yelled back.

Grandpa Thayer shot his son a stare that said he'd rather get his johnson caught in his zipper.

"I need the damned tank to get the deposit back!"

But no matter what, he wouldn't let go of the beers.

Vonda didn't know whether to laugh or swear a blue streak. Balancing her end of the mattress on her lower back and rump, which, to her chagrin, were plenty wide to do the job, she groped around her feet until her fingers scraped cool metal.

"Found it!" she said.

And off they went... Vonda hugging an oxygen tank, Grandpa Thayer adopting two beers, and Jerome packing the mattress, all to join the pie-eyed Wicked Witch in the bathroom.

Who needed flying monkeys to create chaos when they had wind and rain and a hole in the roof a Mini Cooper could pass through, not to mention Caroline and Charlotte waiting in the wings to beat morale to death should it rear its ugly head?

Vonda staggered toward the safety of the master bathroom, positive at that moment she would never watch *The Wizard of Oz* again without breaking out in a cold sweat and unrestrained cackles.

As for the cabin... most of the structure still stood, albeit somewhat gutted. At least, that was her impression at first blush. They would have to wait until daylight to truly assess the damage and decide whether to consider repairs.

If this was as bad as it got, they would count themselves lucky. In a few hours, the storm would be out of their area and the tornadoes it spawned along with it.

The worse would be over.

A few hours was nothing. Vonda could stand on her head for a few hours.

Nothing could possibly make things worse.

22

Never let the truth get in the way of a good story.
—Old Farmer's Advice

Oh, the sweet taste of freedom.

Freedom from debt to Paddy Malone, that is. Remy Broussard's five-grand payoff was done, cooked, and ready to serve. At least, as far as he was concerned.

The breakthrough came to him when the cabin's master bathroom had become the Bermuda Triangle of the Thayer menagerie. Everyone disappeared inside, and whether they'd be seen again was being hotly debated at that moment by Remy's in-laws.

Talk about crazier than a bedbug. Remy felt he now knew what it must've been like to command the wheelhouse of the *Titanic.*

Because space was at a premium in the bathroom, he roosted on the toilet tank, forearms propped on his thighs. He braced his feet on the edges of the plastic toilet lid and flanked his pregnant wife, who leaned back against his bare calves for support while nestling an anxious cat in her lap.

No one paid Remy any mind, so while they talked over each other he seized the opportunity to survey the bevy of familial devotion. He mentally handicapped which of them stood to get booted to the curb before Labor Day.

At first, he considered Miss Ludie the across-the-board pick, perched as she was on the vanity stool in a white floral housecoat, swaying in a boozy haze and lending her drumbeat of doom to the chorus. But on second thought, Mother Vonda wasn't one to abandon a grunter, no matter how sorry that person might be. So, as much as Remy hated to see Miss Ludie stay, he chalked up the old dingbat as the also-ran of the field.

The next possible contender lingered at Miss Ludie's elbow. Grandpa Thayer leaned his bony butt against the bull-nosed edge of the vanity, looking fetching in a fluffy, knee-length pink bathrobe.

His ex-wife had yanked the robe off the hook on the back of the door and not-so-gently shoved it in his cadaverous rib cage a few seconds after his scrotal sack waved at them like Topo Gigio from the front of his stretched-out briefs. Above the old man's right eye, a purpling egg rose on his forehead, probably a souvenir from the sheared roof.

The growing knot gave his profile the prominent browridge of a Neanderthal man. Combine that with his gray pallor and boozy smoker's cough, and Remy figured there was no way the geezer would live to be as old as he looked. So Remy scratched Gramps, too.

Might as well scratch Charlotte, Caroline, and Amelie while he was at it. Mother Vonda would never turn out her girls. Period. End of discussion. No matter what the girls did, no matter how big a pain in the ass they were, no matter how bad things got in the world, her girls were her babies and would be until the day Mother Vonda died.

That left Jerome as a walkover.

In Remy's estimation, his father-in-law's continued survival as his father-in-law was dicey, especially given the convo Remy had overheard earlier in the kitchen between Jerome and Mother Vonda.

Their marital situation was beautiful, just bee-you-tee-ful. While other bettors in Malone's pool would probably wager on Mother Vonda directing the boot to one of the outlaws, Remy's money was riding on Jerome.

Go ahead, spin the wheel of fortune. For Remy, it was game-on. All he had to do was hang tight, wait out the storm, and let Jerome's midlife shenanigans take their own sweet course.

Like fishing over a weed bed using crankbait on medium-heavy tackle, Remy loved it when he was sitting on a sure thing.

A study conducted in 1992 concluded a correlation existed between falling barometric pressure and the onset of labor. Then in 1996, a similar study concluded that very same theory had no juice.

If only those old boys doing the research had asked Vonda. They could've saved themselves time, not to mention a boatload of grant money, money better spent studying something productive, like methane emissions in cow farts or the sex life of the Japanese quail.

But no one ever solicited Vonda's opinion for much of anything. It was probably her lack of scientific sophistication that always managed to get her brand of on-the-job wisdom overlooked when it came to professional journals.

Vonda was still on her current learning curve when she cracked open her eyes. She immediately identified the sound that had invaded her power nap as Miss Ludie's teeth gnashing together. Her choppers emitted a peculiar sucking sound sometimes, especially on the days she popped them in her mouth without sufficient goop to secure their hold.

" 'Bout damned time you woke up," Miss Ludie said.

Vonda's neck muscles were in spasm, and no wonder. She sat planted cross-legged on the hard bathroom floor, with her back bent at an angle a pretzel would envy. The side of her head felt imprinted with the ogee lip of the even harder bathtub.

Her left butt cheek had gone numb, or maybe it had fallen off. Vonda wasn't sure which.

No telling if minutes or hours had passed since she'd given in to stress and fatigue. The Coleman lantern atop the vanity blanketed the dark bathroom in the same glacier blue light as before, and the wind outside battered with the same triumphant ferocity.

The air was thick and humid, smelling as ripe as a damp

beach towel. Vonda gingerly raised her head, testing that her neck wouldn't snap in two, and saw Miss Ludie reflected in the bathroom mirror. The old gal wrestled teeth that kept popping out like champagne corks.

Rubbing her gritty eyes with the heels of her palms, Vonda said, "Where is everyone?"

"Gone to shit and the hogs ate 'em, I reckon. How the hell should I know?"

Vonda lowered her hands to better focus on her mouthy mother-in-law, but the vigorous rubbing had made her vision cloudier. Miss Ludie was a diffused blur ringed with blue-white light.

"Give that to me again," Vonda said, "maybe this time without the editorial."

"They're busy pluggin' holes," Miss Ludie said, not contrite enough to resist a further dig. "This damned shack's in worse shape than Swiss cheese. A helluva fix you got us into, that's for damned sure."

"Me? How—?"

"I'm hungry," Miss Ludie said. "What's for breakfast?"

"Whatever you want to fix," Vonda muttered without thinking.

To her surprise, Miss Ludie hefted herself off the stool, saying, "Well, hell, why didn't y'all say so instead of lettin' me sit here starvin' to death?" She pointed toward the floor. "You keep an eye on Earth Mother there while I see if there's a kitchen left to rustle somethin' up in. Probably not a damned thin' that ain't blown to hell and back . . ."

While Miss Ludie lumbered across the room in borrowed black flip-flops, grumbling to no one in particular, Vonda's gaze followed where the old gal had pointed. There, on the floor between them, Amelie reclined on the cool tile.

Sage green bath towels were rolled and tucked under her neck and bent knees. She opened her mouth, but a grimace accompanied a quick intake of breath and derailed her train of thought. That's when Vonda's vision cleared, and she heard the other shoe drop with the impact of a sledgehammer.

Crap, crap, crap.

Lord love a duck, Vonda recognized that puckered face, had worn one like it herself once or twice. In one swift motion, Vonda knelt beside her daughter, sandwiching Amelie's hand between hers and squeezing reassurance.

"How long?" Vonda said.

"A couple of hours now," Amelie said.

"How far apart are the contractions?"

"Twenty minutes, give or take."

"Your water break?"

"No, not yet." Amelie offered a weak smile. "Never a dull moment, huh? I'm sorry, Ma."

"Sorry? For what, punkin?"

"The bad timin'."

"Puppy dogs and babies," Vonda said, shaking her head. "They never do what you want, when you want 'em to do it."

"Goddamned husbands, neither," Miss Ludie chimed in from the doorway. "Y'all want coffee if I can find any?"

"Sure," Vonda said, sorry to have to look a gift horse in

the mouth. "I do, but there's no way to make hot water yet."

"I declare, you'd think Mister Coffee's been around forever. Y'all are spoilt." Miss Ludie turned to head out, and Vonda thought she heard the old gal muttering in her wake, "Pussies, a bunch of goddamned pussies . . ."

Vonda turned her attention back to Amelie, saying, "I can't believe they left you on the floor. Let me help you to the bed."

Amelie shook her head.

"It's cooler down here," she said. "Really. Feels better on my back, too. The bed's too soft."

Vonda arched a skeptical brow, saying, "I dunno about that, but if you're sure? I hate to have to tell my grandson or granddaughter about bein' born on the bathroom floor."

"What happened to goin' back to our roots? To bein' pioneers through this storm?"

"The floor's a little too primitive for me."

"I'm fine for now, Ma." Amelie cracked a smile. "Relax. I don't plan to be down here for the duration. This baby ain't comin' anytime soon. Let me catch a nap, and then I'll move."

"Do the others know?" Vonda said, but gauging by the racket that sprang up behind her, it was a moot question.

She whipped her head around. There, crowding the doorway and looking as wilted as overwatered plants, stood Remy, Charlotte, and Caroline, all talking at once.

"They know now," Amelie said.

Remy sported an anxious grin and said, "It's true? The baby's comin'?"

Charlotte glared at her cell phone, shaking it and saying, "No bars. No bars at all. No 9-1-1. How we gonna help her?"

"I know," Caroline said. "Remove her jewelry and check for tight clothes."

"That's snakebite, doofus," Charlotte said, giving her sister a swift elbow in the ribs. "Why am I talkin' to you? Whaddaya know about babies?"

"Why, Miz Charlotte," Caroline said in a singsong voice, "we don't know nothin' 'bout birthin' no babies."

"Whoa!" Vonda rose, blocking their way. "Time out. Y'all stop your clownin' and take a deep breath."

She offered a pointed stare and a wave of her arms, urging each one of them to comply. They all quieted and sucked in a cleansing breath, even Amelie.

"Now, blow it out," Vonda said, still coaxing with hand gestures. "Slowly. Good. Doesn't that feel calmer? Who's got a watch? What time is it?"

Remy checked his wristwatch.

"A little after six-thirty."

"Two hours' sleep," Vonda said, frowning. "No wonder I feel like I've been schwacked in the head. My sheep can't count . . . uh, where was I?"

"Six-thirty," Remy prompted.

"Right. I dunno where my mind's gone. Okay, here's the situation: We've got the whole day ahead of us. We're in good shape."

"We are?" the girls said in unison.

Vonda nodded and said, "It's too early to hit the panic

button—babies don't come that fast, especially first babies. Right now, Remy needs to come and sit with Amelie because he's her coach."

"Whaddaya want us t'do?" Charlotte said.

"First, find the cat and haul his little tookus in here. There's too much broken glass in the rest of the cabin for him to cut his paws to shreds. Next, fool with Remy's television. See if a station'll come in and let us know what the storm's doin'."

Charlotte saluted and said, "Aye, aye, Cap'n. Your wish is my command."

"Yeah," Vonda murmured, "you say that now."

"And me?" Caroline said. "What can I do?"

"You, my little lovely, are helpin' me get your grandparents settled somehow—"

"We were already helpin' Gramps find hisself some dry clothes."

"Any luck?"

"Some. We done found him a T-shirt and shorts. No undies, though."

"Thanks for that graphic. Guess they got blown into the yard. Well, no help for it now. Let's see what's worth salvagin' in the kitchen then. Say, what's your daddy doin'?"

"Huntin' up a tarp."

Vonda nodded, even as she acknowledged reluctant appreciation for Jerome's willingness to help now that he was there with them. Once she had traded places with her son-in-law at the doorway, she angled back.

"And, Remy?"

"Yessum?"

"Don't forget to keep track of Amelie's contractions."

He checked his watch again and said, "Will do."

Charlotte had waited for Vonda in the bedroom, beyond earshot of the expectant couple. Dipping her chin and speaking low, she said, "It's gonna be okay, ain't it, Mom?"

Vonda wasn't sure if Charlotte was talking about the baby's arrival or the storm's departure, but it didn't really matter which.

"Of course, sweetie." She tucked strands of long, damp hair behind Charlotte's ear. "Everythin's gonna be fine. You'll see."

Out of habit, Vonda smiled then. Faking optimism was second nature for her—after all, she'd cut her marital teeth on white lies.

As for Vonda's earlier thought that nothing could make their situation worse . . . Shoot, she'd just watched that notion go up in smoke.

Poof.

23

It's not what you're called that matters,
but what you answer to.

—Old Farmer's Advice

The eye of the storm had passed over, leaving sullen skies, the dull roar of residual rain bands, and gusting winds to greet the new day.

With every passing hour, Stella posed less and less of a threat to the areas near the coast. But farther inland, her advancing winds and heavy rains were still dangerous and made travel south too iffy for any vehicles except emergency responders.

Most of the Thayers squirreled themselves away in the master bedroom, since the majority of the cabin was a waterlogged shambles. They were cut off from the world. No phone. No electricity. No news of life outside their little corner of hell.

They did have one working toilet, the one last bastion of civilization, for which a grateful Vonda thanked the plumbing gods. Even if they had to use a bucket to make the toilet flush, a bucket was better than the alternative.

Miss Ludie and the girls entertained themselves playing hearts on one of the queen beds, while Remy and Amelie claimed squatter's rights on the other bed. The strength of Amelie's labor remained steady, but over the course of a couple of hours, the frequency of the contractions had barely moved to fifteen minutes apart.

Amelie was holding up remarkably calm, which helped ease the family's concerns. Whether her calm was real or an act, Vonda couldn't decide.

Like mother, like daughter?

Maybe.

Lord knows, Amelie had learned at the knee of the master how to plaster on a happy face and make it look convincing.

Grandpa Thayer preferred the barrel chair in the corner, with his feet resting on the end of the bed near the napping tabby cat. Despite the stress and pain the geezer had endured, he appeared relaxed and peaceful, close to vegging out, as he thumbed through a pile of outdoor magazines he'd salvaged from a wall rack next to the toilet.

Jerome had set himself the task of seeing about hooking up the generator that was stored in the carport's utility room. And Vonda had just stepped into the bedroom with a paper plate full of pork sandwiches and boiled eggs made with the leftovers in the slowly defrosting fridge.

"Dinner is served," she said with a flourish of paper napkins. She set the food on the nightstand between the beds.

"Take what you want, but eat what you take. Amelie? Juice or Jell-O?"

Remy sat with his back propped against the headboard. In front of him, Amelie slowly dialed the television's tuner wheel while Remy massaged her aching lower back.

"Orange juice?" Amelie said.

Vonda shook her head, saying, "Would you like tomato or maybe tomato? Or you can choose our daily special, which is . . ."

"Tomato," sang a chorus of voices.

"I love it," Vonda said with a crinkly smile, "when the peanut gallery gets in on the act. Your choice, little mama?"

"Jell-O, please. And a bottle of water?"

"Comin' right up."

And then Vonda pivoted on her heel and headed for the box of canned goods they had rescued and stacked on top of the clothes dryer. Amelie returned her attention to the frustrating television. Advancing the tuner wheel garnered nothing except snow or static, and Amelie was about to quit trying when she managed to point the short antenna at the right degree to snare a faint signal.

"Hey, a picture!" She laughed in victory, and then just as quickly sobered. "Omigod, y'all ain't gonna believe this. Look . . ."

The audio faded in and out, mostly out, but it appeared the news report centered on the flooding and wind damage in the area. Gauging by the high camera angle, the television station captured the scene from a remote feed either inside the electric

company's upper floors or atop the courthouse building's parking garage.

Amelie angled the little television, holding on to it with the
same delicate grip as Linus holding his blankie. She was afraid
to jiggle the set too much and wipe out the signal, so everyone crowded around the bed to view the tiny screen. Charlotte craned her neck over Miss Ludie's shoulder and pointed
to what appeared to be remnants of the town.

"What's that? The library?"

"Looks like it *was* the pizza parlor," Grandpa Thayer said.

"Y'all are both wrong," Remy said. "It's the bank. Check it
out. Is that a Ford wrapped around the ATM?"

In front of their eyes, an angry river ran through, over, and
around the town, pounding the brick buildings that still stood.
Murky water climbed as high as doors and windows, sparing
nothing. The occasional school bus swept by the camera's field
of vision, bobbing along among the debris as easily as a rubber
duck sails a bathtub.

It was then Jerome entered the bedroom. He arrived in time
to see Caroline windmilling her arms at the screen and squeal-
ing with all the carefree wonder of immature innocence.

"Oh, man, that's Daddy's office. *Daddy,* there you are.
C'mere. Look! We're on television. Ain't that a hoot?"

And sure enough, when they could hear the audio snippets,
the news anchor used footage of the Thayer real estate office
building as the example of the ravaging flood waters.

Jerome stared at the screen, not moving a muscle, frozen
like a deer winding a hunter.

A sizable portion of the mom-and-pop businesses that populated downtown seemed to have been blown to smithereens. Road signs were twisted in half or gone completely. Ornamental trees were stripped of limbs or denuded of leaves. Traffic light poles collapsed, bringing down electrical lines. One-hundred-year-old oak trees were ripped out of the ground by the roots. Historical landmarks were demolished.

Everywhere the camera panned lay pain.

The truth steamrolled over Jerome: Their community had been hit and hit *hard*, and it might take years to recover.

Into this queasy excursion, Miss Ludie delivered one of her cheerful brain dumps and unwittingly brought her son out of his funk.

"Mold and mildew'll eat through them buildin's now faster'n kudzu," she said. "It'll give ever'body black lung."

"Cripes, woman," Grandpa Thayer said, leaning back in his chair, "are you on crack? Black lung happens to coal miners. Do you see any damned coal mines here?"

"Believe you me," she said, shaking a finger at him, "the health department'll make 'em all strip the walls back to the studs." She nodded for emphasis. "Y'all wait and see."

While they bickered, only one thought popped into Jerome's mind. *Rental space.* Hot damn if the demand for retail rental space hadn't just skyrocketed beyond the supply.

He sifted through this heavenly revelation. Mentally cataloging his square footage inventory generated the same energy and excitement within him as closing a big deal. Jerome all but emptied his digestive system right then and there.

Cha-ching, cha-ching.

What a bonanza.

Goose bumps covered him like a rash. Then, just as quickly as the rousing thought entered his mind, it skidded to a halt.

It didn't matter how much inventory Jerome figured he had. What mattered was how much inventory the storm had left him.

He needed to find out for sure. In real estate, time *was* money.

"Son?" Grandpa Thayer said. "You all right? You look a mite peaked."

"Couldn't be better."

Jerome must not have sounded convincing because his father shook his head.

"Don't go lettin' this setback get you down. What's done is done. Y'gotta look ahead now."

"Good advice," Miss Ludie said with a snort, "from an old goat who never thought beyond one day at a time."

They lit into each other again, yammering back and forth. Rather than Jerome's spirit crumbling under the weight of their squabbling, it rose up as this time he couldn't help himself. He chuckled.

"The old man's right, Mother." And something flickered in Grandpa Thayer's eyes before he shuttered them once more. "Nothin' to do but look to the future, which is exactly what I plan to do." Jerome offered his bestselling grin. "We'll be fine . . . leastways once we get that generator workin'."

"Please don't say it's broken," Caroline said, folding her

hands under her chin in supplication. "Please, please, please, anythin' but broken."

"Okay, I won't say it's broken, little girl."

She breathed a sigh, saying, "Thank you, Jesus."

"The problem is no gas. All the cans are empty."

This news chipped away at Caroline's already strained patience and she let loose with a loud stomp and a screeched, *"Let's go get some."*

Jerome finger-combed his dark hair.

"Let me clue you in, sweetheart. There aren't that many stations in town, and I have no idea if any of them have backup generators for the gas pumps."

As his meaning sank in, Amelie said into the silence, "The convenience store up on the highway does, Daddy. They have to."

Vonda handed her a cup of Jell-O and a bottle of water.

"And you know this how?" she said.

"From the cabbie the night Grandpa arrived. You remember? The guy with the acne?"

"How could I forget?"

"That's why he wasn't in a rush to hit the road before closin'. Said he could gas up anytime at the highway station, 'cause they contracted with the cab company. Same for the city and county." Amelie swiveled her attention to her dad and smiled. "Doesn't that sound like the station has to stay open twenty-four/seven for emergency vehicles?"

An understanding passed between Remy and Jerome a moment before Jerome said, "If we know this, so does half the county."

"Best we get on down there," Remy said, finishing Jerome's thought. "Their supply ain't gonna last long once word gets out."

Vonda and Jerome agreed, then Jerome asked about the winds.

"Accordin' to the latest NOAA report," Remy said, "the storm lost strength in the wee hours and ended up comin' in as a cat four. Should be downgraded to a tropical storm pretty quick, I expect. Winds are steady at seventy-five now, gusting to ninety. Shoot, I've fished in worse."

"What do you think?" Jerome said. "Wait? Let the wind lay down?"

"A couple of hours at the most," Remy said, nodding.

"It's settled then," Vonda said. "Girls? Y'all heard 'em. We'll drive in, too, and top off the tanks, yes?"

"Aye, aye, Cap'n," they sang in unison.

The good news about Stella? She was fast-moving, a hit-and-run, which was better than a few years back when Hurricane Daniel traveled slow and sloppy up the East Coast, leaving flooding and mayhem in its wake.

As soon as the weather service downgraded Stella, the Thayers headed for their cars.

Remy climbed off the bed, saying, "Grandpa? Miss Ludie? Will y'all sit with Amelie 'til we get back?"

Wide-eyed, Miss Ludie shook her head and opened her mouth to say, "If that baby comes, we can't—"

"Of course we'll look after her." Grandpa Thayer shot his ex a glare that dared her to contradict him. "We're her grandparents, ain't we? Don't you worry none. Our little gal'll be fine. Run along now."

When Remy stepped outside, blustery skies filled with intermittent rain kicked up errant bits of bark and pine needles that poked him in the face and neck. Dark head down against the wind, he crossed the breezeway to the carport.

All the vehicles were a mess. Covered with dents, sweet gum leaves, and sandy dirt, not a one of them had a paint job that wasn't scratched down to the metal and pitted from gravel, sticks, and tree limbs turned into missiles.

The worst of the lot, though, was Amelie's Volkswagen. It had had the snot kicked out of it.

Tornadic winds had tossed her hoopty a hundred-fifty, two hundred yards out in the middle of the Bahia grass field, dropping the car on its roof. The windows were busted out, the doors torn off, the body crushed to hell and back, leaving a tangled mass of steel that wasn't much good for anything now except an artificial reef.

"Poor Amelie's gonna be heartbroken," Vonda said, "just heartbroken, when she sees how the wind disrespected her Bug."

Jerome regarded the scene with polite interest, saying, "It was a rollin' wreck."

"She loved that car."

"All that piece of shit lacked was cane poles hangin' out the window."

"Quit bein' so mean."

"You quit bein' so moody."

"We're not talkin' about me. We're talkin' about Amelie."

"If that's the hair you wanna split. Who's gonna tell her?"

"No one. There's no point in upsettin' her. It's not good for her or the baby." Vonda edged her face around Jerome and looked in her son-in-law's direction for support. "Isn't that right, Remy?"

"Ain't what right?" He moved to where they stood, followed their gaze, and surveyed the scene. "Will you look at—*sonovabitch!* How high y'reckon they're gonna raise my insurance premiums 'cause of this . . . ?"

"Probably," Jerome said, "an arm, a leg, and your first-born . . . same as they'll raise us for the cabin."

"Will you two forget money?" Vonda snapped. "Cars are easy to replace. People aren't." And she repeated her worry about Amelie's continued good health.

Duly chastised, Remy calmed down, wiped his damp face on his T-shirt sleeve, and said, "I reckon you're right. Now ain't a particularly good time to hand her bad news. I see no hope for it but to try to make sure she don't notice her Bug." He shrugged. "That's gonna take some doin', but I'll figure somethin'."

"Thank you, Remy," Vonda said, shooting her husband a glare. "I'm glad you, at least, understand a mother's concern."

Jerome raised his hands in surrender, saying, "Whatever. I'll tell the girls mum's the word."

Vonda then set about scraping off the crud from the car

windows, while the girls wielded straw brooms and swept off the bulk of the debris from bumpers and around tires. Jerome was putting two red plastic five-gallon gas cans into the back of Vonda's SUV.

He straightened when he saw Remy head to his pickup, keys in hand, and stepped in his path. With a flat palm to Remy's chest, Jerome strong-armed him, halting his trek.

"Where do you think you're goin'?" Jerome said.

"With y'all. We're fillin' the cars, too, ain't we?"

"*We* are. *You're* not."

"But—"

"No way, José. You're not leavin' my daughter and grand-child in the care of two old farts who can barely remember what day it is, let alone fend for themselves." A flash of irritation lit Remy's brown eyes and his jaw set in a mutinous way that worried Jerome, so he dropped his hand away from Remy's chest. "You saw the television—who knows what roads are passable and what buildin's are left standin'. Let's find out first. I don't know how long it'll take us, but until we get back here, somebody ought to stay. Y'know, in case."

"That's all you had to say, man."

Wincing, Jerome added, "It's just . . . she's my baby, y'know?"

"Not no more, she ain't. She's my wife now."

Jerome sucked in a sharp breath.

"The hell you say. Listen, fucknut, you're a husband only as long as Amelie wants you to be, but she'll *always* be my baby."

"Is that some kinda threat?"

"Hardly. It's fact."

"Try preachin' in your own church, instead of holdin' services with me. Reckon that'd be a nice change of pace?"

Jerome's face became a storm cloud.

"Forget it," he said. "You'll figure it out soon enough, when you have one of your own callin' you Daddy." He turned away, then angled back. "A free bit of advice, son, from a man who's been married more years than you've been alive . . . Sometimes, y'gotta pretend like y'give a shit."

Florida Highway Patrol cars with lights flashing blocked the Interstate's entry and exit ramps, keeping all traffic off damaged overpasses. Without access to the Interstate, travel anywhere in the Panhandle just became harder and more time-consuming.

Once the force of the winds had lessened, the Thayers weren't the only people to venture out in search of supplies, available resources, and a route home.

Jerome led their convoy in his Escalade for safety, a trip that took three times as long as it normally would because of downed power lines and storm debris blocking streets. They arrived fifteenth in line when they pulled into the six-pump gas station.

A combination gas station and convenience store, the one-story yellow concrete block building sat off the four-lane highway that was closest to the Interstate. The cars lined up behind the Thayers quickly grew in number, snaking eastward along the grassy median.

Too antsy to sit, Jerome glad-handed through the growing crowd of customers while Vonda and the girls patiently waited in their vehicles for their turn to gas up. When he strolled back to Vonda's car and tapped on the window, she rolled it down to see his hand out, palm up and fingers wiggling.

"What's that for?" she said, glancing at his hand.

"It's pay, then pump," he said. "Ten-gallon limit."

"Can they take plastic?"

"Cash only. They're not takin' any chances on drive-offs. Why don't you and the girls fill up? I'll go in and pay for all of us. Got any money?"

"Enough."

"Good, give me some."

She pursed her lips.

"The guy always pays," she said, "or so I've been told. Don't you have any money on you?"

"About five hundred bucks, but why should I use all my cash? C'mon, I know you always keep a couple thousand rat-holed away."

"Only because some of us know where the bank is and try to keep a stash for emergencies."

"I'm so happy for you. Now fork over a few hundred. It's my money, anyway."

"How so?"

"I earned it."

"Oh, Jerome, Jerome, Jerome. You really don't want to go there."

"It's true. Did you get your plump little butt up and go to work every day? I don't think so."

Vonda leaned out the window, invading his personal space and not minding how wet he got, as she spoke through gritted teeth.

"Listen, you sorry ass, if you had to pay me for what I do, you couldn't afford me."

"Don't start. I do more by mistake than you do on purpose."

Vonda's hot retort was cut off when a neighbor from the Historical Society wandered over and struck up a conversation. It was from him they learned the National Guard had set up a mobile command post in the old Wal-Mart parking lot and was handing out bags of ice and meals ready to eat.

When the neighbor moved on, Jerome stuck his hand in Vonda's window again and wiggled his fingers. Raised eyebrows prodded her until she yanked her summer straw purse off the passenger seat and jammed her hand in, whipping out a fold-over eel-skin wallet.

Yanking out three large bills from the pocket, she shoved them at Jerome and said, "Here. That's all you get. I'm rationin' the rest 'til the banks are open again, or 'til somebody's takin' plastic. God knows how long a wait that'll be."

Jerome swiped the damp money out of her hand, adding, "When y'all are done here, have Charlotte take the gas cans back to Remy. He'll know how to get the generator set up.

Then why don't you and Caroline make your way over and get us as many bags of ice as you can?"

"Let Caroline get the ice. She can follow Charlotte. I want to run by the house to see how high the water got. Maybe we'll luck out and be able to move back home today."

"Don't count on it. Last I saw, the water was pretty damned high, and you know the drainage sucks over there."

"Doesn't hurt to check."

"Suit yourself, but you're wastin' your time."

"I waste time on a lot of things that aren't worth it," she said, but he ignored her sarcasm. "And you're doin' what, while the rest of us are playin' fetch and carry?"

"Goin' to work," Jerome said. "I've got responsibilities, remember? I'll be along later."

Obviously, he felt that was enough explanation. Without another word to Vonda, he headed inside toward the cashier, calling a cordial greeting along the way to some woman who melted with delight.

Vonda watched him go, fed up and disgusted with herself. What was it going to take for her brain to accept the unalterable fact that Jerome was a snake-oil salesman first, a womanizer second, and a husband a distant third?

Her life stretched out in front of her like one long, emotional desert. She sank farther into her seat.

Didn't she deserve better? Oh, brother, how many times over the years had she asked herself that question?

Too many to count.

At first Vonda had stayed with Jerome because she told herself their differences would work themselves out. Then she stayed because she was a good daughter and that was what her parents expected her to do. Then she stayed out of guilt, because her children needed a family. But now her parents were dead, and the girls were wrapped up in their own lives.

Vonda had run out of reasons.

"Y'know what?" she said to the reflection in the rearview mirror. "She can have him."

And then Vonda hopped out of her car.

Of the convenience store's double glass doors, only the left side was still covered with plywood. The white metal canopy covering the pump area was missing its eaves and the metal was peeled up in several places, but otherwise appeared intact. It didn't help protect against the elements now, because the gusts blew the drizzle sideways.

Most people tried to stand where their vehicle and the pumps blocked the brunt of the blowing rain. Others had the tank on the opposite side and had no choice but to grin and bear Stella's liquid sunshine.

Vonda was one such grinner. No umbrella. No raincoat. No common sense, either, it seemed.

A glance around confirmed that sorry fact. Of the women Vonda could see, some wore shorts and tees, others wore classic Capri pant sets. One loud woman with big hair, lips painted in an exaggerated bow, and flamboyant gestures remained in the store's doorway, dressed for high tea with the Queen in a two-piece ivory skirt suit that looked to be made of silk doupioni.

Every one of the women she could see was more stylish, and much more presentable, than Vonda.

Before the hurricane, did Vonda think to pack an arsenal of her best clothes so, when everything got blown into the next county, she'd have something to wear that didn't look like it came straight out of the refugee rag bag?

Oh, hell no.

She'd opted for wearability and comfort over fashion, figuring she'd be sweating her brains out and likely to get filthy doing it. What a bonehead move.

Next hurricane, the silk jammies, the linen suit, the La Perla undies, the designer shoes, the gold jewelry . . . Oh, yes, she was wearing every damned piece of special-occasion stuff she owned. So what if she was homeless? She intended to look fabulous.

Okay, good strategy for next time. The problem was, this time she not only was homeless, in a manner of speaking, but she looked homeless, too.

Still in the holey nylon white tee and faded blue running shorts she'd worn to bed and sweated in the night before, Vonda had pulled up on the wrong side of the gas pump. What she had done didn't register until she got out of the SUV and couldn't find the gas cap.

Damn Jerome, this was his fault. He'd gotten her temper riled to the point she wasn't paying attention to what she was doing.

There she stood, stringy hair wet, no makeup, chipped nails, fuzzy pits, and legs with the kind of stubble sprouting that inspired porcupines to send fan mail. All she needed was a lichen-covered bridge to squat under to complete the little Sasquatch picture.

Vonda swallowed a groan. With no way to duck down or hide between the car and the pump, she resigned herself to doing penance for her stupidity.

First, she hauled out the two empty gas cans and set them on the wet asphalt to fill. Then, with no other choice, she bent over the nozzle and bravely gave the world a full gander at cellulite only her doctor and bathroom mirror ever saw.

By the time Charlotte helped Vonda hoist the full cans into the back of Charlotte's car, Vonda was drenched, with even her tennis shoes squishy with water.

"Follow your sister over to Wal-Mart to get ice," Vonda said, wiping her face on her sleeve.

"Daddy told me to take the gas to Remy."

"And you will. But I want you and Caroline to stay together, safety in numbers and all that. So it's ice, then back to the cabin. And don't go drivin' through any standin' water."

"*Mom.* We're not babies anymore."

"Well, you never know if there's a downed electrical wire at the bottom of a puddle. You're my babies, and I don't want to lose you two."

"Y'gotta cut the cord sometime, Mom. Don't worry, we have brains. We'll be fine. I promise." And Vonda had no choice but to trust in her girls' best judgment. "Love you, Mom."

"Love you, too."

Vonda reeked of gasoline that had spilled on her hands but

paid it no mind as she waved so long to the girls. Then she straightened to fill her car.

That's when she spied Terrell Barksdale.

Good God in heaven.

Could her life suck any worse than it did at that very moment?

Probably not.

Talk about worlds colliding. Moving with the unfettered ease of a toned and muscled body, the man had the audacity to walk out of the convenience store right in front of her hungry gaze, attractively windblown and replete with sexy mojo.

Vonda tried to remind herself she was a married woman, a *very* married woman, but the voice in her head faded to a mild protest at best. No matter what, the attachment to Terrell was always there.

He was someone she loved. Someone she wished she didn't.

Dark stubble highlighted his square jaw, giving him an air of raw intensity rather than a scruffy look. He wore a white and gray short-sleeved baseball jersey, gray workout shorts, beach sandals, and a butter-soft grin on very kissable lips.

Her stomach did an odd little flutter at the delicious sight.

On one hand, Vonda was thrilled and relieved to see Terrell had come through the storm unscathed. On the other hand, he was the absolute last person she wanted to see when she looked like a swamp rat.

Sure, he could probably regale an audience with memories of Vonda in worse shape—especially one bad perm during sophomore year of high school that left her a Brillo-head—but this was now. And now was different, because Vonda was different.

"Vonda?" he called. "Hey, Von, that you?"

No. No. No speaka da English.

Dying a quick death on the spot would put an end to her blighted morning. Too bad it was a wish unlikely to come true. Maybe if she drove off without a word, he'd figure he'd been mistaken about her identity?

It certainly sounded doable in theory.

If Vonda snuck in the car without uttering a word, she could scramble over the seats to the driver's side without being seen, and crank the engine. Voila! A plan was born.

With no time to waffle, she wheeled around, at the same time clicking the hatchback icon on her keyless entry. The hatch had barely risen before she ducked under it and catapulted herself through the blowing drizzle and into the cargo area of her SUV.

Sweet Mother Mary.

Nothing screamed Plan B like making a three-point splat on the ribbed surface of the hard plastic cargo mat. Whose stupid idea was it to buy the carpet protector from hell in the first place? Oh, wait, that was her idea. Never mind.

As it turned out, her bruises were in vain. No sooner had the hatch clicked closed than she discovered her ploy had failed.

24

You'll find yourself a heap better off if you remember to drink upstream from the herd.
—Old Farmer's Advice

Television coverage stepped up as the reporters and photo-journalists ventured back outside.

Remy and Amelie watched the various stories unfold while Grandpa Thayer dozed in his chair, chin lolling to his chest, and Miss Ludie caught twenty winks, dominating the middle of the other bed like a corpse. They realized they had dodged a bullet when they saw the hurricane damage that was spread throughout the county.

Large parts of the coastal areas were devastated.

The Interstate was on the bad side of strong winds and sustained damage to pilings in several places. For the first time in Remy's life, I-10 was empty, an asphalt ghost town. It was sobering to realize he could shoot a cannon down the four-lane and not hit a soul.

Tornados had cut wide swaths, leaving schools and motels without roofs or walls or both. Apartment buildings had collapsed. Houses and trailers were leveled. Docks destroyed. Boats were thrown into trees. Roadsides became landfills overnight, littered with appliances, abandoned vehicles, and household goods.

Remy wondered how their trailer had fared, then decided not to broach the question aloud and give Amelie one more thing to chafe and fret over. What was, was. He would contact Shorty for a report when the phones were back up.

In the meantime, if they were homeless, they were in good company. After the baby was born was soon enough to deal with another major problem.

Close to noon, Amelie's baby decided to step things up. Amelie's water broke and her contractions became more productive.

When she came out of the bathroom and announced it was time to head to the hospital, Remy wasn't even sure if the hospital was still there. Local communications were all but nonexistent. Cell phones and landlines were still useless, and neither Jerome nor Mother Vonda had returned yet from the highway gas station to give an account of the damage they'd encountered.

Remy assumed they and the girls were delayed due to downed trees and power lines or submerged roadways. But which ones? He had never felt this isolated before, cut off from everyone, not even when fishing in the backwoods and bayous, and he wasn't fond of the feeling.

Amelie flatly refused to leave her grandparents on their own at the cabin, which gave Remy no choice but to cart all three of them. Good thing his pickup was a crew cab. There was no way either one of the elders could manage hopping into the backseat of a two-door king cab.

"I left a note," Amelie said as she waddled her way toward the pickup, "sayin' where we'd be, so nobody wonders. Here's the door key. Don't forget to lock the deadbolt."

Remy halted in confusion.

"Darlin', half the roof is gone," he said, about to mount an argument. Then he noted the familiar set to her chin that told him she was channeling the *Exorcist* again, and he changed his mind. "But, hey, if my sugarplum wants the door locked, by golly, I'll lock it."

"Almost forgot the cat!" Amelie said, turning back to the door. "We can't leave him—"

"Ain't no cat steppin' a paw in my truck," Remy said, putting his husbandly foot down. "And I ain't wastin' time lookin' for him. The little critter's in the cabin somewhere. He's fine, sugar. Hell, he's better off 'n we are. Your ma or sisters can look after his scrawny ass. Now, c'mon. I'm your husband, and I'm tellin' you to get in the truck."

Fifteen minutes later, the tabby cat was comfortably doing an imitation of the Sphinx from atop a folded towel that protected the finish of the truck's center console. His gaze followed Remy's every move, and Remy could almost swear the feline was smiling.

The truck was a late model with four full-sized doors and

running boards. Even so, Remy enlisted the additional aid of a tall stepladder to hoist the old folks into the bench backseat. He gently lifted Amelie and situated her in the front bucket seat atop a few more towels, because she was leaking like a sieve.

Baby or no baby, Remy preferred to keep his custom seat covers from being ruined if he could. Not that he said it to Amelie in exactly those words. He wasn't suicidal, after all.

Thank goodness she was too focused on her cat, her labor, and her grandparents to concern herself about her demolished Bug. She never noticed its absence, or, if she did, she forgot to mention it.

Earlier, Remy had scooted out to move his truck, parking it so the wreck was out of her grandparents' line of view. If they didn't see it, they couldn't ask about it.

Remy's first instinct was to speed to the hospital, but debris and rubble on the streets forced him to drive slower than he was used to. Coming upon unexpected flooded areas obligated him to make a few detours, too. Behind him, Miss Ludie kept up a running dialogue the whole way, talking a lot and saying absolutely nothing.

Between Amelie sucking air through her teeth every few minutes, Grandpa Thayer struggling for breath, and Miss Ludie yammering with people who'd been dead for forty years, it was a nerve-racking ride. The only one mellowed out was the damned cat, and he was engrossed in giving himself a leisurely bath.

Remy's brain started to hurt.

Then, straight out of the blue, a first-rate idea occurred to him.

It was so simple. His idea followed the premise of catch and release. Remy had them, and now he was going to get rid of them.

He turned on the street to the nursing home, fully intending to drive by and boot the old folks out . . . the cat, too, when no one was watching. The home had a nice living room/reception area where the grands could wait until Mother Vonda picked them up, instead of tagging along with him.

It seemed a sound line of reckoning until Remy drove up on a downed oak blocking the road.

"Young man," Miss Ludie said, "do you know where the hell you're goin'?"

"Yessum. I had an idea I wanted to check out."

"Idea-schmidea," Miss Ludie added. "I'm hungry. When's dinner? Vonda always has my dinner ready for me by now."

"Miss Ludie," Remy said, glowering at her in the rearview mirror. "I ain't Mother Vonda."

"That's for damned sure," she said.

"Remy," Amelie said under her breath. "Please?"

"Please what?" he said in a forceful whisper. "She started it."

"She's old, hon."

"Am I'm gettin' younger?"

"Damn, Ludie," Grandpa Thayer said. "Can't y'leave the boy alone? He's doin' his best."

"Y'all hold your horses," Remy said, opening his door. "I'm gonna have a look-see at what's ahead."

Slender loblolly pine trees littered the street behind the fallen oak as if a giant hand had scattered pick-up sticks. Beyond them was the eeriest sight Remy had ever beheld.

Where the nursing home had stood last week was a vacant lot today. Only a concrete foundation and a few scattered bricks were left behind to mark the spot. One lone mattress lay ripped to shreds next to a wind-ravaged azalea bush, and Remy hoped like hell the guy in that bed had made it safely to a shelter.

To put a nice face on it, Remy was saddled with the grands for the duration. When the realization sank in, he said nothing. What could he say? He simply hopped back in his truck, glared at the now snoozing cat, and threw the engine into reverse.

Amelie reached over and gently squeezed his hand, saying quietly, "We're never given more than we can handle."

"I hear you, sugar." Remy tried to smile at her perceptiveness but knew he was doing a middling job of it. "I hear you."

And he almost believed he did.

He was never so glad to see anything as he was to see the two-story redbrick building with the ambulance and police squad car idling in the horseshoe driveway. The hospital had suffered a few blown-out windows, a partly caved-in roof, and more than half of the parking lot was underwater, but gauging by the number of people smoking cigarettes outside, the emergency room appeared open for business.

Thank you, Jesus.

Minutes later, an efficient nurse had plopped Amelie in a wheelchair and disappeared with her behind huge double wooden doors, with orders for Remy to stay put until he was called back. He didn't argue. The hospital was running on its own generator and a skeletal staff, and they were doing their best to work through a bad situation.

Remy displaced two dweeby teenagers to find seats for Amelie's grandparents in a noisy waiting area that was packed tighter than Oprah's girdle. Not only was the ER area being used for triage, but also to shelter the dozen or so elderly folks from the assisted living facility a few doors down the street.

Miss Ludie and Grandpa Thayer wasted no time in making themselves at home, accepting the freebie sandwich and bottled water handed out by Red Cross volunteers. The grands readily mingled with the other gray-hairs, as every one of them, it seemed, launched into mangled details of their experiences through the storm.

When Remy picked out his name above the hubbub, he turned expecting to see the same stoic nurse as before. Instead, he was surprised to see a disheveled older woman staring at him as if he owed her money. A second later, his pickled brain cells registered who was barreling toward him.

"Miz Lolo?" he said. "Hey, y'all doin' okay?"

He leaned down and gave her a friendly peck on the cheek and a light squeeze of the shoulders.

"I'm fine now, Remy. Oh, my, what a night. Marcel fell and wrenched his good leg when we were runnin' out, but the doctor's lookin' him over now."

"Holy smokes, why were y'all runnin'?"

"You haven't heard?"

Remy shook his head, saying, "No, ma'am. We ain't been able to hear much about anythin' happenin' around here since the power went out."

"It was terrible, Remy, just terrible. The gym roof collapsed." Lolo slanted him a curious glance. "Didn't Vonda tell y'all we were goin' to ride out the storm at the school?"

"I'm sure she told the others."

"Well, anyway, we were sittin' there, Marcel and me, in our lawn chairs. We like to be against the wall where we can people watch, y'know, rather than in the middle with all the screamin' kids. We were listenin' to the most god-awful wind you ever heard and, all of a sudden, the walls shook and the ceilin' started fallin' down in chunks and—"

"Was anybody hurt?"

"Of course they were. Roof stuff was flyin' every which way. Poor Mr. Anthony. Oh, Remy, he had a heart attack right there in the middle of all the shoutin' and keeled over on to the floor." Lolo sidled closer and her voice sank to a whisper. "I heard they were gonna airlift him to Pensacola when the winds died down some more. They don't hold much hope he'll make it."

"That's too bad. I'm real sorry to hear that."

"Tell me, y'all came through the storm all right? Why're you here? Is it Amelie's time?"

Lolo drew breath to continue speaking, but Remy jumped in ahead of her.

"We made it through the storm just fine," he said, figuring Mother Vonda could bend her big sister's ear later with war stories about the mess at the cabin. "And, yessum, I reckon we're havin' us a baby today."

Lolo swiveled her gaze around the crowded reception area and then turned back to Remy with a question in her eyes.

"Where'd Vonda get off to? I can't imagine she'd miss her first grandbaby's arrival."

"I'm sure she'll be along directly," Remy said without the slightest idea if that was true or not.

Lolo gushed a bit about soon becoming a great-aunt, then said, "Do you need anythin'? I'll stay if you need me to."

"No, ma'am. Much obliged, but we're good. You go on and look after Mr. Marcel. Tell him I hope his leg's doin' better."

"If you're sure . . . ?"

"Well, y'know, now that I think on it," Remy said, as if hatching the thought for the first time, "there is somethin'. Y'all know what my truck looks like, don't you? Amelie's got this little tabby cat in the front seat . . ."

Once Lolo took herself off down a crowded corridor in search of her husband, Grandpa Thayer moseyed over with his oxygen tank to stand next to Remy.

"She always could talk a body's ear off," Grandpa Thayer said, swallowing a deep cough with the last swig of his water.

"They all can." Remy casually swept stray dark hairs away from his eyes. "It's a genetic flaw. This baby'd better be a boy, or I'm really outnumbered and outgunned."

Grandpa Thayer grunted, a noncommittal noise.

"Boy or girl," he said, "enjoy every minute. Spend as much time as you can with your baby's mama, watchin' your baby grow. One day you'll wake up and he'll be grown, and then it'll be too late to turn back the clock."

Remy heard what the old man wasn't saying.

"Okay, so I'm an idiot for lettin' Amelie go that time," Remy said. "What're you? Perfect?"

"You don't know the half of it."

Canting his head and raising doubtful eyebrows, Remy said, "Word is you weren't much of a father, or a husband, for that matter . . . No offense intended."

"None taken," Grandpa Thayer said with a grin. "Can't argue with the truth. All my life, when I was done, I was done, and didn't look back. I'm sayin' try to learn from my mistakes."

"And if I don't, what? I end up worse than you?"

Grandpa Thayer shook his head.

"Wise up, son. The rules don't bend for anybody—you can only be young, ignorant, and fearless for so long. Trust me when I say bein' with family is better than bein' alone."

He bent double then with a stringy cough that stole his breath. Remy frowned with concern and helped him into a chair, squatting on his haunches in front of him.

"You gonna make it, old man? Should I call a nurse?"

Grandpa Thayer waved his hand in a dismissive gesture.

"No need to bother with a nurse," he said, " 'cause I've set myself a new goal."

"What're you talkin' about. What kind of goal?"

"To see my great-grandchild before they pull the plug on me. I ain't goin' under the grass 'til I do."

The busy maternity nurse popped through the double wooden doors, hollered Remy's name as if she were a drill instructor, and gave a curt motion for him to follow where she led. Remy gained his feet and started after her, but Grandpa Thayer detained him with a surprisingly firm hand to his elbow.

"You got a chance to do it right from the get-go," he said. "It's a gift from God. Now, take it."

And having offered him that bone to chew on, Grandpa Thayer gave Remy a strong shove toward his future.

In a move reminiscent of the *Kilroy Was Here* graffiti Vonda recalled from childhood, she peered over the back of the SUV's third-row seat, ready to perish from humiliation.

What she saw in the opened driver's window sent the high school girl inside her fluttering among the clouds instead. There was Terrell's adorable face staring back at her, his eyes sparkling, and an infectious smile aimed right at her.

"Need some help, Von?"

"Who, me? What gave you that idea? No, I'm good."

It was amazing she actually managed to answer him with a straight face. She cleared the third seat, bent her knees, and made her way over the center console to the driver's seat, her soaked air insoles emitting obscene grunts with every step.

"I see you're all right," she said along the way. "I'm glad. Sis okay, too?"

As romantic gaffes go, Vonda flopped into the driver's seat, figuring she took the grand prize.

"Lost her shed," Terrell said, "her chimney, and her pool enclosure, but otherwise fine."

"Good." Vonda snatched a handful of paper napkins from her stash in the console and started patting her face and arms dry. "I mean, not good that she lost them, but good that's all she lost."

"I knew what you meant. You always hop in your car that way?"

"First time, actually." She offered a weak smile. "I don't recommend it."

Before she could make up a plausible explanation, a stocky man, wearing a blue ball cap and a blue plastic rain poncho that identified him as a store employee, leaned over Terrell's shoulder and spoke to Vonda.

"Ma'am, please? Cars are behind you."

"But I haven't filled my car."

"Ten-gallon limit, ma'am." He pointed his pen to the pump that had registered the qualifying sale. "Please pull forward."

"Oops, forgot the two cans," Vonda said. "Sorry."

She cranked her car and glanced to her fuel gauge. A little less than three-quarters full. Here was hoping it was enough to last.

Terrell swiveled his gaze left and then right, and said, "I'm parked on the side lot. Pull over there."

She did as he asked. No sooner had she cut the engine than he jumped in her front passenger seat and passed her a towel.

"Here, looks like you could use this."

The clean scent of flowers wafted to Vonda's nose as she

accepted the fluffy cloth. She idly wondered what detergent his sister used.

"Gee, thanks. I was hopin' no one would notice."

"Hard not to. You're beautiful even soakin' wet."

His quietly spoken words elicited a contented sigh from her, and she said, "I like it when you tell me somethin' that makes me happy."

"I mean it, Von." He slowly smiled, a sincere and tender regard that gave her another warming sensation. "How was it over your way? I was hopin' the phones would come back, but they didn't. I worried all night."

Vonda recounted the events at the cabin, ending with, "We can't all stay there, sharing one large room, so I was goin' to ride by the house—"

Terrell shaking his head stopped her cold.

"I tried this mornin' when it was safe enough," he said. "Road is impassable. Can't even get close."

Vonda gripped the steering wheel at twelve o'clock, and then dropped her forehead on top of her knuckles.

"I was afraid of that," she said, rocking her forehead until she angled her head to stare him in the eye. "How long do you think before we can?"

"Depends on how bad the floodin' is upstream from the lake."

"A week? Ten days?"

"Don't know." He waved his hand in the air, wiggling his fingers. "Hold on while I whip out my crystal ball and check."

"Sourpuss," she said, sitting back in her seat. "Cut me some slack, will you? I've had a couple of really sucky days. Can you spell stress?"

"Speakin' of . . . what's the word on the dancin' chicken?"

"Who?"

"Jerome."

"Oh, him."

"Yeah, him."

Vonda stared out the raindrop-dotted windshield. The weather seemed to have reached a crescendo and was now slacking off.

"Von, tell me you're not stayin' with the lyin' bastard. Please tell me you've been his live-in servant long enough. You're fed up bein' a doormat."

She snapped her chin around and said, "What else am I missin'? Is that how you see me? A doormat?"

Terrell drew the backs of his fingers down her cheek and softly outlined her jaw, forestalling any further arguing on her part. Delicious shivers radiated down her spine.

"You don't think you deserve happiness," he said. "I'm here to tell you, you do."

Rather than upsetting Vonda, Terrell's words did the opposite. She felt comfort and power in having reached the same conclusion earlier.

It had taken her thirty years, but she finally accepted that she had loved the lie. She and Jerome had no common ground, other than their girls, never did and never would.

Reaching up to Terrell's hand, she interlaced her fingers with his.

"You're probably my only friend with the courage to be completely honest with me about him, Terrell."

He shrugged. "Comes from knowin' you so long."

"Maybe. But I sure hope you never think about leavin' me."

" 'The grass may wilt,' " Terrell said, " 'the flowers may fade, but I'll stand by you forever.' "

Eyes wide with shock, Vonda couldn't believe her ears. Poetry? Here was another facet to the man she hadn't known about.

"My God, Terrell," she said, her voice shaky with emotion, "that's . . . that's the most romantic thing I've ever heard you say."

"I read it on a greetin' card." He grinned. "Y'make me glad I passed on my first choice."

"Which was?"

" 'Like a fart in the elevator, I'm with you for the whole ride.' "

"You're right," she said, scrunching her nose and nodding. "Your second choice . . . mucho better."

They both laughed then, and Vonda congratulated herself on not getting too mushy or doing something foolish like throwing herself at Terrell and coming apart in his arms.

"You're such a dickhead," she said, chucking the damp towel at his chest. "You know that?"

"But you love me anyway."

"That I do. I simply can't help myself. I'm a victim of your sweet-talkin' charm."

"Never a victim, Von. You are most definitely a survivor."

"Well, if I plan to keep survivin'," she said, "I need to get over to the Wal-Mart parkin' lot. Want to come with me?"

"And load up on some of those delicious MREs? No thanks. I had my fill of those in the Army. I refuse to eat any more of them, *especially* the Captain's Chicken meal."

"National Guard has bagged ice, too, I heard."

"Picked up some already." Terrell leaned across the console and kissed her before she realized his intent. "You go ahead. I'll call you as soon as there's service. If you need help talkin' to Jerome—"

Terrell might've considered the kiss over and done with, but Vonda didn't. Not by a long shot.

She shocked him into silence when she grabbed a handful of the front of his cotton jersey, yanked him over to her, and planted a long, thoroughly wet one on his mouth. This wasn't a heat-of-the-moment smooch. Vonda knew exactly what she was doing.

She imprinted her taste on lips that she outlined with bold strokes. His mouth was soft one second, demanding the next, his hunger a reflection of hers.

She inhaled his scent, the essence of fresh rain and the richness of the outdoors that clung to his skin. Her fingers stroked up and down his face and neck with a gentle touch, awakening his physical sensations and giving him something to fantasize about. His mouth was as supple as the wind and as promising as a rainbow, and her thoughts willingly strayed to satin sheets and steamy nights.

An exploration turned into sheer bliss.

Vonda sipped, nipped, drank at his lips, sensual, seductive, alluring, coaxing more from him as the sense of renewal and wonderment climbed and climbed until they were both blanketed in a hot, fluid ache. Someone moaned sweet encouragements, but Vonda wasn't sure which one of them it was.

A minute later, when she released Terrell, she murmured against his sweet mouth, "You're a really good kisser."

"About damned time you found out."

She chuckled, saying, "Don't worry about me. I'll be fine."

"You're better than fine, sweetheart." He wrinkled his brow adorably, staring at her through heavy-lidded languor. "Much, much better."

"See y'later, then?"

"Just try to get rid of me."

After Terrell left the parking lot, Vonda sat a few moments in her car, smiling. She hugged herself, embracing this new person, this new Vonda, a woman with the newfound strength not only to rely on herself but to go after what she wanted.

And what she wanted right now was a little heart-to-heart chat with Jerome Thayer.

25

The end comes, no matter what.
—Old Farmer's Advice

Never underestimate the power of the grapevine.

Once the National Guard set up their mobile command post, the previously empty parking lot became the unofficial place to dish the dirt on the storm, get an earful, or catch up on the scuttlebutt from the outside world. In addition, the owners of the mom-and-pop country kitchen in the center of the strip mall next door had seized the opportunity to make a buck.

They fired up their portable grill and cookers and planned to serve a meat-and-three-veggie hot meal special as long as their freezer held out and the food supplies lasted. How such news spread in the middle of a natural disaster was a mystery in itself.

But spread it did.

It was paper-plate, no-frills dining, but no one seemed to mind. Diners packed the counter stools and the dozen or so tables, with people overflowing to the sidewalk. Some folks had even brought over their own lawn chairs, despite overcast skies and blustery winds. At least the rain had finally stopped.

Business at the little cafe had never been so good.

To Vonda, it looked like half the county was crowding the parking lot. There were four lines of cars, two for ice and water, and two for MREs, and all were stretched a good block or more.

She debated whether she had the patience for another long wait in line when she spotted both Charlotte and Caroline pulling their cars close to the ice stations. That decided it.

Vonda turned her SUV around to head back to the cabin. In her rearview mirror, she caught sight of a blond woman waving a straw hat with a beaded brim. She was dressed in black mules, skintight dark leggings, and an animal-print tunic tee that heightened her pale complexion. Her animated gestures looked all too familiar.

Rolling down the window, Vonda poked her head out and shouted, "Donna Lily? Is that you?"

Sure enough, Donna Lily Wagner shouted back.

She stood next to a white sedan and leaned down to say something to the driver. A second later, Vonda saw Tata MacKnutt's dark head stick out of the driver's side window. She gave a frantic wave, indicating Vonda should park nearby.

After hugs and kisses all around and brief updates about coming through the storm with minds and bodies intact, Vonda asked what her friends were up to.

"We came to eat," Donna Lily said. "I can't look another olive loaf sandwich in the face."

"It's my fault," Tata said. "I bought too much because Miss Fickle Eater here told me she liked it."

Both women favored classic styles, but Tata was the more casual of the two in white cropped pants, a floral-print empire top, and white skimmers.

"I do like olive loaf," Donna Lily said. "Just not for every friggin' meal I put in my mouth."

"Have you seen your house yet?" Tata asked.

"No." Vonda shook her head and gave a dismissive wave of her hand. "The first floor's underwater, that much I know. I'll deal with the house issues when the county clears the road. Until then, I flat refuse to worry about what I can't do anythin' about."

Mouths open, Tata and Donna Lily glanced at each other and then back to Vonda.

"Wow," Tata said. "Listen to the new attitude. What's come over you?"

Vonda shrugged, saying, "I'm findin' a new rhythm for my life. I've put my wants on hold long enough."

"You've decided about Jerome," Donna Lily said, clasping Vonda's bare arm. "Haven't you? Omigod, this is so excitin'. C'mon, girl, join us for veggies at the country kitchen before they sell out, and tell us all about it. I want to hear every detail."

"I can't," Vonda said, digging in her heels. "There's Amelie . . . my in-laws . . . I look like death warmed over. Really, I should get back—"

"Twenty minutes," Donna Lily said. "I know the baby's not comin' that fast or you wouldn't have left her in the first place. C'mon. Twenty minutes."

"Well, maybe not that quick."

Tata nodded, saying, "Amelie's hubby needs a chance to step up to the plate. He has no reason to, if you always do. Think about it. They need some space."

Vonda breathed a heartfelt sigh. The love she felt for her girls was a central and unwavering part of her being, but deep down, she knew her friends were right. It was time to start taking a step back.

"Okay, you win," she said and glanced down at herself. "But I still need to change. I don't know what I was thinkin' this mornin', leavin' these on. Hot flashes had me crazy, I guess."

"You can always walk three paces behind us," Tata said.

Donna Lily poked her in the ribs.

"Just kiddin'." Tata crawled into the backseat of her car and came out with an oversized leather tote, from which she pulled a calf-length black beach cover-up and a pair of matching slides. "Problem solved. Here, put these on. One size fits all."

Vonda held them up, saying, "You always keep these in the car?"

"Only in case I run across a gorgeous middle-aged man who wants to take me for a moonlight swim."

"Happen often, does it?" Donna Lily said, arching her perfectly shaped eyebrows.

Tata snorted. "Sadly, no. But it makes for a better story than sayin' I'm clueless why I have them stashed in the backseat. CRS . . . can't remember squat."

Vonda threw the crinkled cotton cover-up over her old shorts and tee, effectively hiding them from sight, slipped her feet out of the wet tennis shoes and into the sandals, and then borrowed Donna Lily's hat to mask the bad hair day she was having. She chucked her shoes onto the floorboard of her car, then grabbed her wallet.

A swish of lip gloss later and the three women joined the crowd taking numbers outside the café.

The mouthwatering aromas of fried chicken and grilled pork chops swirled in the wind, intertwined with the smell of Dutch oven–baked biscuits and the sharp tang of campfire coffee brewing. Every so often, a relative of the owners would pass among the customers outside, carrying a paper cup of toothpicks and a sampler plate of fried green tomatoes or fried pickles.

Vonda's rump and hips objected to the calories, but her taste buds were tap-dancing with delight. She headed inside to hunt up napkins and was directed to a self-service condiment station beyond the crowded dining counter.

The station sat at the front of a gloomy alcove next to a corridor leading to the back of the building. Over the doorway hung a universal blue-and-white restroom sign with an arrow pointing into the hot darkness.

Someone had taped yellow police crime scene tape across the doorway about chest-high to restrict access. In the middle of the tape sat a cardboard sign with two lines scrawled in black marker:

NO WATER. NO TOILETS.

STELLA GO HOME.

Normally, Vonda would have seen the tape and the cardboard sign and not paid any further attention to the area, but the acoustics in the cafe were terrible. A conversation she heard coming from inside the corridor compelled her to stop and strain her ears to listen.

Granted, it was hard to make out the words over the collective voices of the diners behind her, but this one voice pierced all known objects, pierced right into Vonda's very heart and soul. It was the same voice, the same giggle, saying the same words she'd heard over the phone all those hours ago, when she'd asked Jerome to come home and help her batten down the house.

Vonda couldn't stop the storm, couldn't stop the rain, and she couldn't stop herself from peeking around the corner.

There, against the wall and groping each other like two teenagers under the bleachers after the prom, were her husband and his latest excuse. Avoiding the scene as if it didn't exist wasn't a solution. Nor did Vonda want to pretend not to see.

Just to be pissy, she rounded the corner bold as brass and tapped the woman on the shoulder.

"Hey there, Birdlegs," Vonda said, then shot a smile at her husband. "Hey, Jerome, workin' hard I see."

Startled, the lovers jumped apart and stared speechless at Vonda, as if she'd lost her mind.

"Listen," Vonda said into the pregnant silence, "y'all need to come on out and try some of these tomatoes. They're fabulous. Tata and Donna Lily think so, too. They're right over yonder. See 'em? Give 'em a wave." Vonda stepped back where she had a view of the café interior and pointed toward the outside, waggling her fingers.

Birdlegs, aka Coach Susan, taught and supervised Caroline's cheerleading squad. After two part-time seasons, this was to be Birdlegs's first full year at the high school. She was short, skinny, tan, fit in an all-state athlete sort of way, and young enough to be one of Jerome's daughters.

Strange as it seemed, Vonda looked at the two of them together and felt overwhelming pity well up inside of her for Jerome. He was on a quixotic search for something elusive, and odds were he would spend the rest of his life seeking it, without ever discovering he'd had it within his grasp all along.

That struck Vonda as so very, very sad.

"Did I interrupt anythin'?" she said, tilting her head and smiling her politest PTA president smile.

Not surprisingly, Jerome chose to remain silent. He braced his shoulders against the wall, his brows cobbled together, and let Birdlegs bear the burden of the awkward conversation.

"Mrs. Thayer," Birdlegs said, smoothing her blond hair behind her ears with shaky hands. "We were just—that is, you . . . you're not interrupting anything. Nothing at all."

Index finger tapping her jawline, Vonda said, "Y'know, I didn't think I was, either."

As the awkwardness stretched out, a pathetic mewling sound escaped Birdlegs. She hid her mouth and reddening cheeks behind her hands, garbling her words through her fingers.

"I'm so sorry," she said. "Really, I . . ."

A kind person would've tried to spare the poor girl. A real kind person would've tried to soothe over the shame and embarrassment Birdlegs was so obviously feeling at that unfortunate moment. But a really kind person would've never turned the corner in the first place.

Vonda was human, not Mother Teresa.

"Don't be a hypocrite," Vonda said. "You're embarrassed at bein' caught, and we both know it. Before this, your conscience hasn't bothered you, so please, let's don't pretend it does now."

Dropping her hands, Birdlegs threw a beseeching glance to Jerome, a silent appeal for him to speak up, to come to her assistance, but the bastard remained unmoved and unconcerned. He merely watched to see what would happen, his arms crossed over his chest, his bored expression never wavering.

To Vonda's dismay, she saw some of herself in the mirror of Birdlegs's eyes. Her chest tightened with the knowledge and she suddenly felt angry at herself for conjuring any sympathy for her husband.

He didn't deserve it.

"Take a good look, Susan." Vonda gestured to Jerome. "See who he is, not who he isn't."

"I . . . I think I'd better go," Birdlegs said.

Vonda nodded. "Don't leave on my account."

"No, I—good-bye, Jerome. Mrs. Thayer."

And Birdlegs slipped away into the crowded cafe like a wisp of smoke. Jerome waited until she was out of sight to straighten away from the wall.

"What're you doin'?" Vonda said.

"Me? Nothin'."

"Is that what you call this? Nothin'?"

He shrugged. "This was just messin' around. It doesn't mean anythin'."

"Wrong. It has obviously meant somethin' to her."

"That's her problem, not mine. I was waitin' to see if you'd plant one in her kisser."

"Sorry to disappoint you."

Vonda turned to leave.

"Is that all you have to say? Von—wait!"

She angled back and said, "I suppose you want to tell me you've found a woman who understands you so much better."

"Maybe. Somethin' like that."

"Oh, grow up, Jerome. I don't have time for your games."

"Are y'listenin' here, Von?"

"No, Jerome, I'm not. I don't care. Do you understand? *Say* whatever you want. *Do* whatever you want. I just don't care anymore." With equal parts conviction and sadness, Vonda turned her back on him. "I've got to go, my friends are waitin'."

Vonda rounded the corner first, with Jerome right behind her. She stopped short of colliding into the posse that was waiting for her.

There, huddled by the condiment station stood Donna Lily, Tata, and her sister Lolo. It was apparent from the surprise on their faces that they had been eavesdropping and had heard every word that passed between husband and wife. Not to mention they probably caught a glance at Birdlegs ducking under the tape a few seconds ago.

Her friends did the math. Vonda figured that out when Jerome's smile and hardy greeting to them met with a wall of silence.

For a sticky moment, they all stared at each other, until Vonda forced a smile and held out her arms to enfold Lolo in a hug.

"Hey, how're you doin', big sis?"

"Better than you, it would seem," Lolo said, glaring poisonous darts over Vonda's shoulder at Jerome. "I'm glad I ran into you two."

Hearing an odd note in Lolo's tone, Vonda pulled back from the hug. Jerome had started to slink off, but he, too, was stayed by Lolo's words.

"Is somethin' wrong?" Vonda said. "Is Marcel okay?"

"He's fine," Lolo said. "Or will be with plenty of rest, the doc says. I've just come from the hospital with him, and guess who I ran into there."

"No clue. Who?"

"Remy."

"Our Remy?"

Lolo nodded. "I came in here to grab a bite to go, and I saw the girls, so I thought I'd give you some news. Quit your arguin' and run over to the hospital. If it's not already born yet, we're havin' a baby!"

Connected to tubes and monitors, Amelie was spread-eagled and tired but still calm and confident and determined to breathe with every contraction exactly like they had taught her in childbirth class. Remy was so proud of her.

For his part, he now wished he hadn't spent so much class-time doodling. He gave the effleurage a try but couldn't seem to remember what to rub or where, so he massaged whatever his hand touched and hoped for the best.

Remy stationed himself at Amelie's head, figuring to stay out of the way, and held her hand, perfectly happy he couldn't see what was happening below. On this voyage of discovery, one thing Remy discovered was that—while he could field dress a deer and fillet a fish with the best of them—when it came to his own wife's pain and blood, his nerves were shot and his heart was on the squeamish side.

Her doctor walked into the room, all blue scrubs and surgical mask from head to toe. Remy didn't know her from Adam's house cat. Two brown eyeballs that crinkled at the corners when she laughed were the only things he saw.

The eyeballs invited him to sit next to them and help deliver the baby. But Remy, understandably, declined.

"If you don't tournament fish," he told the eyeballs, "I won't practice medicine."

It seemed like a square deal to him. The eyeballs laughed

and the crinkles appeared again, and not too long after, Amelie started pushing.

The baby arrived with ten fingers and ten toes and a good set of lungs, and Remy thought his heart would burst through his chest. He'd seen newborns who looked as if they'd hit a few evolutionary speed bumps on the way into the world, but this was the first newborn he'd seen who was perfect.

Remy kissed Amelie, her name a burst of happiness from his mouth. He told her how good she had done, and stayed with her, sharing in her joy, energy, and enthusiasm.

Only when the nurses booted him out so they could get everyone cleaned up did Remy make himself leave. He headed to the vending machine closet to buy a soda, and that was when he heard Mother Vonda call his name.

He wheeled around and saw the whole herd of Thayers stepping off the elevator. Mother Vonda and Jerome, Miss Ludie and Grandpa Thayer, the girls, and their auntie Lolo, too, crowded around him in the corridor, all flushed with excitement and talking at once.

Finally, Mother Vonda shushed them and spoke the words on the tip of all their tongues.

"Well?" she said, clasping her hands in front of her. "Do we have a baby yet?"

Remy grinned from ear to ear and glanced at each face before pronouncing, "We have a *nine-pound* baby."

Laughing, clapping, and squeals of joy erupted at the same time. A moment later, Mother Vonda shushed them again.

"And?" she said, grinning. "Boy or girl? Don't keep us in suspense."

Taking a deep breath, Remy then said four quiet words that would change their lives forever.

"We have a son."

Three hours later, Amelie was comfortably tucked in her hospital bed, with Remy reclining on top of the covers next to her. The family had finally left, giving the new parents time alone to get acquainted with their little boy. He was sleeping peacefully in his mother's arms, but Remy now knew that state wouldn't last for long. His son had a healthy appetite and believed in indulging it often.

"Have you talked to Shorty?" Amelie said.

"Not yet," Remy said. "I reckon he'll be checkin' on the trailer tomorrow, since the weather's supposed to be hot and humid. I figured on ridin' over there in the mornin' and seein' what's what."

Amelie nodded and then said, "What about Malone? He doesn't strike me as the forgivin' sort. He's gonna want his money, probably more than ever now if his bar was damaged in the hurricane. Where're we gonna come up with five thousand dollars, Remy?"

"Shhh, don't go upsettin' yourself, sugar. I talked with Paddy already."

"You have?"

Remy nodded. "That's why I was at his place the day y'all

came by and I took sick. He and I worked out a repayment plan of sorts."

"Of sorts? I'm not sure I care for the sound of that."

"Don't worry your little head about it. But to be on the safe side, if that deal falls through, I've got me a ZX 250 Skeeter, with a three-hundred horse Yamaha he can have."

"Oh, no, Remy, not your boat."

He put two fingers to her lips to quiet her.

"It's just a boat, sugar."

"How're you gonna fish without a boat? It's worth ten times what you owe. You can't sell—"

"Try more like fifteen. Thing is, I ain't exactly talkin' about sellin'. I was thinkin' more along the lines of him considerin' that five thousand as a sponsorship interest in my boat." Remy drew a picture in the air with his fingers. "We could paint his logo on the side, have patches sewn on shirts and caps and—"

"Y'think he'd go for it?" Amelie said.

"I don't see why not. It's advertisin', and I'm good for promotin'. I mean, look at me. I'm an upstandin' family man, with a beautiful wife and a strappin' young son." Remy leaned over and kissed Amelie gently, slowly, and thoroughly. "If you'll still have me, that is. Will you, sugar?"

"I don't know, Remy." She looked at him, worry on her face. "Will you do somethin' about the gamblin'?"

"Is that what it'll take?"

She nodded, saying, " 'Fraid so. We've got a baby now and we need to make a future for him. But that's not gonna happen if we're partyin' and spendin' like we're single."

Remy read the truth in her eyes. Knowing this point was not negotiable, he had a choice to make.

He stared at her and at his little boy and realized deep in his heart that the choice had already been made.

"I hear you, sugar, and you've got my promise."

And then he sealed it with a kiss.

It was nearly dark by the time Jerome drove Vonda back to the strip mall parking lot to collect her car. No words passed between them on the ride over. Vonda had nothing left to say.

The wind had calmed down to a breeze tangy with the rich, earthy smells of wet grass and plants. Pink streaks lit the darkening clouds, and the evening was filled with the buzzing sounds of night bugs and nature busy at work rejuvenating herself.

Vonda climbed down out of Jerome's truck and hesitated before closing his door, saying, "I'll run by the cabin tomorrow to collect my clothes and stuff I left there."

"What?" Jerome jumped out of his Escalade and slammed his palm on the hood. "What're you talkin' about? Where're you goin' tonight?"

"I'm leavin', Jerome. Did you really think I wouldn't? I'm goin' to stay with Tata and Donna Lily until your lawyer and my lawyer can iron out things."

Vonda slammed his door shut, and Jerome was around the bumper and in front of her before the echo of the latch died.

"You're serious?" he said.

"Very."

"But what about us?"

"What *us*? There is no *us*. Not anymore. I don't think there ever really was."

Jerome's expression fell and he backed up a step, as if he were intimidated by her resolve. Just as quickly, his expression changed to a wry grin.

"Can't we start over?" he said. "We can go to Venice on a second honeymoon. You'd like that, wouldn't you? Sure you would, you've always wanted to go to Venice, see the canals, ride the gondolas, eat the pasta. I could take a week off, maybe ten days—"

Apparently, the closer in him really believed he could do the deal. Vonda offered him a sympathetic grin.

"It's way too late to bargain, Jerome. Save it for the lawyer."

He jammed his hands into his pockets.

"What about the girls? Have you given a thought to them, to how they'll feel, to what you're doin' to them? You haven't, have you?"

Vonda groaned, saying, "You're determined to be a big, flappin' melodramatic douche bag, aren't you? Amelie already knows. I'll talk to Charlotte and Caroline tomorrow."

She unlocked her car door and tossed her wallet to the center console.

"You're gonna leave me, just like that? Tonight? Isn't that a little selfish? What am I gonna do with the parents? I can't work and look after them."

"Poor Jerome." Vonda gave an inelegant snort. "You have issues, don't you?"

He seemed to take exception to her tone and changed tack.

"I love you, you know," he said. A lone tear trickled down his unshaven cheek. "I don't know what I'll do without you. Come back to me, Vonda?"

She bowed her chin and collected her thoughts, then looked up at him.

"You're the father of my children," she said. "Because of that, you're someone I'll always care for. But I'm not in love with you, Jerome, and I haven't been for a very long time."

His tears dried up and he flashed her a sheepish smile. She smiled back, grazed his face with her fingertips one last time, and settled herself behind the wheel of her SUV.

"So what happens now?" he said, leaning his forearms on her opened window.

She glanced toward the country kitchen cafe and back to his face, and said, "You go back, talk to your parents—and I mean really talk—and see if assisted livin' might interest them. Then you patch things up with Birdlegs—or not—as you choose."

"What're you gonna do?"

He was fishing for information that Vonda didn't feel was his business anymore. She put her car in gear, and Jerome backed out of the way.

"Happiness is a journey, Jerome, not a destination. I plan to play, laugh, and enjoy bein' alive. Maybe you should do the same."

"You're crazy," he called, waving good-bye as she pulled away. "I love you."

"I know."

And for her fifty-first birthday, Vonda thought she might like to try skydiving.